SUDDEN DEATH

EVA MACLEAN

By Eva Maclean

The Detective Miranda Murphy Series

Dead Matters
Dead Cool
Sudden Death
Dead Drop

Vinci Books

vinci-books.com

Published by Vinci Books Ltd in 2025

1

Copyright © Eva Maclean 2023

The author has asserted their moral right to be identified as the author of this work in accordance with the Copyright, Designs and Patents Act 1988. This work is a work of fiction. Names, characters, places and incidents are the product of the author's imagination or are used fictitiously. Any resemblance to actual persons, living or dead, places and incidents is entirely coincidental.

All rights reserved. No part of this publication may be copied, reproduced, distributed, stored in any retrieval system, or transmitted in any form or by any means, including photocopying, recording, or other electronic or mechanical methods, nor used as a source for any form of machine learning including AI datasets, without the prior written permission of the publisher.

The publisher and the author have made every effort to obtain permissions for any third party material used in this book and to comply with copyright law. Any queries in this respect should be brought to the attention of the publisher and any omissions will be corrected in future editions.

A CIP catalogue record for this book is available from the British Library.

Paperback ISBN: 9781036700720

Printed and bound in Great Britain by Clays Ltd, Elcograf S.p.A.

Prologue

WHEN HE HAD MADE the decision, when he knew that he was going to do it, he went through the rest of the steps in something like a dream. He felt a bit sick and his knees were shaking, but he kept walking. It was as if this was an appointed task which had been given to him and he was trusted to carry it out – just like Frodo. And when it was over, when he had done this thing, he would never have to be afraid again.

He had bought the rope from the hardware store. They didn't know him there. Nobody had asked him his age, or what it was for, so that was good. And he knew how to tie the right knot. They had practised it in Cubs.

There was nobody around in the woods. The sun shone through the trees and he heard a dog bark in the distance, but it sounded far away. All the others would be in school, they'd be having playtime soon, and he hated playtime. When he came to his favourite tree, standing there, waiting for him, he stopped for a moment and thought of all the people he would miss. He hoped his mum would be OK. He hoped it would be quick.

Chapter One

DETECTIVE INSPECTOR MIRANDA MURPHY was walking Barney on Hampstead Heath on a Saturday morning when the call came in on her mobile. Maybe actually walking was only a small part of it. The bigger part, certainly as far as Barney was concerned, was plunging into the boggy area created by the torrential rain of the last three days and bathing luxuriously in the mud. Trying to stop him was a failed mission. What was it with dogs and mud? Perhaps he thought it was good for his complexion.

Murphy hadn't been expecting any call from the station because, as far as she could remember, she wasn't on the rota for this weekend. When she queried this with the despatcher, she was told that Inspector Fulbridge had called in with flu and somebody had to attend a flat in Dalston where a body had been found. Great. She had to get this filthy dog home and then get to work. Right now, he looked like a dungheap with eyeballs. Checking that there were no swimmers nearby, she threw his ball into the Ladies Pond and he dashed in after it, causing a bunch of ducks to retreat in alarm. That would get the worst of the mud off. Of course, he picked up another layer of slime on the way out. Nobody had told her that there would be so much bloody housekeeping involved in having a dog. She didn't remember the children being this much trouble, but that was probably selective memory.

An hour later, having left the heaving mass of filthy fur with James and Clive, she was on her way to Queensbridge Road, Dalston. The car still smelled a bit whiffy, so she had all the windows open. 2C was a second-floor flat in a purpose-built block in a side street just off the main road and the entryphone was answered by PC Julie Fraser. Julie and her partner had responded to the original call and he was in the kitchen making the tea. Murphy pulled on her plastic overshoes and gloves and started by texting Wilcox. No reason not to ruin his Saturday as well.

The deceased was a young man of about twenty-seven, wearing jeans, T-shirt and trainers. His eyes were closed, there were no obvious marks of violence, and the way in which he was slumped in the armchair looked pretty natural to Murphy. For a moment she wondered if he wasn't just asleep, but the rise and fall of the chest was definitely absent and one of the paramedics she had encountered on the way in had shaken his head in a way that told her all she needed to know. What looked like a suicide note on the coffee table in front of him appeared to give further confirmation.

His flatmate who had made the 999 call was sitting in the kitchen. She introduced herself as Sophie Carter and told them that the deceased was called Liam Webster. She was a fragile-looking girl with red hair and exceptional bone structure. Her mascara had run catastrophically and wiping a tissue across her face wasn't improving the look. Murphy could see her hands shaking and encouraged her to drink the tea that Julie was placing in front of her.

Slowly Sophie told her story. Liam had been living here about a month. She had just arrived back from spending the night with a friend in Oxford and she had found him lifeless.

'I couldn't wake him.'

'Did you move him at all?'

'No, I wouldn't have been able to move him, he's too big for that, but I did shake him and then I looked for a pulse and there was nothing there. He was stiff.' She shuddered and bit back a sob.

Wilcox appeared in the doorway at that moment, looking as if he'd just been pulled off the pitch, which he probably had. The combination of football strip, tracksuit bottoms and overshoes and the streak of mud on his forehead seemed to shock Sophie out of her grief, and she almost smiled.

'Kevin, good to see you,' said Murphy. 'Hope you weren't about to score the winning goal.'

He shook his head. 'Nah, they were trouncing us.'

'Alright' said Murphy. 'Sophie, do you have contact details for Liam's next of kin?' Sophie shook her head. 'This is now a possible crime scene, so you will have to leave. When you're ready, we'd like you to go down to the station with Julie and make your statement, so we can get it all written up and signed.'

Sophie picked up her jacket and handbag and turned as she went out of the door. 'That note...' she said, 'I know how it looks. But he never seemed to me like that sort of person. What if he didn't kill himself? What if somebody else was involved?'

The door closed behind her. Wilcox exchanged a look with Murphy. 'Shock,' he said. 'People say weird things.'

FRANK, the pathologist, arrived at that moment, banging the door open, sliding across the carpet on his plastic overshoes and almost smacking his case into the coffee table.

'So, no Linda today?' said Murphy.

Frank shook his head. 'The boss doesn't do Saturdays.'

'Smart woman,' said Murphy. 'I guess she has more clout than me.'

'Definitely dead,' said Frank, kneeling in front of the body, 'but you'll have had that from the paramedics. No immediate sign of what caused it. No injuries that I can see. No sign of poisoning. We'll know more when we've done the PM. Rigor well established, wearing off a bit. Time of death will be between the last time he was seen and when his body was found.'

'Thanks a heap, Frank,' said Murphy. 'Even Linda sometimes gives me more than that.'

'You're joking. Linda says we can only accurately tell time of death if the victim was wearing a watch which smashed when he fell over, and you can't even be sure about that. What she'd say if I stuck my neck out and gave you a time of death in advance of the PM, well, we won't go there.'

Murphy admitted defeat and turned her attention to the rest of the evidence. The flat had two bedrooms and it was not difficult to see which belonged to Liam. Both were relatively untidy, but one had male underwear strewn on the floor and the other had a bra draped over the mirror. Neither of them gave any kind of clue as to why Liam Webster was sitting dead in an armchair.

'I've got his phone and laptop,' said Wilcox, when she returned to the sitting room. 'Can't get into them yet.'

'We'll need to get into them to find out how to contact his family,' said Murphy. 'And the other item to secure is that.' She pointed to the note on the coffee table, written in small neat caps.

I'M SORRY ABOUT THIS, I COULDN'T TAKE ANY MORE. AXIOM IS NEVER GOING TO WORK.

Chapter Two

MURPHY AND WILCOX drove back to the station in her car. Wilcox sank as low as possible in his seat and braced his feet under the dashboard, which was his usual precaution. Then he found this made it impossible to get his head far enough out of the window to escape from the smell.

'I've had Barney in here,' Murphy explained. 'And he'd been rolling in God-knows-what, so that's the less than fragrant atmosphere. So, you'll have to choose between sudden death and asphyxiation.'

At that moment the taxi in front decided to change lanes without warning and sudden death immediately looked the more likely option. Wilcox hurriedly withdrew his head. 'Well anticipated,' said Murphy. 'If that hadn't gone our way, your head could have been severed at the neck.'

Something about the careless way she said this made Wilcox feel decidedly unnerved, but he saw that they were now approaching the station and a few minutes later he was able to make his escape.

Sudden Death

After getting past the duty sergeant, who brightened up when he saw Wilcox and offered some impenetrable joke about the offside rule, he tracked down Fiona, the technician who had drawn the short straw and had to work this Saturday. The phone was unlocked in a matter of minutes.

'Just like that, access to all his secrets,' said Murphy, putting down the statement she was skimming. 'It always seems like the worst sort of prying. Anyway, enough of the scruples, we need to find his next of kin as Sophie didn't seem to know. I guess you don't ask for next of kin information when you take in a flat mate. Here we are, mother and father in Gravesend. Can you send the uniforms out to inform them? Poor people. And I think we'll have a few words with Sophie while she's here. This statement doesn't say much more than she told us in the flat. Let's see if we can get her to expand a bit.'

Sophie was sitting in the least ghastly of the interview rooms, Wilcox was pleased to note, and had been given tea (more tea!). If she had her wits about her, she wouldn't drink it, but it was the thought that counted.

Wilcox started the tape and intoned the preliminaries. Sophie looked a bit alarmed.

'Don't worry,' said Murphy. 'We're not charging you with anything, but we have to keep a record of all our interviews. Can you just explain the domestic set-up between you and Liam Webster. I gather he's not your boyfriend.'

Sophie shook her head. 'No, we're not in a relationship,' she said. 'It's my flat and he's my lodger – or he was my lodger. I originally bought it with my ex-husband and when we divorced, I bought him out – with a bit of help from my mum. There's quite a big mortgage so I need to have somebody else in to help with the bills. Liam's been living with me for about a month. Before that I had a girl called Alex, but she got married and moved out.'

'And you decided to pick a man this time. Any reason?'

She shrugged. 'Not really. Well maybe. Perhaps I thought I would feel safer – as a woman – having a man around the place. No, that's wrong, I don't think I need a man for protection. I just liked Liam. I met him and he seemed like a nice guy, very easy going. I could see I would have no problem getting on with him.'

'And is that how it worked out?'

'Yes. Pretty much. We don't see a lot of each other, but we get on OK.' Her face fell. 'I mean we got on OK.'

'Alright. Now can you just tell us again what happened this weekend.'

Sophie sighed. 'I went up to Oxford after work on Friday to see my friend Cass, we were at university together. I've already given you her contact details.' She looked towards Wilcox, who nodded. 'We had dinner and drinks and I knew it would be late so I stayed over.'

'Did Liam know you wouldn't be back Friday night?'

She thought for a moment. 'I don't think he did. I don't remember seeing him Friday morning. He must have gone in to work early. I would probably have told him if I'd seen him.'

'So you came back Saturday morning,' said Wilcox.

'Yes. I got the train arriving into Paddington at 11.13. Then I got the Elizabeth Line to Liverpool Street and the 149 bus. I got home just after 12.'

'And you called emergency services straight away?'

'Yes, as soon as I realised he wasn't going to come round. It was a shock to see him like that.'

'What did you think when you saw the note?'

'I was really upset that he was so unhappy living with me that he would kill himself. I still don't believe it.'

'Did you recognise the handwriting?'

'No, but then I've never seen his handwriting. And it was all in caps.'

'Yes, that's right,' said Murphy. 'What's your job Sophie?'

'I'm an engineer,' she said. 'I work for Sevills – they're a big contractor.'

Something stirred in Wilcox's brain. 'So you worked on Crossrail?' he said.

She smiled briefly and nodded. 'Yes, that was a really great project. I felt so lucky to be part of it. Liam's a kind of engineer too – or he was. He was a data engineer. We had that in common.' Her smile died. 'We were both engineers, but very different jobs.'

'Did you meet any of his friends or family?'

Sophie shook her head. 'No, nobody. But then, we hadn't been sharing the flat for very long.'

'Alright Sophie. I think that's all we need to know for now.' Murphy gathered up her papers. 'Thank you for your time. We're still going over your flat so you can't go back there at the moment. Do you have somewhere else to stay?'

'I can stay with my mum in Bethnal Green.'

'That sounds like a good idea. Just write the address here for us in case we need to talk to you again.'

WHEN SOPHIE HAD GONE, they escaped from the interview room. Murphy stretched and put her feet on her desk. Everything felt stiff and the morning dog walk seemed days ago. Was it really just this morning?

'We've got her on CCTV at Paddington,' said Wilcox,

coming out of the control room. 'She's definitely getting off the Oxford train, she couldn't have been that side of the barrier otherwise. And we've got her a bit later at Liverpool Street. So that seems to check out. Julie's shuffling through the CCTV from Queensbridge Road.'

'OK. Let's go see.' Murphy eased her feet down carefully and they left the CID room.

The image was grainy but three men could be seen getting out of a taxi on the corner of Queensbridge Road at 1.30 am on Saturday morning. The taxi remained in place and ten minutes later two of the men reappeared and got back into the taxi, which then drove off.

'Let's look at that again,' said Murphy. 'Looks like the one in the middle, being supported by the other two, is Liam, as he doesn't reappear. They drop him off and then ten minutes later the other two come out and they set off again. He's definitely drunk or incapable in some way.'

'So that's the last sighting of him alive,' said Wilcox. 'Wonder if he was alive when they got back in the taxi?'

'Well those are the two individuals we need to track down,' said Murphy. 'What have SOCO come up with so far?'

'They're still processing samples. Liam's parents and sister are coming to identify the body. Sophie's already identified him, but it's better to have next of kin. It was explained to them that there would have to be a post-mortem. They're very upset.'

'Of course they are. At least it wasn't a violent death, so there are no marks on the body. I don't know how much better that will make it for them. We'll have to go see them after the PM. I don't have anything I can tell them until then. I'm going home now, to apologise to my lodgers for dumping a dirty dog on them. Can I give you a lift?'

'No, I'll get the tube.' Wilcox shook his head emphatically.

Murphy set off on the drive home, negotiating the Saturday afternoon traffic and remembering she hadn't done any shopping. A bark greeted her as she put the key in the lock and she prepared herself for the onslaught of dirty claws and matted hair. What she saw instead was a glossy creature that looked like it had emerged from a grooming parlour.

'Blimey. He smells amazing.' She buried her nose in the back of his neck.

'Jo Malone bath scrub,' said Clive. 'Heavenly. And I put conditioner on his hair – coat I mean.'

'Thank you so much,' said Murphy. 'I was only expecting the hose in the back garden.'

'Yes, we started with that,' said James. 'And that got off the worst of it off. But he still wouldn't have been fit to sit on the sofa. He seemed to really enjoy his bath.'

'I'll bet he did,' said Murphy. 'Attention. It's what we all want. Or most of us.'

Chapter Three

SOPHIE OPENED the fridge door quietly and took out a small can of tonic. A squeeze of lime, a few ice cubes, just pretend it's a G&T. A real one was what she felt like right now, a hit of something powerful, followed by the slight dulling of the senses, but she knew the danger of solitary drinking – that smooth snowboard slide downhill into unconsciousness. Not going there again. And being at her mum's didn't lend itself to drinking. Her mum couldn't drink with those drugs she was on.

She took the drink into the sitting room, made sure the door was shut and kicked off her shoes. She picked up her phone and tapped out a number. Cass picked up on the first ring.

'Hello, my love. Is everything OK?'

'Not really, Cass. Are you able to talk?'

'Yes, no problem. I'm sitting on the grass outside the Bodleian eating a tuna and cucumber sandwich, just like a lazy tourist, so fire away. Has something happened?'

Sophie felt her throat start to close up and she forced

herself to breathe. 'It's my flatmate, Liam. I told you about him.'

'Yes. You did. Why? What has he done?'

'He's dead.'

'Dead – is that what you said?'

'Yes.'

'But how?'

Sophie blew her nose hard and got her voice under control. 'I don't know. The police have been and he's been taken away but they're not saying anything. I found him when I got home on Saturday morning. He was just sitting there.'

'That's awful, Soph. I'm so sorry. Do you want to come back here for a bit?'

'No, I need to stay around, the police may want to talk to me again. I just needed to talk to somebody. I can't believe this has happened. I think it's my fault, Cass.'

'How can it possibly be your fault?'

'It just feels that way. Bad things happen around me. Have done since I was young. Now this poor young guy moves into my flat and a month later he's dead.'

There was a snort. 'That's rubbish and you know it is.' Cass sounded very firm and Sophie could picture her rolling her eyes. Cass was like the opposite of a drama queen, which was why she was so valuable. 'One really bad thing happened to you Sophie, which would have driven anybody off the rails, but it didn't affect anybody else. You are not responsible for everything that happens to other people.'

'OK, I guess I was getting a bit carried away there.' Sophie relaxed her shoulders. Cass's commonsense attitude always helped to dispel the worst of her fears. 'But,' she continued, 'Liam dying like that, just out of the blue, it makes no sense. I'm worried he had something to do with it.

You know. Him. It's like I poked the hornet's nest and this is what came out.'

'Sophie, give yourself a break. It's really sad that this poor chap has died, but you weren't there when it happened and it's nothing to do with anything you've done. Back away from it and let the police sort it out. Are you at home right now?'

'No. I can't go back there at the moment. The police are searching the place. I'm at my mum's. She's upstairs having a nap, which is why I'm keeping my voice low. I don't want to worry her. She knows about what was going on with him, but I haven't told her about Liam yet.'

'I'm glad you're at your mum's. It's better than being on your own right now. Are you going in to work on Monday?'

Sophie shook her head and then remembered she was on the phone. 'No. I just phoned my boss and he said not to worry. I guess it's good that I'm in an industry that has people doing stuff at weekends. He put in the call to HR – amazing that he tracked one of them down on a Saturday. They've given me a few days off. Sort of bereavement leave. HR weren't sure if bereavement leave applied to flat mates, so they compromised and gave me half the allowance. Pretty generous really, considering I had the full allowance last year.'

'That's all good, love. They're taking care of you, and so they should. Now do me a favour and do some stuff that makes you feel better for the next few days. Don't sit around worrying.'

Sophie smiled. 'Yes, you're right. I think I'll go hit the wall. Nothing like a bit of adrenaline to put things in perspective.'

Chapter Four

MURPHY REGULARLY THREATENED Kevin Wilcox with having to attend the next post mortem instead of her, but somehow, she always found herself here in the end. She wasn't sure why, there was nothing to recommend it, apart from the fact that it always put her off her next meal, so maybe there were weight loss benefits. If pushed, she would have said that she liked hearing the findings as they were arrived at, directly from the horse's mouth, as it were. And the horse whose mouth she most respected was Linda Fleming. Fleming was of an age and professional reputation that meant she didn't take bullshit from anybody, whether that was the receptionist or the Chief Constable. It was a position that Murphy hoped to reach in the fullness of time. In the meantime, she concentrated on making sure her mask was securely fastened over her nose, practising breathing through her mouth and reminding herself that lots of pathology students would kill (well, maybe not!) to be standing here instead of her.

The body was wheeled in on a trolley, unzipped and

transferred to the table. Liam looked very defenceless without his clothes. Linda walked around him, switched on her microphone and began speaking.

'A well-nourished male, mid-to-late-20s, maybe a little bit too well-nourished, but nothing serious. Tattoos on both arms, otherwise no wounds, marks or scars.' She raised his eyelids. 'No sign of suffocation.'

She picked up the scalpel, which was the signal for Murphy to transfer her attention to the ceiling. The next half hour was chiefly composed of noises and a few smells. The squelching noises as the organs were pulled out, the drilling noise as the top of the skull was removed, and the burning smell as the blade cut through the bone.

'Let's have a look at the stomach contents.' Murphy had no desire to look at the stomach contents and looked away again as Linda poured them into a dish.

'Beer, by the smell of it, quite a lot of beer. There could be other alcohol as well, maybe vodka, that doesn't really smell, we'll have to test for it. And particles of meat. That would have taken a while to digest, so it's pretty recognisable.'

'One of those dodgy kebabs on the way home,' said Murphy, feeling it was time to contribute something.

'Yes, could well be that,' said Linda, 'though I doubt it's the kebab that killed him.'

'Heart,' she announced finally, carving into the offending organ as if it was the Sunday roast. 'It's slightly enlarged and the arteries are narrowed in a few places. The enlarged heart can be genetic. It wouldn't of itself kill him, but it could be a contributory factor. Frank did the bloods after he'd attended the scene, clever chap, and the lab must have put on a sudden spurt because the results have just come in. Let's see.' She picked up a tablet and swiped.

'Alcohol, a fair amount of it, MDMA, one or two tabs. None of that would usually have been fatal, but it does happen. The MDMA suggests clubbing. Was that what he was doing?'

'Yes, he was brought home in a taxi from somewhere, possibly a club.'

'Well, the MDMA and the exertion may have precipitated a short-circuit which stopped the heart pumping. Some people are more affected by drugs than others. MDMA can cause death from heatstroke, leading to respiratory collapse. It also raises blood pressure and heart rate, which seems the more likely explanation here. But we have to bear in mind that it could have happened anyway, without any precipitating factors. What we call sudden cardiac death – SUD.'

'What, you mean anybody's heart can just stop like that, for no reason?'

Linda nodded. 'That's right. It's pretty rare, but it can happen. It can happen to anybody. So, I guess we should all make the most of the time allotted to us.'

Murphy was silent for a moment, pondering this, then recalled herself to the job in hand. This was about poor Liam Webster, not her or anybody else. She turned back to Linda.

'So his heart stopped. Is it always fatal?'

'Theoretically no, but in practice, usually, yes. If someone had got to him with a defibrillator within five minutes, he might not be lying here, but that's a bit of an ask in most cases. And of course, he would have given the immediate appearance of being already dead so anybody who was not a medical professional would have assumed nothing could be done. He would have had a better chance of survival if he had stayed in the club, or wherever else he was - there might have been a doctor in there making an exhibition of himself, or herself.'

'So possibly natural causes?' said Murphy.

Linda nodded. 'I would say misadventure. Death from natural causes is an unusual event at his age, but not impossible.'

'Nobody could have done anything to bring this about?'

'If so, they were bloody clever. Maybe somebody gave him the MDMA when he'd been drinking alcohol but the results would be unpredictable. Would anybody else have known about the state of his heart? He probably didn't know himself. It has more the look of a completely random occurrence.'

'How about suicide?'

Linda gave her a sharp look. 'Can't see how. It's pretty unusual to dance yourself to death and he hadn't taken enough alcohol or MDMA to definitely cause a fatal event. It wouldn't be a very convincing effort. Why are you thinking suicide?'

'We found a note.'

Linda raised her eyebrows. 'Well, that is interesting. Believe me, he would have been in no state to start typing up his justifications.'

'It was written.'

'On paper? With a pen? How quaint. Even less chance of that. You're thinking he realised he was dying and scribbled something? No. Just no.'

Chapter Five

WILCOX HAD BROUGHT his car in and he volunteered to drive to Gravesend. Murphy was happy with this. The journey out on the A2 was not exactly scenic, so she reclined her seat and prepared for a short nap. This was made difficult by Wilcox's use of the satnav.

'Can't you shut that woman up?'

'She's keeping me updated on the traffic.'

'What do you need to know? There's traffic. We're in it. If there's a holdup ahead, we'll get held up. That's it.'

'If there's a holdup, she'll tell me how to get round it.'

'But she'll be telling everybody else the same thing. And we'll all be snarled up together somewhere else.'

Wilcox shook his head and said nothing. Murphy closed her eyes and endeavoured to shut everything out.

After what seemed like no time at all, the robot told them to turn left at the next junction and Murphy sat up and endeavoured to pay attention.

'I've never been to Gravesend' she said.

'I've been looking it up,' said Wilcox. 'It's quite a historic place. Pocahontas is buried here. It's not known where exactly, because the church was destroyed in a fire.'

'Is that so? Which is Reverend Webster's church?'

'St Matthews. Just round the corner here. The vicarage is next door.'

The door of the vicarage was opened by a slight woman with unruly greying hair and an expression of utter defeat. Murphy could understand that. Whatever news they were bringing would do nothing to alter the fact that she had last seen her son on a trolley in the morgue.

They introduced themselves and Mrs Webster led the way to a sitting room where her husband was waiting to greet them. He was a more substantial figure than his wife and looked, Murphy thought, like the sort of vicar that his flock would have found very approachable, even the sort of vicar they could have had a joke with. But not now, maybe not ever again.

'Thank you for coming all the way out here' he said. 'I'm not expecting any good news, but we appreciate hearing it in person.'

'I understand that' said Murphy, as they sat on the sofa. 'We have the initial results of the post-mortem and it is the opinion of the pathologist that Liam's death was due to misadventure. He had taken a moderate amount of ecstasy, but nothing that should have been fatal. However, the drug, combined with alcohol and exertion in the club could have been sufficient to cause his heart to stop beating. But the heart can also stop beating without any precipitating factors. This will all be stated at the inquest, but it's best that you know beforehand. In the absence of any other indicators, his death could be classified as due to natural causes. That means that, as far as we can tell at the moment, there will be no need for an inquest. I will confirm this to you in the next day or so and then you will be able to go ahead with the funeral.'

'But that can't be right,' said Mrs Webster, straightening up with the appearance of somebody now mustering her remaining resources. 'How can it be natural to just die at his age?'

'It's not common,' said Murphy, 'but it does happen. Did he ever show signs of having a heart condition?'

They both shook their heads. 'He was a healthy child' said his mother shakily. 'Don't remember ever taking him to the hospital.'

'What the pathologist found was that his heart was slightly enlarged and there was some narrowing of the arteries,' said Murphy. 'These factors may or may not have contributed to what happened, but the event was what is called sudden cardiac death. Something short-circuits and the heart just stops pumping.'

'So, he didn't kill himself?' said the vicar.

Murphy shook her head. 'We don't think so. In the opinion of the pathologist, it was unlikely that he or anybody else could have brought that result about.'

Reverend Webster's shoulders sank back down. 'Thank God for that. I couldn't bear to think that he was so unhappy and we didn't even know about it, that he would have wanted to kill himself. But we were told there was a suicide note?'

'Yes. That is a puzzling aspect.' Murphy opened her case. 'This is a copy of the note. I appreciate it's all in caps, but do you recognise anything about the handwriting?'

They both stared at it for a few moments.

'No,' said Mrs Webster finally. 'Nothing about it looks familiar.'

'I agree, I don't recognise it at all,' said her husband.

'AXIOM is the name of the project he was working on. He told me a bit about it, but I didn't really understand very much. He was a clever chap. Very good at maths.' He swallowed hard and Murphy could see that he was holding back tears.

'We're looking into it,' said Murphy. 'It looks like somebody else wrote it, but we don't know why. We'll let you know what we find out.'

'AND THE PERSON I want to talk to next,' Murphy told Wilcox as they set off back down the A2 to London, 'is his sister, who might know things that the parents don't know. She runs a café in Finsbury Park. It should still be open.'

Wilcox sighed. 'OK. We should be right on time for the rush hour.'

Wilcox's prediction was correct. The journey from Gravesend to Greenwich was no trouble. The miles flew by. The journey from south London to north London took twice as long, confronted at every turn by snarl-ups and roadworks.

'What about this then?' said Murphy as they rounded a corner and met three lanes of stationary traffic. 'Why isn't your woman getting us another route? Isn't that what she's for? She's gone very quiet all of a sudden.'

'It probably happened since she was last updated' said Wilcox stiffly, as the lights changed long enough to allow the three cars in front to get through and then slammed back to red in front of them.

'What particularly pisses me off' said Murphy, 'is that they're not even doing any roadworks here. They've packed up and gone home. There's no actual hole still in the road but they've left the traffic management up. They just do it to wind up motorists.'

After what seemed like an eternity, they made it onto the Old Kent Road.

'Hooray' said Murphy. 'Back in Monopoly land. OK, I know the way from here.'

The next half hour consisted of a spirited argument between Murphy and the sat nav, which had suddenly sprung back into life, with neither of them prepared to give ground. Eventually they made it to Finsbury Park and Murphy climbed out and stretched, noticing that Wilcox looked a bit weary. Probably had a late night.

Bella Webster was a tall young woman with spiky silver hair. Murphy liked the colour a lot, but reflected that it was really only available to the young. On an older person it was in danger of looking natural. Bella was on her own in the café, wiping down surfaces and clearing up.

'I thought about closing the café for a few days when I heard,' she said, 'but then I wondered what I would do all day just sitting around thinking about it. It's easier to keep busy. I've spent some time with mum and dad, but nothing I can do is going to make any difference. Anyway, I'm closing in a few minutes and then we won't be disturbed. Would you like a coffee before I switch the machine off?'

'I'd love one,' said Murphy looking admiringly at the gleaming Gaggia. Wilcox shook his head, yawned and waved his water bottle.

'This has been a terrible loss for you,' said Murphy, when Bella had returned with her coffee and switched the door sign to Closed.

'It certainly has.' She folded her arms and leaned across the table. 'And my poor mum and dad. They are heartbroken and I can't help them, nobody can. Liam and I were very close as kids, but then we grew up and went in different directions. I didn't see that much of him the last few years. Maybe once every few months he'd come in here for a coffee and a chat. So, we didn't exactly make time for each other, but I always knew he was there. And now, of course, I wish I'd spent more time with him, thought more about him, contacted him more, showed him how much I cared about him. All that stuff. There are people I only really know through Facebook that I spend more time interacting with than I did with Liam.'

'I don't think that's what's important,' said Murphy. 'The point is that if he had ever needed help, he'd have come to you, you'd have been there.'

'But I wasn't, was I?' Bella grabbed a paper napkin from the pile on the table, wiped her eyes and blew her nose. 'Something really bad happened to him and I wasn't there.'

'It probably wasn't a situation in which anything could have been done,' said Murphy. 'I wanted to ask you if Liam had any kind of drug history. I thought you'd know more about that than your mum and dad.'

Bella shook her head. 'Liam was never in with the druggy crowd. That was more me than him, to be honest and he used to give me lectures about it – how dangerous they were and did I want to end up a crack addict. All that sort of stuff. I think he was right about drugs – apart from anything else, you don't know whether what you're taking has been adulterated. But that wasn't Liam's thing. He was into rugby and cricket, so drinking was the thing, not drugs.'

Murphy took a sip of her coffee. 'He had only taken a moderate amount of ecstasy and that may have had no bearing on what happened. For some reason his heart stopped. It's referred to as sudden cardiac death. It's unusual in young people, but it happens. Don't feel bad that you weren't there. Even if you had been in the room with him and you'd been a trained nurse, it's very unlikely that you'd have been able to save him.'

'You're saying he just – died?'

'Yes, that's what happened.'

Bella shook her head slowly, as if in disbelief. 'He didn't kill himself.'

'We don't think so,' said Murphy.

Bella burst into tears. 'Oh My God. I'm sorry. I just thought… I'm just so glad he didn't.'

'No, it looks like he didn't,' said Murphy. 'I think that's some comfort to your parents too. But we did find what looked like a suicide note, and if you're up for that I'm going to show it to you.'

Bella nodded wordlessly, wiped her eyes and blew her nose again.

Murphy pulled the note out of her case and put it on the table. Bella stared at it and frowned.

'Do you recognise the writing?'

She shook her head. 'No that's not his writing. I've probably only ever seen random bits of his writing, because everything we've done for years has been on keyboards and screens, but if I think of birthday cards and stuff like that, no there's nothing familiar about this. Even though it's in caps, I can see it's not Liam's writing.'

'That's what we thought,' said Murphy. 'Your parents said the same thing. We're going to go back through his flat, see if we can find anything else that he's written, but this looks at the moment like it was written by somebody else.'

'But why would anybody do that?' She looked at it again. 'AXIOM. I think that was the name of the project he was assigned to. He mentioned it once, like there were problems with it, but I didn't pay much attention. I really wish I had, now that it's too late. This seems to suggest that he killed himself because of the project. That's absurd. He would never have killed himself. Even if the project failed. Why would that matter so much?'

'That's what I want to find out,' said Murphy. 'We'll make enquiries at his workplace, see what comes up and we'll let you know. If anything else occurs to you, give us a ring. Thank you for the coffee.'

'The thing is,' said Wilcox, as she fastened her seatbelt, 'there's nothing left for us to investigate. It looks like he died of natural causes. In that case, no crime has been committed. The fake suicide note is irrelevant, it's not a crime to have written it. We should really leave it and move on. That's certainly what Bellweather will tell us to do.'

'But I want to know,' said Murphy. 'Don't you want to know? That note had no fingerprints on it, so somebody didn't want us to know who had written it. Now that we've dealt with the family, I want to talk to those guys who brought him home and find out what happened. We'll have to wait until the morning for that, but let's have another quick look around the flat for now.'

An exhaustive search of the flat didn't turn up any handwritten material. No diaries, calendars or wall charts with things scribbled on. No shopping lists or to-do lists.

'Bella was right,' said Murphy. 'Nobody writes anything down these days. It's all on their phones. Let's knock on a few doors while we're here.'

There were five other flats in the block. Two didn't answer and two claimed to have seen nothing. But a young man in the flat across the hall had also come back late on Friday night and seen two men leaving the flat.

'They were young guys, pretty pissed, I think. Didn't look at them too closely, maybe they had beards. I didn't think they looked suspicious. One of them called out 'You get some sleep, mate' or something like that, just as they were closing the door. That's what I remember.'

'You saw them,' said Murphy. 'Did they see you?'

'Yeah, sure.'

'And did they call that to the person in the flat before they saw you, or after they saw you?'

He frowned. 'After. Yes, I'm sure it was after they'd seen me.'

Chapter Six

THE SOCO TECHNICIAN reported that they had found four different DNA samples at the flat. Liam, Sophie and two others. None of them on any databases.

Murphy entered Liam and Sophie's names into the PNC, just on the off-chance.

'Well, well,' she said.

'Don't tell me,' Wilcox said. 'They've both got form.'

'Actually, neither of them has got form. But Sophie's crossed our path before. She made a formal complaint two months ago about somebody stalking her. Let's see, she gave his name as Daniel Webb. There was no threat of violence, so it doesn't seem to have rung any alarm bells. She was advised to keep a diary and any other evidence, contact the stalking helpline and report back in a fortnight, which she didn't do. So, it was assumed that the problem had resolved itself and no further action was recommended.'

'That maybe explains why she wanted a male flatmate,' said Wilcox.

Murphy nodded. 'Maybe poor Liam was supposed to

keep her safe. We'll have another chat with her when we've finished looking into exactly what happened to him. Is his laptop unlocked yet?'

Wilcox nodded. 'Yes, I've been going through his social media. A pretty perfunctory LinkedIn profile and, other than that, just Facebook, which I'm looking at now.'

A few minutes later he looked up.

'There's nothing much here' he said. 'A Facebook post about a month ago about moving into a new flat. Something about wanting Tottenham to beat Arsenal. As it happens, they didn't. Arsenal thrashed them. I could have told him that was going to happen. Hope he hadn't put any money on it. Nothing much since. A few movies that he's been to and recommends, somebody else has come back and said, no mate, I thought it was crap. He's liked a couple of other people's posts. Somebody's selfie travel shot from Cape Town, somebody else's dog-doing-something-clever video. But nothing else from him. No reference to going to anywhere on Friday night. Nothing unusual. He wasn't a very active user. We could start checking into all his Facebook friends, but do we really want to do that?'

'OK' said Murphy, 'maybe we'll leave Facebook for the moment. So, let's see. He was alive when he arrived back in the taxi, we know that, but was he alive when the two men were seen leaving? Julie was chasing up the taxi driver. Let's go see if she's got anything.'

Julie Fraser was next door putting her coat on and logging off. She stopped when she saw them and picked up a pad on her desk.

'I should let you know' she said. 'Bellweather came in half an hour ago, just one of his little wanderings around. He asked me what I was working on and I had to tell him. He was pissed off. He said it was a waste of resources as there was no suspicion of foul play and he'd be having a word with you about it.'

'Him and his words,' said Murphy, waving a hand. 'They just go over my head these days. Anyway, what have you got?'

Julie scanned her pad. 'The taxi driver was called a nice guy, older person. He said he picked up these three guys outside a nightclub in Graham Road. He can't remember the name of it. He confirms Liam was alive – well, he said they were all alive, drunk but alive - but one of them looked worse for wear. He was asked to wait while they took the most drunk one indoors, flat in Dalston. They kept him waiting about ten minutes and then he dropped the other two off. He's given us a description of the other two, one blonde and one dark, apart from that neither of them seemed to have any distinguishing features. Except the dark one had a beard. He says he had no reason the think anything was wrong, except all three of them were inebriated, but that's not unusual on a Friday night. He was mainly thankful they hadn't been sick in the cab.'

Chapter Seven

LIAM WEBSTER WORKED for a US-owned company called Frexon, located in Islington, on the Caledonian Road. That much they had been told by his parents. The website stated that Frexon stores customers' data and also corrects and upgrades it and produces reports. It said a lot of other things about open-source and version control, which Murphy decided she didn't need to know. It was very high-tech, that much was clear, and it claimed to employ over 100 data scientists and engineers in six countries.

The building was the usual glass and steel construction with a large, empty floor area, obviously intended to give an impression of space and light and air – and money. The list behind the reception desk told them that Frexon was on the third floor. Murphy smiled and waved her badge at the porter behind the desk, who looked somewhat taken aback, and they headed for the lift.

The Frexon receptionist had very black hair tied in three bunches on top of her head and a ring through her nose. She looked Murphy and Wilcox up and down as if they were a phenomenon she had not previously encountered. When Murphy showed her badge, she waved them to a sofa while she summoned somebody to help them.

'Why did she look at us like that?' she whispered to Wilcox.

'Because we're old,' he whispered back. 'Or, at least... you are.'

'Well, I'm glad to have that clarified,' she whispered back as a young woman in artfully ripped jeans and a man's waistcoat approached them.

'Hello. I'm Claudia Woodley. I gather you have some news for us about Liam.' She led the way to a pair of sofas sectioned off by glass screens.

'It's not so much that we're here to bring you news,' said Murphy. 'We're here to ask you questions.'

'Well, OK.' Claudia seemed to take the rebuke in good part.

'Liam Webster was found dead in suspicious circumstances on Friday night,' said Wilcox. 'So we are looking into all aspects of his life and that includes his job.'

Claudia Woodley sank slowly into a seat. 'Liam's dead?' She stared at them.

'Yes, I'm afraid so. That means we have to establish exactly what happened to him.'

'Yes, yes of course you do. Oh, my goodness. I don't know what to say.'

'Perhaps,' said Wilcox, 'you can tell us, to begin with, how long he had worked here and what his job involved.'

'Right.' She sat up straight and took a deep breath. 'Liam joined us about two years ago. He's been working in my section. We undertake projects to format and organise data. That makes it useable for analysts and data scientists.

In practice our work and that of data scientists overlaps quite a lot.'

'And your section is working on something called AXIOM?' said Wilcox.

Claudia Woodley was silent for a few moments. 'How would you know about that?'

'We saw a note in his flat which referred to it. Perhaps you can tell us something about it.'

'It's pretty confidential,' she began. Murphy raised her eyebrows.

'OK.' Claudia sighed. 'AXIOM is a project to integrate existing storage facilities with AI. Artificial Intelligence' she added.

'And who were Liam's closest colleagues?'

'He was in a team with Ben and Alfie. Ben Riley and Alfie Worthington.'

'We'll need to speak to them,' said Wilcox. 'But first, perhaps you can tell us a bit more about Liam, how he was, whether he had any problems, how he was doing at work.'

'You don't mean that he…?'

'We're still not sure what happened' said Wilcox, 'so we're grateful for any insight you can give us.'

Claudia breathed deeply. 'Liam was a good guy' she said. 'I guess I have to say 'was'. It feels really weird, I can't believe he's not coming back. Anyway. He worked hard and he was thorough. He got on with everybody, as far as I know. And I would have said he had a very happy disposition, but now of course… we don't know. Maybe there were things bothering him that he never talked about. And to be honest, there's not much personal chitchat goes on here. We have very tight deadlines, so people have their heads down most of the time. I'm so sorry this has happened and we'll miss him.'

'Yes, we understand,' said Wilcox. 'Perhaps now we could speak to' he checked his notes, 'Ben and Alfie.'

'I'll go and fetch them.'

'And perhaps you could find us an office,' said Murphy.

Claudia nodded. 'OK. I'll see what I can do.'

'This chatting on the sofa is all a bit cosy' she said to Wilcox, as Claudia walked away. 'I like to get my interviewees sitting across a table from me, paying attention. Especially when I have interesting questions to ask them.'

Claudia returned a few moments later and escorted them to a corner office with a large desk. It was constructed of glass partitions, but did appear to be at least partially soundproofed.

'This will be OK,' said Wilcox looking around, as Claudia left them. 'You can threaten them verbally without anybody hearing, but if you try any physical roughing up, everybody will be able to see and health and safety will know about it.'

Murphy was prevented from replying by the arrival of two young men. Ben was blond and clean-shaven, Archie had curly black hair and a beard. Both looked apprehensive.

Murphy smiled at them and gestured to the two seats on the other side of the desk.

'Thank you, Ms Woodley,' she said pointedly. Claudia sniffed and withdrew, closing the door behind her.

'OK' said Murphy. 'She will have told you that Liam has been found dead. Now that the boss has gone, you can both tell me what you've been up to.'

They turned and looked at each other. 'It's very shocking.' said Ben 'We've been up to nothing,' he added.

'OK, let's approach it another way. Tell us what happened Friday night,' said Murphy.

'We usually go for a drink after work on a Friday,' said Ben.

'So that's what you did?'

He nodded. 'A bunch of us. We went to the King's Arms, just round the corner. About 6.30.'

'OK,' said Wilcox. 'So that's you two plus Liam and who else?'

'Tim — he's one of the analysts — and Becky from Finance.'

'What happened then?'

'We all stayed in there about an hour, maybe hour and a half. Then Tim and Becky went home and we stayed about another hour or so. Then we went to get a kebab.' Murphy nodded. This agreed with the PM findings.

'OK, so you hung around a street corner and ate your kebabs,' she said. 'Then what?'

'Then we decided to go clubbing,' said Archie. 'Place called 'Martha's'. It's in Hackney. Graham Road. Had to queue for about an hour. Then we had a bit of an argument with the doorman, because they only wanted to let in women. But we got in eventually.'

'And what happened in the club?'

Ben shrugged. 'We danced a bit, not so much, had another drink.'

'Drugs?'

They both shook their heads.

Wilcox sighed. 'Come on,' he said. 'The price they charge for drinks in those places, drugs are the cheaper option. And we know Liam had taken ecstasy.'

Now they were both nodding. 'Just one tab each,' said Ben. 'Then the dancing became a bit more enjoyable. We left about one, maybe a bit after that — all three of us were pretty wasted by then.'

'And then you took a taxi,' said Wilcox.

'How do you know?'

'We know because we've got you on CCTV.'

They both looked alarmed at this.

'Now carry on and tell us the rest,' said Murphy.

'The taxi dropped Liam off first,' said Archie.

'And you both escorted him inside.'

'That's right,' said Ben. 'He was pretty incapable, so we got him up to his flat. He collapsed into an armchair. And then we left.'

'Just like that?' said Murphy. They nodded. 'So that would have taken what, about four minutes?'

They nodded again.

'Only the taxi driver says he waited ten minutes,' she said, 'so that's six minutes unaccounted for.'

'It was probably a bit more than four minutes,' said Ben. 'We were in bad shape, so none of us were moving fast.'

'And what shape was Liam in when you left?'

'He was OK,' said Alfie. 'Probably half-asleep.'

'What can you tell us about this?' Murphy placed the copy of the note on the table.

'Nothing,' said Ben.

'Nor me,' said Alfie. 'Did Liam write it?'

'I'm rather thinking,' said Murphy, 'that one of you two wrote it.'

They both shook their heads vigorously.

'Why would Liam have written something like this?' said Wilcox. 'If he had written it.'

'Dunno,' said Alfie. 'Except maybe he was a bit worried about AXIOM. I guess we all are – a bit.'

'Why? What's wrong with it?'

'It's had a few problems,' said Ben. 'Data corruption, bit

of data loss. And a bit over budget, a lot over budget. But it's always like that with projects.'

'OK,' said Murphy. 'Let's have a couple of sheets of paper.'

They looked at each other and then some sort of agreement seemed to pass between them. Ben opened the drawer to the printer sitting on the desk and extracted two sheets.

Murphy placed them in front of Ben and Alfie with two biros, taken from a container on the desk. 'This is just like school, isn't it? Name on the top of the paper, then copy out this note in your best capitals. No cheating.'

For a minute it looked like they were going to refuse, then Archie picked up a biro and Ben did the same.

''Very good' said Murphy when they had finished. 'Now we'd like to take your fingerprints and DNA for elimination purposes. Is that OK?'

'But you know we were there,' said Ben.

'Yes,' said Wilcox. 'But somebody else might have been there after you. So, we need to eliminate your DNA and prints.'

'I DON'T REALLY KNOW why we bothered with all that' said Wilcox, as they left. 'It certainly put the wind up them, but for what? He probably died of natural causes, after all.'

'One of them wrote that note,' said Murphy. 'And didn't you think it was odd that they didn't ask us how Liam died? He could have been shot or stabbed, for all they know.'

'I think they're actually not all that clever,' said Wilcox. 'Despite all the brainy data science stuff. And I don't know how we're going to get all these samples we've taken analysed. We have no budget for it.'

'Leave it with me,' said Murphy. 'I'll think of something.'

Chapter Eight

SOPHIE WAS ON THE WALL. The wall was good. It required complete mindfulness, everything else was swept into abeyance. And it required commitment. You had to commit to each move before you made it. You had to give the body an unequivocal command if you wanted it to obey. Anything hesitant and you were done for. The time for hesitation had definitely passed. Life was what went by while you were wondering what to do. It was surely better to make a decision and take action, and then regret it later, if necessary, than it was to pass all that time as a bystander, regretting what you hadn't done. If you just clung to the wall for too long without moving, you were done for. Your limbs would stop obeying.

Bouldering today, no ropes. Just you and your fingertips. You had to know how to fall, but that was part of the fun. Not that anything felt much like fun at the moment. But this served a purpose. Hanging in there with your body kept in place by the strength of your fingertips and your toes, it concentrated the mind. Kept all those other thoughts out of the way.

She was doing a harder route today. One she'd never done before. Almost vertical. Very small grips. Not much to get your fingers around. When you were feeling a bit self-destructive, a bit self-harmy, it was amazing how far you could go outside your comfort zone. Falling from a greater height would give her some relief. It beat cutting anyway, she wasn't going back to that.

She edged along and grabbed carefully at the handhold above her head. Locked her fingertips into place. Stop, breathe, consolidate. She swung one of her legs across and then followed with the other. So far, so good. She concentrated on the feeling in her arms. Really gripping hard with the fingertips was making her forearms ache, but she was used to that, it was a good ache. It meant she was building up muscle. Building powerful hands and forearms. All the better to open jars with. And do other things.

The guy on the wall next to hers went up past her. Effortlessly, like a giant spider. No brainer really. His arms and legs were longer than hers. She'd been stationary for too long. Time to stretch for the next handhold. Her fingers were getting a bit damp, should have used more chalk. The next one was hard, very little to hold onto, but what the hell. She swung her body across. Her fingers slid off and suddenly she was falling.

Chapter Nine

MARTHA'S CLUB was located in a basement in Graham Road, not far from Victoria Park. The sign was blue neon and probably looked good lit up at night. In daylight you could see the pigeon droppings encrusted on it. The steps down were littered with cigarette ends and the odd nitrous oxide canister, and the handrail was coated in a grey deposit.

'This shows how bad the pollution is here,' said Wilcox, looking at his palm and fishing in his other pocket for a tissue.

'I guess that's right,' said Murphy. 'Lots of hot little hands will have been clutching it last night and taking away all the muck, and now there's a new layer already.'

A bang on the heavy black door didn't produce any response, but dim lights could be seen through the window.

'Give it another go,' said Murphy. Wilcox banged harder and a voice from within yelled 'Go away. We're closed.'

'Police!' Murphy yelled and a few minutes later they

heard the bolts being drawn back. A rumpled man with a protruding belly and a grubby T-shirt glared at them.

Murphy smiled warmly at him as they showed their badges. 'Good man. For a minute there I thought we'd have to go back for the battering ram.'

'Wassitabout?'

'Perhaps you should invite us in Mr..?' said Wilcox.

'Terry,' he grunted and held the door open.

Murphy found that it took a few seconds for her eyes to adjust to the dim lighting. The ceiling was black and there were wires and cables and bulbs everywhere. It reminded her of the health and safety module she was supposed to have done. Not your ideal working environment. A middle-aged man in jeans and a white shirt peeled himself away from the bar and came towards them, hand outstretched.

'It's OK, Terry,' he said and the man with the belly lumbered off. 'Ian Fallowell' he announced, turning his attention to Murphy, and the introductions were made.

'Are you the owner, Mr Fallowell?' asked Wilcox.

He rubbed his hands together. 'That's right. Me and my business partner, we're joint owners. So how can I help you?'

'We're making enquiries about one of the customers you had in here on Friday night,' said Wilcox.

'I couldn't begin to tell you who was in here on Friday night. Place was rammed. I wouldn't know anything about any individual customer. Why? What's he done?'

'He's done nothing,' said Wilcox. 'He's dead.'

'What?' His face froze for a few seconds, then he frowned and crossed his arms. 'Nothing happened here on Friday night. It was a normal night.'

'The person in question spent the evening here, then went home and was found dead the next morning. We're going over his movements to establish exactly what happened.'

Ian Fallowell shrugged. 'But, like you said, he went home. Nothing happened to him here.'

'He had drugs in his system,' said Wilcox, 'which we think he probably obtained here. Were you personally here on Friday night?'

'Not for the whole evening, no. But there were plenty of people on duty here. We have a minimum staffing requirement. Health and safety, we're very particular about that. We'd have known if anything untoward had happened.'

'We'd like to look at your CCTV,' said Murphy.

He nodded and sighed. 'Wait here a minute while I go and sort out the discs.'

'Doesn't look too glamorous in daytime, does it?' said Wilcox, peering around.

'Certainly doesn't,' said Murphy. 'But then it doesn't need to. Probably looks like a really cool venue at night. Nobody notices the dirty windows when the sun's not trying to shine through them and people dancing and waving their arms in the air don't look down at the floor too much.'

Ian Fallowell reappeared and motioned them into an office with a desk and two screens.

'This is the front door and this is inside' he explained. 'I've set them both to Friday night.'

'These queues at the front door are really helpful,' said Wilcox. 'People having to stand there for ages. Gives you a good chance to spot who they are.'

Liam could clearly be seen queueing with Ben and Alfie at 10.37. None of them were making any attempt to hide from the camera. Footage inside from a few hours later showed them dancing energetically.

'They've had themselves sorted,' Murphy pronounced. Ian Fallowell said nothing.

'So what do you do about drugs?' she asked.

He shrugged. 'We don't frisk people on the way in, but we look out for any dealing. People go to the toilets to swap drugs, but we can't have CCTV in there for obvious reasons.'

Liam could now be seen sitting down and fanning his face, which was pink and shiny. Ben joined him and then Alfie appeared with drinks. 'Still looks OK' Wilcox remarked.

Murphy nodded. 'Let's speed it up a bit, look at where they leave.'

At 1.09 the trio could be seen making their way out and the outdoor camera picked them up hailing a taxi. None of them looked like they could have walked a straight line.

'And here's our driver' said Wilcox as the taxi drew up and they staggered towards it.

'OK,' said Murphy. She turned to Ian Fallowell. 'I'd like a copy of these discs.'

'You can take the originals,' he said. 'We'd have overwritten them tomorrow anyway.'

'Fresh air and sunlight,' said Wilcox, taking a deep breath as they made their way back up the steps.

'Sounds like you're not a clubber at heart, Kevin,' said Murphy. 'That's worrying in one so young.'

Chapter Ten

THE ADDRESS SOPHIE had given them for her mother turned out to be a ground-floor flat in a purpose-built block just off the Bethnal Green Road.

'I don't really understand what we're doing here,' said Wilcox, as they got out of the car. 'It looks like no crime has been committed.'

'There are just two things snagging my attention,' said Murphy. 'Like who wrote the note and why Sophie wondered whether somebody could have killed him. So just humour me for a bit longer. As soon as we've cleared those up, we'll get back to the knives and drugs, I promise.'

He shrugged and rang the doorbell.

Murphy smiled at the spy hole and held up her badge and the door was opened by Sophie who smiled uncertainly at them.

'Just a quick chat' said Murphy and Sophie held the door open for them. She was wearing track pants and a T-shirt and Murphy's attention was drawn to he left forearm, where there were a series of white scars.

'Come through' she said. 'My mum's in here.' She led the way into a comfortably-furnished room where all the seating was grouped around the TV.

The woman in question was sitting on the type of riser recliner armchair recommended for the elderly. You just pressed a button and it slowly tipped you out. Murphy had always promised herself that, no matter how bad her knees got, she would never have one of those. Stowed behind her armchair was a wheelchair, so in her case, the need was definitely justified.

'I'm Eileen Frensham, and I'm afraid I can't get up' she said as they introduced themselves. Another woman rose from the sofa – middle-aged with grey hair, but obviously able-bodied. 'This is Glenda,' said Eileen.

'Glenda Morrison' said the woman and they all sat down. Eileen grabbed the remote and muted the sound on a quiz show running on the television.

'Glenda's my carer' she said. 'The woman who makes my life possible.'

'Arthritis?' asked Murphy and Eileen nodded.

'Most people who have arthritis don't have it as badly as I do' she said. 'It came on very suddenly. If I try to stand, my hips are very painful and the swollen joints in my hands make a lot of normal tasks difficult. Some days I wake up and feel much better, other days the pain is really bad. I'm on cortisone, which is not great and has lots of steroid side effects, but it stops my joints from seizing up completely. Glenda takes me out in the wheelchair every day, which gives me some fresh air and I was so lucky to find this place on the ground floor. Stairs are out of the question for me now.'

'It's good to meet you both,' said Murphy. 'We just wanted a quick word with Sophie.'

'We can talk in front of mum,' said Sophie. 'She knows everything that goes on.'

'OK,' said Murphy. 'When we spoke to you at the flat, you said that you found it hard to believe that Liam had committed suicide. You thought somebody else could have killed him. Why did you say that?'

Sophie was silent for a moment. 'Because he wasn't somebody who would have killed himself. But maybe I was wrong. I hadn't known him that long, after all. Did he kill himself?'

'We're still investigating,' said Murphy, 'so I can't say much yet about how or why he died. Is that the only reason? Or did you have somebody in mind?'

Sophie was silent.

'We are pretty certain,' said Murphy, 'that Liam did not write that note. So, if you think somebody else could have been responsible for his death, I'd be interested to know who you had in mind.'

'I think you should tell them, Sophie,' said her mother.

Sophie sighed. 'It was just an immediate reaction,' she said. 'I was upset, probably in shock, so I just said the first thing that came into my head.'

'But presumably it came into your head for a reason,' said Murphy. 'And I'd like to know what that was. Who were you thinking about?'

Sophie was silent. 'Was it Daniel Webb?' asked Murphy.

'How do you know about him?'

'We're the police,' said Murphy. 'We know everything. Actually, we don't, but we do manage a certain level of record keeping. You made a police report about him stalking you.'

'That was nothing really, it just...'

'It was not nothing,' interrupted Eileen. 'I visited her flat and found one of his letters lying around. I made her report it to the police.'

'OK. Now tell us exactly what has been happening with him.'

A look passed between Sophie and her mother. Sophie cleared her throat. 'He's been kind of stalking me.'

'What, following you around?'

'Sometimes. But it's like he doesn't so much follow me as appear in places. And write me letters. But it's not so serious really.'

'Sounds serious enough to me,' said Murphy. 'And that made you think he could have killed Liam?'

'No, not really, it was just me being stupid. I think I was a bit hysterical after I found Liam. As I said, he sends me letters and in his last letter he referred to Liam. Not by name, he doesn't know his name. But that's what I thought of when I realised Liam was dead.'

Murphy frowned. 'Have you got this letter?'

'I've been throwing them away' said Sophie, 'but I think I still have the last two.'

She reached behind the sofa for her handbag and scrabbled around in it, emerging with two folded and dog-eared sheets of paper.

Murphy unfolded them and Wilcox looked over her shoulder.

'Laser printer' he said. 'Nothing to identify where they came from.'

Sophie, my darling.

I'm sitting here just thinking about you. About your wonderful pre-Raphaelite hair and your blue eyes – and the rest of you. I want to run my fingers through that hair and soon I will. That's a very cool area you're living in. Lots of street life. I had a drink in the Duke of Kent. I wondered if I might see you in there. Is that your local? And do you do your shopping in the Tesco Metro on Dalston Lane?

So much yet to discover about each other...

And one dated a week later:

Well, I've seen your live-in man darling. I'm of the opinion that he's just a flatmate, nothing more. I don't think you can be after his body. Very poor muscle-tone, I don't think you could actually prefer him to moi. He'll have to go in the end, of course. Or perhaps you can move in with me and we'll let him stay on and pay us rent.

What do you think?

'Interesting' said Wilcox. 'Doesn't put his name. Gives him a bit of deniability.'

'There were a couple of earlier ones,' said Sophie, 'and the first one did have his name, but I chucked them away.'

'That's a shame,' said Murphy. 'Keep anything that arrives from now on. How did you meet this guy?'

She hesitated. 'On Tinder.'

Murphy nodded. 'OK. That's a perfectly valid way to meet somebody. And what happened?'

'We went out for drinks. It was just once. Then I decided that I didn't want to see him again. I sent him a message to tell him that. Not in those words of course, I was very tactful about it, or I thought I was. I hoped he wouldn't be too bothered but I guess he was cross.'

Murphy folded her arms. 'Oh, he was cross, was he? He'll have to get over himself. These letters suggest he's been spying on you, following you maybe. Were you aware of that?'

'Well, I never actually spotted him following me, but I guessed he could be. Perhaps he's good at it. He did turn up in places where I was once or twice, once in a bar when I had arranged to meet somebody and another time, he passed me when I was running, so maybe he'd followed me.'

'That's smart as well,' said Wilcox. 'He can claim coincidence, just happened to be in the same place, whatever.'

Murphy frowned. 'And do you have any reason to think this guy could be violent?'

She shook her head. 'No. He's never threatened anything violent.'

'But he's got you scared?'

'Yes, I suppose he has. But no, not really that. Not so much scared, but certainly on edge. I keep wondering if I'm being watched. I think he's amusing himself at my expense, but I'm a bit afraid of what he might do.'

'Have you been back to the police about this?'

'I only went once, when it first started. They told me to contact the stalking helpline and to keep a stalking diary.'

'And have you done those things?'

She shook her head. 'No. I guess I should have done. I didn't want to take it that seriously. I didn't want it to be a thing. I hoped he'd just get fed up and leave me alone.'

'If there's no indication that he could be violent, the police won't have rushed round to see him,' said Murphy, 'but it's important that you keep a diary, keep all the letters, maybe take a photo if you see him hanging about. All of this evidence is important if we want to bring charges against him. Do you have an address for him?'

'No, not a home address, but I know where he works. He told me. Couldn't wait to tell me. He has his own company. I think it's called McEwan and Webb in Holland Park somewhere. It's certainly something and Webb, anyway.'

'And what do they do?'

'They're estate agents. Quite posh estate agents, I think. That was the impression I got anyway. He was telling me all about the expensive houses he has sold.'

Murphy raised her eyebrows. 'Really? Maybe I'll pay them a visit. The other thing I came to tell you was that you can go home now. We've finished with the flat.'

'That's great.' Sophie's tone belied her words.

'You don't look like it's great. Are you scared to go back?'

'A bit, but I'll be fine.'

'Get yourself another flat mate as quickly as you can, and if anything happens or you get any more letters, pass them on to us.'

She nodded. 'Thanks.'

Glenda escorted them out. 'I'll keep an eye on things' she said.

'That will be good,' said Murphy.

'Why are we getting involved in this?' asked Wilcox, as they got into the car. 'It's not in our remit. We don't think Liam Webster was unlawfully killed.'

Murphy shrugged. 'No, that's right.' Her expression hardened. 'But I don't like what I've just heard. Women deserve not to be stalked and harassed and I'm going to make sure he knows that.'

Chapter Eleven

MURPHY ARRIVED HOME – on time, for once – to see Susannah sitting in the kitchen. Her sister looked annoyingly at home, draped across a chair, while the others bustled around her. Murphy hung her coat up, kicked off her shoes and dropped her keys in the bowl.

'Why do people always come round here at dinner time?'

'Don't worry Murph, there's plenty to go round,' said James.

'Artichoke barigoule,' said Susannah brightly. 'I'd never attempt such a thing myself, so it's great to go somewhere else and eat it.'

'It's a triumph,' said Clive as he brought the dish to the table. 'Even if I do say so myself.'

Murphy washed her hands and then reached across and detached one of the leaves. 'It's very good' she admitted, as she bit the end off. 'So, who's cooking at your house?' she asked Susannah.

'Simon. He's making shepherd's pie for the girls. He's become more domesticated these days.'

Murphy smiled inwardly. Since his disastrous fling-with-a-younger-woman episode, Simon had been working hard at redeeming himself. Susannah might have forgiven him but Murphy was withholding judgement.

'That's a good development, isn't it?' she said 'Glad he's making himself useful. I like the idea of men tied to the kitchen.'

'I wouldn't regard myself as tied to the kitchen,' said Clive with a sniff as he dished out.

'No,' said Murphy. 'In your case it's a labour of love. That's why you can do better than shepherd's pie.' She turned to Susannah. 'Now, is this visit due to anything specific or have you just come to see us?'

Susannah chewed and swallowed before replying. 'Mum. It's about Mum.'

'Why? Is there something wrong?'

'No, not as far as I know. But she's taken up with some man.'

Murphy felt a stab of surprise. Their vague, diffident mother had been devastated by the unexpected death of her husband several years earlier, but had come through and re-established herself as a working artist. But as for a new relationship, at her age…

'Really? Who is he?'

Susannah frowned. 'From what I've been able to gather, from the little she told me, she met him on a trip to India in the spring and they've kept in touch. He's called Mark Bingham. He has a house in Brighton, so she's spent some time there over the summer. He's retired, I think.'

'And that's all you know?'

'That's all I've been told. My investigation techniques are probably not as good as yours.'

'Have you googled him?' said James.

'Actually no,' said Susannah. 'That's a good idea. Although, at their age, there's probably not much of a profile.'

'But it's altogether a good thing, isn't it?' said Clive. 'Good for her. It means she has company. You don't have to worry so much about her.'

'That's true of course,' said Murphy. 'But Susannah probably thinks we should check he doesn't have a wife in the attic.'

'Looks like he's not on Facebook' said Susannah, scrolling on her phone. 'But is that a bit suspicious in itself?'

'Not necessarily,' said Murphy. 'Not everybody bothers with it. I don't for a start. But he should be on something, I suppose. LinkedIn maybe?'

'There are a few people called Mark Bingham, but none in Brighton.' Susannah was still scrolling.

'But what are we actually worrying about here?' said Murphy. 'Mum has had a rough few years. She's entitled to be friends with whoever she wants. Do you think he's planning to steal all her money?'

Susannah shrugged. 'If he was after money, I don't think mum would be a prime target. I'd just feel happier if we knew a bit more about him. I thought maybe you could look him up.'

Murphy stared at her. 'Look him up? What? On the PNC? Are you out of your mind? All attempts to access the PNC are recorded. I'd be busted back to traffic in less than the time it would take Bellweather to organise the disciplinary action. And that would be pretty fast.'

'Forget it. It was just a thought.'

'It's a thought to put to the back of your mind,' said Murphy.

'Maybe you should just ask to meet him,' said James. 'That's the old-school way of doing it.'

'That's right,' said Clive. 'Remember what it was like when you were teenagers and you had to introduce your boyfriends to the parents? I have memories of that, scarred me for life. But it's just the other way around now. You're the responsible adults.'

'That's right,' said Murphy. 'I hope he hasn't got a motorbike. Maybe we'll impose a curfew on her.'

Chapter Twelve

IT WAS CROWDED in the Washhouse Bar, but Sophie liked being in busy places, where she could just disappear into the mass of everybody else. When she was doing physical things, when she was at work, when she was really tiring herself out, then she was strong, in control. The crap going round in her head was kept at bay. The rest of the time she liked to be where stuff was happening, where she could just be an onlooker, with her attention fixed on anything external to herself.

There was plenty of external stuff to focus on here. The building was a huge brick construction which had been built centuries earlier as a laundry, with high ceilings to relieve the pressure of the steam. Looking around carefully, Sophie could see where internal walls had been taken down and replaced with steel beams. It was a proper job; the integrity of the building had been preserved. Although, considering that generations of exploited women had sweated in here over boilers and washboards and irons, integrity was perhaps a misnomer.

Sudden Death

When she had finished analysing the building, she had another sip of G&T and turned her attention to the clientele. All of them were young, some quite a lot younger than her, and she flicked her gaze around them quickly. Two men further down the bar were having an animated conversation while concurrently, furtively, looking around – looking for women. One of them looked a bit like Daniel Webb and she looked him up and down, scanning for weak points. Bit of a round tummy. That was bad. No muscle there to protect the internal organs. A hard right-hander in there would get right through to his diaphragm and then, while he was still bent over, a swift uppercut with the left. That would tilt him backwards, ready for a knee to the...

'Sorry I'm late.' A breathless Freya erupted from somewhere and they hugged.

Sophie smiled. 'No problem. You're always late, so I know what to expect. It's factored in.'

'God, am I really that bad? I think actually I am. How I hold down a job is a mystery to me.'

'You hold down a job because, despite your appalling timekeeping, you're still better than all the rest,' said Sophie, turning round to attract the barman's attention.

At that moment, the Daniel Webb lookalike and his friend slid along the bar towards them, one of them holding his debit card between two fingers. Sophie couldn't believe it. Now that Freya was here, they calculated that there was one each, so they had decided to move in. Maybe the creep had noticed her looking at him and thought it was because she fancied him.

'We can buy our own drinks, thank you' she told them.

He smiled, the one with the debit card.

'We just thought you looked interesting and maybe we

could chat to you for a bit.' That was the other one, trying his hand at being disarming.

'That would be lovely,' said Sophie, insincerely, 'but I'm afraid this is a business meeting.'

His face fell. Dismay cloaked in good humour, and swiftly replaced by annoyance.

'OK. Right.' They retreated back to the other end of the bar.

Freya was trying hard not to laugh. 'You were a bit hard on them, Soph. They didn't mean any harm.'

'I thought I got rid of them quite elegantly.'

'I must admit, it worked pretty fast.'

Sophie smiled. 'And would you have wanted to waste a couple of hours, or even half an hour, chatting to them, listening to them going on about their jobs and their vehicles and their extreme sports, when we've come here to talk to each other?'

'Point taken. And how have you been?'

Sophie hesitated. Freya was a recent friend, recent as in last year. That meant there was no messy backstory. They had met at Sophie's previous employer, where Freya still worked. Two young professional women. They knew nothing of each other's pasts, it was all present tense, no baggage. So, Freya was relaxing to be with. Sophie wouldn't be telling Freya how she really felt, the confused thoughts and emotions that rattled round in her head. She could pretend all of that didn't exist. It belonged to some other person, not the person sitting here now.

'Pretty much OK' she said. 'The new project's going a bit slow and lots of squawking going on about the budget. As far as I can see, it's going to go over, but we could have told them that in the first place. And I'd prefer to be back in the City. Oxford Street is horrible now, full of cheap rubbish shops and those oversized confectionery outlets that are probably a front for organised crime. Nowhere to go for lunch.'

Freya laughed. 'Talking of lunch, we got taken out to lunch by the new CEO yesterday and guess what? He's only just arrived and he's off again already. He starts paternity leave next week – his wife's having their first.'

Sophie felt something inside her clench. She smiled. 'I guess it's good that he's doing that' she said. 'I think a lot of men are not actually that keen on paternity leave. It can be tougher than staying at work. Who's taking over while he's away?'

Freya took a large swig of her drink. 'Well, that's another issue. Alison thought it should be her, and I thought so too, but they've given it to Matt. I mean, nice guy and all, but between you and me he doesn't know his arse from his elbow, so I'm going to be the one digging him out when it all goes wrong.'

'The thing to do when it all goes wrong' said Sophie, 'is to make sure you're not in the frame. Make sure you do that.'

Chapter Thirteen

DANIEL WEBB'S office in Holland Park was on the first floor of a regency building with a stucco front and large, very clean windows. The parking situation was not so favourable, but Murphy scribbled a note and put it under the windscreen. Maybe it would work.

'It won't work,' said Wilcox. 'Traffic wardens are wise to that. Nice area though. Office rents won't be cheap round here.'

'You never know,' said Murphy. 'It might be really squalid inside. But somehow, I don't think so.'

They announced their arrival to the entry phone and a minute later they were buzzed up. Opening the door on the first floor they were met by an enormous 3D model in the middle of the open-plan area.

'Looks like a church,' Murphy remarked to the handsome and artfully dishevelled man who was regarding them with folded arms and a quizzical expression.

'Yes. It is a church. Deconsecrated of course. Big project.'

'Lots of expensive flats?'

He nodded. 'A certain amount of social housing, it's *de rigeur* these days, but mostly expensive flats.'

Murphy looked him up and down. 'And you must be Daniel.'

'The same.'

'DI Murphy and DC Wilcox.' They showed their badges. He didn't look worried.

'You're an architect Daniel?'

'Not at all. Nothing so accomplished. My partners – Stanley and Audrey – they're the architects.' He waved an arm in the direction of two desks at the end of the office and the occupants waved back. 'I just manage the money and argue with the builders. We're selling off-plan to keep the wolf from the door, as they say. Now, to what do I owe the pleasure?' He led the way to the corner furthest away from Stanley and Audrey where two sofas were positioned perpendicular to each other.

'Sophie Carter,' said Murphy, looking carefully at him as she said it.

He smiled. 'Ah, the lovely Sophie.'

'Yes. She's been telling us something about you. Can I have your version of how you two met?'

'How we met,' he repeated musingly. 'Well, that's easy enough. She made the first move. That's what women do these days you know. She clicked on my Tinder profile. And we fell in love.'

Murphy raised her eyebrows. 'That's the women's magazine version, is it? Her recollection is a bit different on the 'fell in love' bit. And you clicked her back, or matched with her?'

'That's right.' he smiled. 'We became a matched pair. Like songbirds.'

'But it seems that she no longer wants to be part of this arrangement.'

'Is that what she's told you? That's just part of the game for her. She's playing what they used to call 'hard to get'. It's a ploy to keep me interested. Which I am, mostly.'

'What she says is that she's no longer interested. And you've been harassing her, writing her letters.'

He shrugged. 'How does writing letters amount to harassment? I've been writing her letters because I'm too busy to see her. She should appreciate that I've taken the time to write to her. Who says the art of letter-writing is dead? She's probably cross because I've neglected her. Anyway, I've only written her a couple. How many have you seen?'

'Two,' said Murphy.

'Well then.' He shrugged.

'From the letters I've seen,' said Murphy, 'you like to keep an eye on her. Have you been following her around?'

He shook his head. 'Give me a break. I don't have time to run round following people. Is that what she said? Does she have any evidence? I'm sure she'd love me to be following her.'

'In the last letter you sent Sophie you referred to her flatmate.'

'Did I? Maybe I did. I don't know the guy's name or anything about him, but I know he exists. Why? Has he complained about me as well?'

'He's dead.'

'What?' His mouth started to open and he shut it hurriedly. 'Dead how? And that's why you're here? You think that I had something to do with it?'

'Not necessarily,' said Murphy. 'But your behaviour is

encouraging us to look upon you as a person of interest. What were you doing on Friday night?'

He seemed to be thinking for a moment. 'Working late and then having dinner with Stanley and Audrey. At Germain in Notting Hill. Frightfully expensive and not really worth it, even if we are putting it on expenses. I don't recommend it. But this is ridiculous. I can't seriously be a suspect for anything. I didn't even know the guy.'

'I think you would be well advised to steer clear of Sophie Carter. It's best not to draw our attention to you, don't you think? We'll leave it there for the time being.'

They made their way out and the door shut behind them with a click.

'We may have overstepped the mark,' said Wilcox. 'I mean letting him think he's under suspicion for the death of somebody who probably died of natural causes. I'm not sure how we explain that one.'

'I'm not telling anybody about the PM results yet,' said Murphy. 'Something could still crop up to contradict what Linda said.'

'But what you really came here for was to warn him off Sophie Carter - and that's not our case.'

'It's not anybody's case and that's the problem. Nobody has the right to stalk women, not on my watch.'

Chapter Fourteen

WELL, *my love, I gather your faithful protector is no more. It may have seemed like a good idea to point the police in my direction, but it won't do you any good. You were the person in closest proximity to him, weren't you? Why did you do it Sophie? Did he force himself upon you? Or maybe he refused to force himself upon you? Maybe you weren't his type?*

Don't worry, I won't say a word. In fact, when the two clodhoppers arrived to beard me in my den, I said nothing. I didn't tell them any of the little secrets I've found out about you. Because you do have secrets, don't you Sophie? So now you have nobody to look after you. Let me offer my services instead.

xx

'I wasn't planning to show it to you' said Sophie 'I had just chucked it in the bin along with the rest of the junk mail I picked up from the flat.'

'I picked it up out of the bin and opened it,' said Eileen. 'Load of disgusting innuendo. It was I who insisted she call you, or I would have done it myself. I can't believe he's right in the head.'

'I don't know what he means about the secrets' said Sophie.

'Don't worry about it,' said Wilcox. 'Standard gaslighting technique.'

'It's a nasty little note,' said Murphy. 'And I don't mean the clodhoppers bit. He must know you'd be showing this to us and he's demonstrating that he's not bothered. Thinks he's bombproof. Any other appearances?'

'Yes, just one. He was around outside the site when I left last night, standing across the street, just looking at me. He didn't come over, he just stood there. It felt like all he wanted was to unnerve me. I made a point of not running, I didn't want him to think he had scared me. I ignored him and walked down the street. As soon as I was out of sight, I went down into the tube station. He didn't follow me.'

'You handled that well. But you shouldn't have to be handling it. It's ridiculous behaviour. Why do you think he's so interested in you?'

Sophie shrugged. 'I can't imagine. He's not in love with me. He hardly knows me. He's just having fun at my expense. Maybe he has nothing much else going on in his life.'

'Talking to him,' Murphy said, 'he gives the impression of being very pleased with himself, but that can be just a veneer. He's either disturbed in some way or he has some other agenda. He didn't seem like somebody disturbed. He seemed very relaxed. I'd say what he needs is something to disturb him. We may have to pay him another visit.'

'I think you should,' said Eileen, rising painfully to her feet and putting her arm around Sophie. 'He shouldn't be able to go round frightening women like that.'

'I'm not frightened mum,' said Sophie. 'I'm less frightened than you are. I think we should forget the whole thing. I'm able to look after myself.'

'He seems to thrive on attention,' said Murphy. 'And if he doesn't get it, he doesn't like that. So, I'll give him some attention. Let me have another word with him.'

Chapter Fifteen

MARK BINGHAM MUST ONCE HAVE BEEN an attractive man, Murphy thought, looking at him across the restaurant table. Actually, maybe he still was. Still had all his hair, not running to fat, clean-shaven. And it looked like he had all his own teeth. Having monitored Bellweather's scary veneers closely for so long, she figured she could spot them at a glance. She hoped her mother had not been seduced by a good-looking face and the ability to tell a story. He was telling one now.

'...and when they pulled the pipe out, half the wall collapsed.'

'As long as you didn't find a body behind it,' Susannah laughed. Murphy thought that only people who had never been confronted with a body could imagine it was amusing.

'As a matter of fact, I did have that thought,' Mark replied, 'just for a moment. But thankfully not. Although the cavity would have been big enough to hold a body.'

It was time to weigh in, get some information out of

him. 'How long have you lived in Brighton?' Murphy asked, tearing a piece of bread.

'Nearly ten years. I really love it there. I'm a keen swimmer so I wanted to be near the sea and, when I got close to retirement, I thought it was time to make a move. Eastbourne's where lots of people retire to, but I didn't want to mix just with retirees. Brighton is a much livelier place, great shops and pubs and restaurants.'

'The idea of retirement is a bit scary' said Murphy, 'but it also sounds like a lot of fun, in certain ways. Sometimes, when I have a bad day at work, I think I could make a pretty good fist of it.'

'It's great as long as you're fit and well,' said Valerie. 'Otherwise, you'd be stuck at home all day watching TV or getting sucked into social media.'

'You're not on social media much, are you, Mark?' Susannah was now doing her bit.

'Ah – you've checked me out. Well of course you would. I'd do the same myself. I used to be on Facebook – which is probably the platform of choice for somebody my age – but not anymore.'

He probably hoped that would be the end of it. Not as far as Murphy was concerned.

'What prompted you to leave?'

He sighed, then continued. 'To be honest, something unfortunate happened. This is embarrassing, but I've started now, so I might as well finish. About nine months after my wife died, I went onto Tinder and matched with a woman in London. We had a couple of dates but I soon decided she wasn't the right person for me. Nice woman, but I wouldn't have wanted to spend my declining years with her. I went ahead and told her this, not in those words of course, and hoped we could part amicably. Not a bit of it. She was absolutely affronted and the next day she posted a long, scurrilous comment on my Facebook page, hinting that I might have had something to do with my wife's death. I didn't, in case you're wondering, but my wife was wealthy in her own right, so that seemed to lend credence to it. I blocked her, of course, but she got one of her friends to repost it and then I started to get comments from other people on Facebook – people I didn't really know but they'd somehow ended up following me – and I just took the decision to be done with it all. I closed my Facebook account, took down my Tinder profile and decided to stay away from women. I came to the conclusion they were too dangerous.'

'You didn't think of suing this woman?' asked Susannah.

Mark Bingham shook his head. 'Not for a minute. That option is just for people who have time, money and headspace to burn. I put it behind me and kept my head down. I figured I'd learned a lesson. And then I met Valerie, which was such a wonderful and unexpected thing.'

'You don't know yet how dangerous I can be' said Valerie, smiling up at him.

'She's right,' said Susannah. 'Don't underestimate her.'

'I think it's true that women are a lot stroppier these days' said Murphy, 'but that's probably no bad thing. And most crimes are still committed by men.'

Chapter Sixteen

MURPHY'S DAY began with two phone calls. One was from the Crown Prosecution Service lawyer in charge of taking forward a rape case on which Murphy had spent hundreds of hours. 'Bugger,' she said, as she put the phone down. Wilcox looked up enquiringly.

'They are not pursuing the case against Christopher Dakin. Usual story. Examination of Molly Wright's phone has put the wind up them. Too much evidence of casual sex, therefore her claim that sex with Christopher Dakin was non-consensual is less likely to be believed. Or, at least, the CPS are not 100% certain of winning, so they won't do it.'

Wilcox nodded. 'We thought that might be the case, didn't we?'

Murphy shrugged. 'Yes, but I guess I still hoped they'd do the right thing. It's justice denied, that's what it is. After the whole physical exam and the rest of the horrible stuff that a rape victim has to go through. And I really hate this idea that if a woman has an active sex life, then she's fair game. If she's slept with Tom and Dick, how can she claim she didn't want to sleep with Harry? We'll have to go and see Molly and tell her.'

The second phone call was from Linda Fleming.

'That's as expected' said Murphy, as she put the phone down. 'Liam Webster's death is confirmed as due to natural causes, so no need for an inquest. That might be some comfort to his family. They can get on and arrange the funeral.'

'The only anomaly is the suicide note,' said Wilcox.

'Yes. I haven't forgotten that. I think there's only one answer really.'

MOLLY WRIGHT CAME to meet them in her lunch hour, hurrying briskly out of the beauty salon where she spent her time microblading eyebrows and administering Botox.

'It makes me feel worse than the rape,' she said, stirring her coffee shakily. 'I wish now I'd said nothing about it.'

'You were very brave,' said Murphy, 'and I can only apologise for the CPS decision. It's not the one I would have made, obviously. I hope you can recover and move on, although I know it won't be easy.'

'What I want most of all is never to see him again,' said Molly. 'That's the best I can hope for now. But I must admit, although I would have gone ahead with it, I was really scared about the court appearance, about being cross-examined by the defence and having all of my life spread around for everybody to hear about. I wasn't looking forward to that.'

'No, of course you weren't,' said Murphy. 'I think the worst outcome would have been for you to have gone through all that and for him then to have been found innocent. That would have been worse, and it could have happened. That's what the CPS did not want to risk.'

'Thank you for coming to tell me in person,' said Molly as they left the coffee shop.

'You're welcome,' said Murphy. 'You take care now.'

Chapter Seventeen

DANIEL WEBB HAD a small but functional flat in one of the better streets in Shepherd's Bush. The stairs were properly carpeted and looked like somebody was responsible for keeping them clean. He seemed completely unfazed when Murphy rang the bell and yelled 'Police.'

'Par for the course round here,' he said, opening the door to them with a smile. 'No shame in being visited by the police. I guess it will be different when I move to Holland Park.'

'Do you get a nice flat in the church?' asked Murphy, seating herself unasked on the leather sofa.

He spread his arms. 'Of course. Developer's perks. To be honest, I won't be sorry to leave Shepherd's Bush. When you talk about places that resist gentrification, Shepherd's Bush is right up there. It's a top-level resister.'

'Maybe people like it the way it is' said Murphy.

Daniel widened his eyes as if this was a new one on him. 'I guess that's possible, there's no accounting for tastes of course, but without change there's no growth.'

'And no money to be made,' finished Murphy.

He laughed 'I see you've got me bang to rights.'

'Perhaps more than you realise. We're investigating a matter of stalking. I think you know what we're talking about. And we've been given your latest missive.' She handed it to him.

'Well, my love, how are you coping in that flat on your own? I looked through your window last night – you looked very alone. You were wearing that blue shirt that I like. I was hoping that you would undress before you drew the curtains, but it was not to be.

No matter, we will be together in the fullness of time. Eventually you will have to stop denying it.'

'The lovely Sophie' he sighed theatrically. 'I don't think of it as stalking, not at all. I'm still hoping to win her round, you know. I'm just a man in love and what's wrong with that?'

'I don't much care how you think of it and what's wrong with that is that the woman in question isn't interested.'

He shook his head. 'But that's where you're wrong. We have a special bond and she knows it. She is interested, she just doesn't want to admit it to herself. She'll come round in the end.'

'There won't be any 'in the end'. Is there some part of that which you don't understand? You're to stop contacting her now or it will be my job to make you stop, and I have a number of resources at my disposal to enable me to do that.' She stood up. 'We'll see ourselves out.'

'That was a fast exit,' said Wilcox, as he closed the front door behind them.

'I didn't want to give him a chance to get the last word in. He's got plenty to say for himself.'

'He's an entitled asshole.'

'That's one way of putting it, but not how I would

recommend phrasing it in your report. Funnily enough, I'm finding him a bit different to what I expected. I thought I would be creeped out by him, but that wasn't the vibe I was getting. There's something else going on.'

THE CID ROOM was busy when they arrived back. Conversations were buzzing all around and looking through the glass they could see that Bellweather was in a meeting in his office with two members of the drug squad.

'What's going on?' asked Murphy. 'Are they arresting him?' Wilcox shot her a warning glance.

'One of our known dealers – Jesse Finch – he was shot last night,' one of the DCs told them. 'You know the DCI. He's always keen to have a hand in when guns are involved. Thinks he's in *Line of Duty*.'

'I can kind of understand that,' said Murphy. 'Bit more exciting than chasing after people who've offended each other on Twitter.'

At that moment the meeting came to an end. Bellweather emerged and came to stand in front of Murphy's desk.

'Daniel Webb,' he pronounced meaningfully.

'Yes,' said Murphy and waited for what was sure to come.

Bellweather bared his teeth. The Hollywood veneers were looking a bit tarnished, Murphy thought. That was the trouble with all these expensive plug-ins, they had to be maintained. 'I've just taken a call from the IOPC. His father has made a complaint about you. Accused you of harassing his son.'

'It's more his son doing the harassing,' Murphy replied.

'Has he committed any offence for which you can arrest

him right now?' Murphy shook her head. He drew breath and carried on. 'I thought not. In that case drop whatever you've got going on there and get on with some work – like last night's mugging.'

'He's been stalking a young woman,' said Murphy.

'Has he committed an offence under the terms of the Act for which you could arrest him as of this moment? No, he hasn't. So, unless you want this escalated into a disciplinary offence, drop it.'

'How did Complaints move so fast on that?' Murphy wondered aloud, when Bellweather had swept back into his office.

'Didn't you know?' said Julie Fraser. 'That chap Daniel Webb. Probably not to be messed with. His dad's a councillor. Retired barrister or some such. Lot of clout in City Hall.'

'Interesting,' said Murphy. 'I wonder if his dad knows about the creepy letters he writes. I would guess not.'

Chapter Eighteen

RITCHIE PULLED Sophie's arms behind her back, lifted them and applied pressure. She could feel the ache travelling up to her shoulders and circling around the back of her neck. That was what she needed to feel.

'OK, that's good' she said.

He released her arms and briefly squeezed her shoulders. 'Alright, let's do some lunges.'

Sophie rested her fingertips on the armrest of a bench 'In loving memory of Elsie, who loved this park' and positioned her feet. She knew how Elsie had felt. The park was a stable part of her life now, one of the places where she could focus her attention on her surroundings and stay out of her head.

She got together with Ritchie at the same time every week, all year, whatever the weather, freezing cold in the winter, sweating in the summer, as long as stuff wasn't actually falling from the sky in buckets. It made a change from the gym. She already spent too much time there.

'What's happening with your stalker?' he asked, as she

concentrated on bending her knees and keeping her shoulders back. 'Still hanging around?'

'He's backing off a bit now. I've finally managed to get the police interested, or rather my mum has.'

That wasn't the truth at all, she reflected. She was now massively regretting getting the police involved. She was going to sort it out in her own way and having them involved would just complicate things. If she wasn't careful, she'd end up where she'd warned Freya not to be – in the frame.

Of course, Ritchie knew and understood none of this. He pulled one of her shoulders back. 'That's good, that's progress. Did they suddenly remember it's their job?'

Sophie turned around and changed legs. 'Actually, it was a coincidence really. I told you about my flatmate dying, didn't I?' He nodded. 'It was an awful thing to happen, but that was what brought them round to the flat, and this time they were more interested in hearing about my stalker. Or at least one particular police officer was interested. Probably because she's a woman.'

'However it happened, it's good that they're paying attention, although it doesn't say much for the men on the police force. Do they think you're in danger?'

She shook her head. 'No, and nor do I. He's a harmless creep really. It's just the way a number of different events have come together.'

'You shouldn't be staying in that flat alone until they've sorted it out. You might think he's a harmless creep, but harmless creeps can develop into something worse. This guy could be violent.'

'The police moved me out of my place initially. I had to stay with my mum while they searched the flat. And I haven't gone back yet, I'm going back tomorrow. Actually, he's a jerk but he's probably less capable of violence than I am. I'm not scared of him in any physical sense, I just hate the way he worms his way into my thoughts. I don't know what he's thinking and I wonder if he knows what I'm thinking. He kind of claims he does and that creeps me out.'

'He's messing with your head,' said Ritchie authoritatively. 'That's not OK. If the police don't deal with him, maybe we should pay him a visit. I think I know people who know some people.'

Sophie laughed. 'That sounds well mafia.'

'Of course.' He smiled. 'It sounds like something out of a bad movie, but I think it works. Let me know if you want an intervention. OK, plank.'

An intervention, Sophie thought, well here's to interventions. Ritchie didn't know the half of it.

She got down and lay on her front on the mat, supporting herself on her toes and elbows. Some guy in the US had done this for over eight hours, which was a record. She wouldn't be able to do it for eight minutes. No way. It was hard, but she concentrated on what she hoped it was doing – strengthening her spine and her abdomen, making her stomach like a rock, able to withstand a hard punch. She rolled onto her back and did some crunches, listening with one part of her brain while Ritchie narrated the plot of the superhero movie he'd seen the night before. Spoilers didn't matter because they both knew she'd never watch the film. Maybe Ritchie could be the man she was looking for, he ticked a lot of boxes. But no, better not to mix things.

Chapter Nineteen

MURPHY THOUGHT they'd better do as they were told and put some attention on last night's mugging. After a few phone calls and a lot of holding on the line, Wilcox ascertained that Ian Wells had been sent home from the hospital. He may have been deemed fit for discharge, but he took a long time to answer the door to his flat and he was moving very slowly, more of a painful shuffle. He was a stocky individual with a shaved head and a beard. Looking at his scalp, Murphy could see that there was a large bald patch, so shaving his head was probably a matter of necessity rather than a fashion statement.

He held the door open without enthusiasm and waved vaguely in the direction of three armchairs. Murphy took the least sagging one and tried not to sink too far into it. All that fuss at work about health and safety and ergonomic seating and then she spent her days visiting places like this where the furniture was calculated to do her back in.

Ian Wells sat down gingerly in the nearest chair and winced as he went down.

'I wasn't expecting to see the police again,' he said. 'I spoke to them last night.'

'Yes, I know you spoke to them at the scene,' said Murphy, 'but you were not in good shape, so we wanted to talk to you again today, see what other details you might remember. Were you concussed?'

He shook his head. 'No. I did hit my head on the pavement, but I was wearing a beanie, so that may have helped cushion the impact. The hospital didn't find any signs of concussion, no headache or vomiting, so they let me come home last night.'

'And what are your injuries now?' asked Murphy.

He sighed. 'Dislocated knee.' He indicated the damaged joint and lifted it slightly with two hands. 'They put it back in place in the hospital and that hurt a lot – worst pain I've ever experienced. Thought they'd give me a general, but no, just bloody gas and air. Still hurts, come to that.'

Murphy smiled and decided not to point out that women often have to endure far worse with just gas and air. 'Anything else?'

'Lots of bruising, bruised ribs mainly. They think one of them might be cracked, but that makes no difference really, it just has to heal – and painful groin.'

So that's why he was shuffling around. 'They kneed you in the balls?' asked Murphy and he nodded.

Wilcox winced. 'And they took your phone and wallet?' he said.

Ian Wells nodded. 'I did the 'find my phone' thing and it tracked it to a rubbish bin in Islington, just off the Caledonian Road.'

'That will just be where they threw your sim card,' said Wilcox. 'They will have held onto the phone. Probably sold it on eBay.'

'That's what I figured. I cancelled the bank cards as soon as I realised. They were probably able to buy a bunch of groceries or whatever, but they wouldn't have had the pin to withdraw any cash.'

'So, not so bad, apart from the injuries' said Murphy. 'Can you tell us about the attack?'

'I'd been drinking with some friends' he said. 'At a pub called The Grenadier near Euston Station. I've been there a few times. It wasn't that late, only about 9.30. None of us was up for a late night. We left the pub together and then we split up and I took a short-cut round the back of Eversholt Street. I was walking home, it's not far and walking round at night doesn't worry me. I can take care of myself. I saw these two guys in balaclavas coming towards me. Obviously, it wasn't cold enough to be wearing a bloody balaclava, so I knew there was something going on. I decided to give them a body swerve but when I turned to go back the other way there was another one behind me. The three of them grabbed me. One of them punched me in the gut – really hard – and when I straightened back up, they kicked me in the balls – twice. I went down and they were kicking my ribs and my arse. I guess that was when they lifted my phone and wallet. Then I heard somebody shout and they disappeared. I couldn't get up; I was so winded. I just lay there and somebody called the police and ambulance.'

'Nasty,' said Wilcox. 'But luckily no knives. And can you describe these people at all?'

He seemed to be considering this. 'They weren't that big or tall,' he said. 'I'm no lightweight, and I reckon I could have taken them on if there were just two of them, but three was too many. They were everywhere. There was too much going on all at once.'

'And it sounds like they knew what they were doing,' said Murphy.

He nodded slowly. 'Yes, they definitely knew the moves.'

'What were they wearing?'

'They seemed to be all in black – trousers, sweatshirts, boots. The hoods were up and I couldn't see their faces. Two of them had balaclavas and I think the other one just had a mask over his mouth – like cyclists wear.'

'Interesting,' said Murphy. 'You didn't hear their voices at all?'

'Nah.' He shook his head. 'Nobody said anything. It was a silent attack.'

'Now tell us, who's pissed off with you at the moment?'

He shrugged. 'I dunno. Nobody. I was just minding my own business.'

'You haven't had any feuds, arguments, online spats, breakups with girlfriends?'

He shook his head. 'Nothing like that.'

'Do you have a girlfriend?' asked Murphy.

His face seemed to freeze. 'Not at the moment, no, and I don't see what that has to do with anything.'

Murphy smiled. 'The thing is, so many things have to do with something. You'd be surprised what we turn up when we start poking around into things.'

He frowned. 'Well I don't think you need to poke into this any further,' he said. 'I'm not going to press charges anyway.'

'Oh, I think you should, if we find the perpetrators,' said Murphy, standing up. 'And we're certainly going to be looking for them. I think what happened to you is what we would classify as ABH. Maybe not grievous bodily harm but certainly actual bodily harm. If they'd broken your ribs, I'd go for GBH. We can't have people going round behaving like that. We'll certainly be looking into it and we'll let you know what we come up with.'

He shuffled to the door and let them out.

'He didn't look too pleased to have us on the case,' said Wilcox. 'No gratitude at all. Most burglary victims would be overjoyed if the police actually turned up and showed that much interest.'

'No, he didn't, did he?' said Murphy. 'And I think we'll find that it's because he has stuff of his own to hide. Did anything occur to you about the assailants he was describing?'

Wilcox stopped and thought. 'They were small but they knew how to fight. Kids maybe.'

Murphy nodded. 'Maybe, but the fact that they made a point of kicking him in the balls twice made me think of something else. I wondered if maybe they were women.'

Chapter Twenty

MURPHY KNEW she was making a career-threatening move going back to see Daniel Webb, after having been warned off, which was why she had come alone. Being partnered with her wasn't doing much for Wilcox's career as it was.

She hesitated before ringing the bell, but she knew she was going to go ahead and the door was opened a few moments later. He would have spotted her through the spy hole, she was certain of that, so he must have decided to see what she had to say and how much amusement he could extract from it.

He was wearing what tends to be described as 'loungewear' – sloppy t-shirt and track pants, stuff to slop around in after work – his feet were bare and his hair looked like he'd just emerged from the shower. She could tell from his raised eyebrows when he opened the door that he knew exactly what the position was. His dad would have told him. For a moment they stood and stared at each other, then he slowly smiled. He knew he had the upper hand.

'I've been told to keep away from you,' said Murphy, 'as you will have been told, so this is the last time you'll see me. And I don't need to come in. But I have to ask you this one question which is bugging me.'

He smiled again. 'Sure. Go ahead.'

'Why were you pretending to stalk Sophie Carter?'

'Pretending?'

'Yes, pretending. You know what I'm talking about. You gave it your best shot, but your heart wasn't really in it. You're not a stalker, not at heart. Nobody else has ever complained to the police about you stalking them. And I've seen a fair few stalker notes. Yours just don't ring true.'

He frowned. 'Why? What's wrong with them?'

'They don't fit your personality for a start. You're not a person massively in love with somebody else, you've probably never been in love with anybody. You might be massively in love with yourself, but that's another matter. And stalkers tend to be unhinged to some degree, or at least needy. I'm not picking that up. You don't need her. All I'm picking up is a cynical attempt to gaslight. What I want to know is, what did you think you were doing?'

He folded his arms and leaned against the door frame. 'I guess it was a bit bad of me. I was just responding to the situation as it unfolded. I didn't start it, remember. She was the one who contacted me on Tinder, clicked on my profile. I didn't make the first move, she did. And then she has the cheek to toss me aside. To be honest, that's never happened to me before. So, I thought I'd give her a fright. It was a laugh, really. Some of what I wrote was bonkers. 'In the fullness of time.' Hilarious. Who actually says that?'

Murphy shook her head. 'OK, you've had your fun. If that's how you cope with rejection, you're the one who needs help. Frightening young women is not a laugh and it has to stop right now. If she gets one more sighting of you, one more communication, we'll be back here and we'll be a lot less polite.'

He shrugged and said 'Take care now' as she set off back down the stairs. That pissed her off, as he knew it would. She was tempted to run back and kick him in the shins, but was stopped by the vision of Bellweather's face and the expression of sheer satisfaction that would appear on it as he commenced the disciplinary process for assaulting a member of the public.

Chapter Twenty-One

LIAM WEBSTER'S funeral took place two days later in the church in Gravesend where his father was the vicar. It was a modest building, dating from the 1930s. No soaring Norman arch or flying buttresses, but a beautiful organ, by the sound of it, and a substantial congregation.

Murphy had no strictly official reason for being at the funeral. Liam was not a victim of crime and the investigation, such as it was, had ended. But she wanted to see Sophie and also two other people that she guessed would be there. She had compromised by leaving Wilcox back at the station to get on with the mugging cases, which were what they were supposed to be working on.

Mr and Mrs Webster had expressed a small measure of relief when they were told that they could now bury their son, but their appearance at the actual event showed the heavy toll taken by the loss. His father was conducting the service. Murphy couldn't imagine anything worse. She supposed he could have asked for another vicar to take the service, but he had decided to do it himself. It was a brave effort and, when he talked of giving Liam back to God, she could hear his voice wavering.

His mother looked sunken, leaning heavily on her daughter, and at one point Murphy, sitting at the back of the church, could see her shoulders shaking.

Bella stood up and did the eulogy, during which Murphy learned that Liam had been a mainstay of the cricket club and had done cycle races for charity. Four of his schoolfriends had carried the coffin in, which Murphy thought signalled more powerfully than anything else that he was loved and respected. At the end they sang 'Abide with Me' and Murphy found herself as moved as everybody else.

Afterwards she lingered in the churchyard and spotted Sophie, whose mascara was running again.

'You'll miss him, won't you?' she said.

Sophie nodded. 'I didn't even know him for that long, but he was a good guy, lovely to have around. And too young to just die like that.'

'It's an untimely death, that's for sure. I can tell you now that Liam didn't commit suicide. I had to wait until it was confirmed before I could tell anybody other than close family. He died from natural causes.'

Sophie was weeping again. 'Thank God' she said, although she didn't look particularly thankful. 'I hated to think that he would have killed himself. But how can it have been natural causes, at his age?'

'Sometimes,' said Murphy, 'the heart just stops. It's very rare but it can happen.'

Sophie shook her head. 'Poor Liam. Why should it have happened to him?'

'Nobody can answer that,' said Murphy. 'I also wanted to let you know that I don't think Daniel Webb will be bothering you anymore. He was really just messing you about. I think he wanted to wind you up. I'm not sure why.'

Sophie looked alarmed. 'I don't know why either,' she said.

'He doesn't like being rejected,' said Murphy. 'That's what he told me anyway. I guess not enough women have rejected him. Hopefully more will in the future. Anyway, he should back off now.'

'I wondered if something had happened,' said Sophie slowly. 'I haven't had any letters since that last one I gave you and I haven't seen him hanging around. I guess he's got the message. So, thank you for whatever you've done. I'm glad I won't be seeing him again.'

She didn't look particularly glad, but Murphy acknowledged that the occasion didn't lend itself to expressions of satisfaction. Sophie looked if anything lost and vulnerable, and somehow unnerved.

'How are you getting on?' Murphy said. 'Do you have any family besides your mum?'

Sophie shook her head. 'My dad died quite a few years ago and then my mum got ill. It was very sudden. She's quite badly crippled, as you saw, but she's OK as long as Glenda comes in. Otherwise, I'd have to move back home and I guess I'm selfish, but I just didn't want to do that. I don't think I'd be much good as a carer.'

'I can understand that,' said Murphy. 'You have your own life to lead. Excuse me now.'

Ben and Alfie were attempting to make good their escape when she caught up with them.

'Come with me you two,' she said, and led the way to her car. They followed meekly and she stopped and leaned against the bonnet.

'We've had the results back from your little writing test,'

she said, hoping they wouldn't ask to see any evidence, 'and now I want you to explain exactly what you did and why you did it. We can do that here or down the station. I don't mind.'

There was silence for a moment. They both looked at their feet and then at each other. Ben was the first to speak.

'We brought Liam home,' he said. 'He was very drunk, and we were too. When we got him inside, he collapsed into the armchair and at first we thought he'd fallen asleep. We tried to rouse him, shouting at him and shaking his arm, but it was as if he had gone into a deep sleep. I wondered if we should try to get him into bed, but then we thought he'd be OK sleeping there.'

'After a minute or so,' said Alfie, 'we were still stood there wondering what to do and I noticed that his chest wasn't moving, so I checked his pulse and there was nothing there. We tried to rouse him, but we couldn't. I held my phone up to his mouth and there was no breath. He was dead. We didn't know what to do.'

'What you should have done,' said Murphy, 'was call an ambulance. It's unlikely the paramedics could have saved him, but you would at least have done the right thing. But you didn't do that did you? You did something else - something disgraceful and self-serving.'

'Yes,' said Ben. 'It was an awful thing to do and I've really regretted it – we both have. Been thinking about it all the time.'

'Now tell me why you did it.'

'It doesn't seem to matter so much now,' said Alfie, 'but Frexon has this kind of unwritten policy. They don't like failure. Whenever there's a failed project, somebody has to walk for it.'

Murphy looked at them both and slowly shook her

head. 'So you decided that, as Liam was dead anyway, he could walk for AXIOM. And you could both keep your jobs.'

Alfie nodded. 'Yes. It was an awful thing to do.'

'Too right it was,' said Murphy. 'You even tried to make it look as if he was still alive when you left. And now you turn up to his funeral, as if you care. Do you realise how much additional pain you have caused to Liam's family? Your fake suicide note led us to suspect Liam had been murdered, and that frightened the life out of his flatmate. And you did it for a completely stupid reason. I'm not sure how far this will go. If I have my way you will both be charged with perverting the course of justice.'

At that moment her phone started ringing. 'I'll catch you two up later' she said and walked a short distance away.

It was Wilcox. 'You'd better come back,' he said. 'It's Daniel Webb.'

'Really? What's he done now?'

'He's been found dead. Looks like murder.'

Chapter Twenty-Two

'HE WAS FOUND EARLIER this morning by the milkman,' said Wilcox, as they stood there in their gloves and plastic overshoes and looked down at the body, curled up in an alley just off the Uxbridge Road. He pointed to where a milk float was parked, just visible at the end of the alley on the other side of the street.

'Let's have a quick word with him first,' said Murphy. 'He'll be wanting to get on his way. Lot of people waiting for their milk.'

The milkman was sitting in his cab smoking a cigarette. His hand was shaking.

'Not what I expect to see on my round,' he said. 'Couldn't believe it at first.'

'Thank you for doing the right thing and calling it in,' said Murphy. 'I'm sure it was a shock.'

He nodded. 'That's for sure. At first, to be honest, I thought he was a drunk sleeping it off. Then I had another look and I saw the blood. Poor guy.'

'Did you touch him at all?' asked Murphy.

'I didn't want to touch him, I really didn't. But the call handler asked me if he was breathing so I put my hand on his chest to see if it was moving at all. It wasn't. And his eyes looked dead, it was obvious he was dead.'

'Did you see anybody else around?'

He shook his head. 'No. Never normally see anybody around at this time.'

'I think that's all for now,' said Murphy. 'We've got your details, so we may be in touch again. Thank you for waiting.'

He nodded and started the motor. A minute later he departed the scene with an incongruous tinkling of bottles.

'Looks like he died last night,' said Wilcox as they walked back to the crime scene.

Linda Fleming was bending over the body. 'Hate these morning jobs' she said. 'I'd have sent Frank, but the bugger's on holiday. Young Kevin's probably right. I'd say he died last night, simply because that's when the perps tend to be up and going about their business. Can't get any closer than that for time of death. Death caused by blow to the head. That didn't take much working out. Any other conclusions will have to wait for the PM.'

She closed the victim's eyes then stood up and stripped off her plastic suit. 'Tomorrow afternoon,' she said. 'I've got three more backed up. No more killings, please.' She snapped the locks on her case, picked it up and made her way back to her car.

'OK,' said Murphy, dragging her attention away from her last sighting of Daniel, very much alive. 'What else do we know?'

Wilcox shrugged. 'Not much. His phone and wallet are still here, wallet still contains all his cards and quite a bit of folding money. So not a robbery. SOCO have found nothing useful so far - apart from a bit of straw, which may be nothing to do with anything.'

Murphy looked down at the body. Blood had stopped leaking from the head wound and was now starting to congeal. She was glad Linda had closed the eyes. The expression she had seen on his face when she first looked at it was one of utter surprise. He didn't know what hit him.

'He looks vulnerable lying there,' she said. 'Walking home from work is such an innocent thing to be doing – if that's what he was doing. And he's been lying there all night, out in the open. Maybe he wasn't that easy to spot, tucked into this alley, but I wonder if anybody else passed by and thought he was just drunk, or decided they didn't want to get involved. I've been treating him as a perp, and now he's a victim. Of course, people always look innocent when they're dead.'

Wilcox was looking at her strangely. Time to pull herself together

'Well, this is certainly not suicide,' she said. 'Let's get the wheels in motion.'

She signalled to the mortuary staff to remove the body and they set off back to the car. Uniformed officers were despatched to notify the family.

'WHAT'S WRONG?' said Wilcox, closing his eyes as they swerved round a bus and narrowly avoided a collision with a motorbike.

'You mean my driving's worse than usual?'

'No, your driving's perfectly normal – for you. But there's something else wrong. You're really bothered by this one.'

Murphy sighed. 'Yes, I am. The last conversation I had

with him ended with me threatening him with consequences. I didn't like him, I thought he was a bad apple and a danger to that girl Sophie. I never thought of him being in any danger.'

'The fact that he's dead doesn't change any of that,' said Wilcox. 'Bad people can be victims as well as good people. Whatever you said to him won't have caused somebody else to kill him. That's just how things happen. And I think you should slow down for these lights.'

There were no parking spaces left at the station, so Murphy parked on the street, flashing her badge at a parking warden who was circling like a shark.

Inside they found Bellweather in a state of acute paranoia.

'How do you think it looks?' he barked. 'This young man is harassed by the police, to the point that a complaint is made to the IOPC, and now he's dead.'

'You think it looks like we killed him?' said Murphy. 'I'm not sure my alibi will hold up.'

He narrowed his eyes. 'I think it looks like we need a swift solution to this one, that's the least we can offer his family. Otherwise, disciplinary measures will be in order. I think it looks like you need to pull in that girl who caused all the trouble. She's got to be the prime suspect.'

'I saw her earlier this morning,' said Murphy. 'She seemed same as normal.'

'But you don't know what she was up to last night, do you?' Bellweather fired back. 'Get her in an interview room and find out what's going on, or I'll put somebody else onto it.'

Murphy nodded and put a call through to Sophie. 'She's still off work. She's at her mum's house' she told Wilcox. 'We'll go and pick her up from there.'

EILEEN WAS upright leaning on crutches when they arrived at the flat.

'I make myself walk – or shuffle – around for twenty minutes every day' she told them. 'Sometimes it hurts a lot, but I don't want to end up completely immobile. So excuse me not sitting down.'

'That's no problem,' said Murphy. 'It's Sophie we've come to talk to.'

'We can talk in front of mum,' said Sophie. 'She knows all about the Daniel business. Although he seems to be leaving me alone now.'

'Yes,' said Murphy. 'The reason he's been leaving you alone is because he's dead.'

Sophie stared at them and slowly lowered herself onto the sofa.

'Dead?'

'Yes, he was found this morning. So, as somebody who recently had dealings with him, we'd like you to accompany us to the station and answer some questions.'

Sophie looked shocked. 'Me? But I haven't done anything.'

'We're not suggesting you have,' said Wilcox. 'But this is a murder investigation, so we will be questioning anybody who was involved with Daniel in any way. It's normal procedure.'

'OK.' Sophie looked across at her mother.

'You're wasting your time pursuing my daughter,' said Eileen. 'She wouldn't hurt anybody. Doesn't even kill flies.'

'I think that's probably not the point, mum. I don't mind answering questions. I'd better go with them.'

'Off you go then,' said Eileen, lowering herself into her seat. 'Glenda will be here in half an hour. Call me later.'

Wilcox was glad that he was driving for once. Sophie

was obviously alarmed at being taken to the police station. There was no need to make her fear for her life in the process. When they arrived, he set up the least unpleasant of the interview rooms and asked one of the PCs to fetch her some tea. Hopefully, she wouldn't actually drink it, but it would serve to make the atmosphere less threatening. At one point he looked across and saw Murphy regarding him quizzically. She never missed anything.

When the preliminaries had been completed, Murphy began the questioning.

'Sophie, I'd like you to begin by telling us how you spent yesterday evening. From about six pm.'

Sophie seemed to gather herself. 'OK. I was doing overtime yesterday, so I left work about six o'clock. That's a site near the Barbican at the moment. We have to clock out as it's a building site, so there'll be a record of that. I came home on the tube. Central line to Liverpool Street and then overground to Dalston.'

'And you went straight home?'

'Yes. Well, no actually. I stopped in Waitrose to get something for dinner. Then I went straight home.'

'So that would be what time?'

'About ten to seven.'

'OK. Then what?'

Sophie sighed. 'Then I had a shower, put something in the microwave, listened to the news. That was just depressing of course. Then I sat and watched Netflix and went to bed. It had been a long day and I was pretty tired.'

'Did you meet anybody else during the evening?'

She shook her head. 'No. So I have no alibi. I doubt they'd remember me in Waitrose.'

'And you didn't go out at any point?'

'No.'

'And did you hear anything from Daniel Webb during the evening?'

'No. Not at all.'

'How about this morning?'

'This morning? I got up about 7, made tea, listened to the news, had another shower, got dressed, ate a banana and went to Liam's funeral. You'll know that – you saw me there. 149 'bus to London Bridge and train to Gravesend. When I got back, I was off work for the funeral anyway, so I went to see mum.'

She was sounding a bit more feisty now, Wilcox was pleased to note. He couldn't see where else Murphy could go with this and she now apparently had the same thought.

'OK Sophie. I think that's all we need to know for now' she said. 'But we do need to get access to your phone and laptop and we are getting a warrant to search your flat. We will get it all done as quickly as possible. Will you be able to stay with your mum for a few days?'

Sophie nodded wordlessly and handed over her phone. 'The laptop's in the flat' she said, with a bit of a wobble in her voice. 'I don't need it for work right now, but I will in a day or so.'

'Don't worry, we'll make sure it's done quickly,' said Wilcox. 'We'll get it back to you as soon as possible.'

'OK' said Murphy. 'DC Wilcox here will take you back to the flat to collect whatever you need and then you can give him your keys and he'll drop you off at your mum's.'

Wilcox guided her out, not missing Bellweather's head swivelling round as they went past. They'd thrown the book at her. Surely that was enough?

Chapter Twenty-Three

'SO WHERE'S SHE GONE NOW?' Bellweather demanded.

'You wanted her thrown in the cells?' asked Murphy. 'We're confiscating her phone and laptop and we're going to search her flat. I think that'll do to be going on with.'

He grunted and walked off. Murphy logged onto the PNC and searched for Ian Wells, the mugging victim.

After a few minutes his name came up. Arrested for beating up his girlfriend three weeks ago. Case dropped when she decided not to press charges. No wonder he was a bit cagey. Definitely worth looking into. The girlfriend might be at home now. It was worth a try. Murphy noted down the address and headed for the car park.

Sandra Fuller had a flat in a housing estate in Islington. It was one of the better-looking estates and had plenty of car parking space, which was a plus. Murphy calculated the odds of returning to find wheels missing and decided to risk it. The flat she wanted was on the tenth floor and the stairs looked a better bet than the lift. How people managed when they didn't want to use the lift (or it was out of order) and they had to get their shopping upstairs, she couldn't imagine.

The door was answered by a young woman in gym gear with a little boy wound around her leg.

Murphy showed her badge and was reluctantly invited in. The flat was clean and well-furnished with a layer of toys strewn around.

'Go and play with your Lego, Finn,' said Sandra. 'Don't worry, we'll be going out soon.'

'He's got a playdate,' she explained.

'I won't keep you long,' said Murphy. 'I just want a quick word about Ian Wells.'

Sandra tossed her head. 'Oh, him' she said dismissively. 'One of my mistakes, and I'm not going to repeat it.' Murphy's attention suddenly drifted over to the dining table on which rested a bright red pair of boxing gloves.

Sandra was following her line of sight. 'Yes, they're mine' she said. 'Should have taken it up ten years ago.'

Murphy sat down and checked that Finn was out of earshot. 'He beat you up, didn't he?'

Sandra nodded. 'He's not Finn's dad and I should have kicked him out the first time. But I bought all the apologies and expressions of remorse. Second time, I came to my senses and called the police. There are no black eyes or anything, he's too smart for that.'

She pulled up a corner of her top and Murphy could see the bruises around her ribs.

'Nasty' she said. 'But you dropped the charges.'

'Yes, I felt I had to, in the end. The police explained the procedure. I would be subjected to cross-examination by the defence, if it ever got to court. And the chances are it wouldn't. I just didn't want all that hanging over me, over me and Finn. So I decided to drop it and take up boxing instead.'

'And have you seen him at all since that time?'

'No, not at all. I don't ever want to see him again.'

'The thing is,' said Murphy, 'Ian Wells was attacked in the street on Thursday night.'

Sandra sat down slowly. 'And you think that I…? No way, I wouldn't go anywhere near him. Was he badly hurt?'

'Nothing from which he won't make a full recovery,' said Murphy, 'and he's not too keen on us investigating it, but I'm interested to find out why somebody picked on him.'

Sandra shook her head. 'I really don't know,' she said. 'Couldn't it just be something random?'

'Yes, he could just have been in the wrong place at the wrong time. Can I ask where you were Thursday night?'

Sandra shrugged. 'I was just here. Me and Finn. We don't go anywhere during the week, because he has school and I'm at work. I do a four-hour shift in a bakery, Monday to Friday, then I collect Finn and we come home.'

'OK. That's fine,' said Murphy. 'Do you know of anybody else who may have had an altercation with Ian? Anybody who didn't like him?'

'I wouldn't know. I never met any of his friends. I don't think he had many of them.'

'How about your friends?'

She laughed. 'He never met any of mine either. Just as well really. I guess we hadn't cemented our relationship. He showed his true colours early on, when it was easy for me to disentangle myself.'

'How about social media?' said Murphy. 'Did you post anything about your relationship?'

Sandra looked worried for the first time. 'I did post something on Facebook when I split up with him. But that was just for moral support. Lots of people responded, said good for you girl, stuff like that.'

'Did you know all these people? The ones who responded?'

'Not well, no. Some of them I didn't know at all. You know how it is, you pick up followers over time and you can't really remember where they came from.'

Murphy definitely didn't know how it was, but she nodded as if she understood.

'OK.' She sighed. 'I think that's all for now Sandra. I shouldn't need to bother you again.'

Going down the ten flights was decidedly easier than going up had been and she remembered Wilcox telling her that going down was actually better exercise than going up. Win-win.

Chapter Twenty-Four

DANIEL WEBB'S flat was not a crime scene, so had not been gone over by SOCO. Murphy always felt that searching premises told her a lot about a person, but maybe it was just that she was a nosey cow and liked looking in other peoples' cupboards. She pulled her gloves on and got down to it.

Daniel's cupboards weren't telling her a great deal, apart from the fact that he didn't keep much stuff. What fell out when they were opened was mostly wires and cables, plus a couple of adaptors. The walls were pale grey, the art on the walls was bold and modern and the lighting was a complicated arrangement of beams hanging from the ceiling from which lights were suspended. It all looked a bit overdone for the Shepherd's Bush flat, but of course he was planning to move into a much grander flat in Holland Park, where he would have more scope for cool interior design. The lights would look better there. Except of course that wasn't going to happen now.

There were no shelves anywhere. 'No photos. No books' she said, looking around.

Wilcox pointed to the equipment sitting in front of the TV screen. 'He was a gamer,' he said. 'They don't bother with books much. Or maybe there's an e-reader somewhere.'

The kitchen looked like it had been newly fitted out and at some expense. It had a range cooker with six gleaming gas rings and one of those taps that did hot, cold or sparkling water. Clive kept saying they should have one of those at home, but they weren't cheap. There was a shiny red proper coffee machine, not one of the ones with the little pods. Murphy gazed at it in admiration and tried twisting a few of the knobs. Wilcox cleared his throat behind her and she hurriedly stepped back.

'Not much cooking goes on here,' she said. 'I swear nothing's ever been heated up on those gas rings. Must have eaten out or lived on deliveries.' She checked the bin and pulled out a pizza box, a wine bottle and a carton from an expensive Thai restaurant.

The kitchen cupboards contained tea bags, coffee beans, muesli and a few condiments. The sriracha sauce had left a red ring on the bottom shelf. 'He must have a cleaner' she continued. 'Maybe not a very good one. It won't be a demanding cleaning job.'

She opened the fridge. Beer, water and milk. An unopened packet of butter. And a lemon. That was it. None of that told her anything.

The bathroom had a shower but no bath. It was an expensive shower, probably high pressure, and the shower gel hadn't come from the supermarket. There was a mirrored cabinet which contained shaving and dental stuff, a few vitamins and painkillers. No drugs, prescription or otherwise. And there at the back, alone and forgotten, a women's deodorant. That was the only sign so far of any female occupation.

Wilcox was shuffling through the record collection. 'The vinyls are quite good stuff,' he said. 'The CDs are music and movies. Fairly eclectic tastes – some old rock stuff, blues, jazz, reggae, a bit of rap. No Ed Sheeran or Taylor Swift, no Abba. The movies are mostly action stuff.'

'Yes, I don't see him as an Abba fan,' said Murphy, heading for the bedroom. The unmade bed was king-size as she would have expected, the sheets looked like high thread count and the scattering of clothes on the floor were the first real evidence of occupation. He had thrown his clothes on the floor unaware that he would never have to pick them up.

The clothes and shoes in the bedroom closet were all top quality. Cashmere and merino wool sweaters. Tyrwhitt shirts. Lobb shoes. Nike trainers of the type that couldn't just be bought in a shop.

'That's right,' said Wilcox when she pointed to them. 'You have to purchase those through an agent. They don't want the hoi polloi running round in them. Look what happened to Burberry.'

Murphy thought privately that what had happened to Burberry was that they had made a lot of money and they should have been glad about that and not complained. It was obvious from everything here that Daniel Webb was considered a high-net-worth customer. It would have been worth somebody's while to take his bank cards. Why hadn't they done that?

Chapter Twenty-Five

FOR ABOUT A YEAR she had been threatening Wilcox with having to attend a post-mortem and Murphy decided that his time had now come. For one thing, he'd never get promotion if he hadn't attended any PMs, and God knows being partnered with her had already blighted his chances enough. But also, it was time to toughen him up a bit. So, there he stood, in his apron, shower cap and plastic overshoes, looking like he wished he was somewhere else. She looked at his wary expression when the body was wheeled in and hardened her heart.

Daniel Webb looked small and vulnerable lying naked on the table. Linda Fleming was looking weary. 'Third one today' she said. 'I'm thinking of going on strike. Who keeps killing all these people?'

'If we knew that,' said Murphy, 'we could just take them off the streets and take the rest of the month off.'

Linda pulled on her gloves and switched on her microphone. 'Fit and well-nourished' she said. 'No sign of any underlying conditions.' She ran her hand along the jaw.

'The bone has healed here, maybe an old fracture, but nothing to do with his death. Bit of a waste really, somebody knocking off a healthy specimen like this. Massive head wound, which looks like the cause of death. OK let's have a look inside.'

She picked up the scalpel and Murphy found herself in something of a quandary. Her usual practice was to look away when the knife went in and keep her attention on other things while the grisly bits went on. She was sure Linda was well aware of that, but had never commented on it. But now that Wilcox was here, she had to set an example. He would be horrified enough by the whole procedure. What would he think if he saw her not able to look at what was going on?

She stole a quick look at the body and then looked quickly away again and pretended to be studying an x-ray pinned to the wall. Linda was carrying what looked like the stomach over to the bench. She sliced into it and poured out the contents.

'Nothing much here' she said. 'He hadn't had a meal in the previous six hours.'

'So he hadn't had dinner' said Murphy, venturing a glance. 'Maybe that narrows it down a bit.'

'Can't smell any alcohol' said Linda, 'but we'll know about drink or drugs when the bloods come back. Anyway, doesn't look like it was drink or drugs that killed him. Now let's look at his skull.'

She picked up the electric saw and sliced off the top of his head. Murphy was never able to look at this bit and she didn't even try.

'Blunt instrument trauma,' said Linda. 'Fractured skull and a massive bleed on the brain. Death would have been almost instantaneous.' She pulled the brain out and squinted at it.

'What sort of weapon?' Wilcox asked and Murphy glanced round to see him peering with apparent fascination at the bloody hole in the top of the head.'

Linda frowned. 'Quite difficult to say. Something quite narrow, not more than an inch wide. There must have been a fair amount of swing behind it, but it wouldn't have needed that much strength, the momentum would have done the job.'

'Like the edge of a cricket bat maybe?' said Wilcox, holding his thumb and forefinger apart and squinting at the gap.

Linda looked up at him and nodded. 'Exactly like that. A swipe to the boundary.'

Chapter Twenty-Six

'THAT WAS SO INTERESTING! When do you ever get the chance to look at a brain? All those lobes slotted in together. It's a perfect piece of construction. I wonder if she'll find anything in the bloods.'

Murphy said nothing and concentrated on driving. Wilcox was starting to annoy her now.

'It should be the next turning off here,' she said.

'That's right,' he checked his phone. 'Two hundred yards on the right.'

The house they pulled up in front of was in a stucco-fronted three-storey terrace close to Regents Park. Wide steps led down from the gleaming front door to a small paved area with shrubs growing in large pots and then down further to a basement. It was actually four-storey if you counted the basement, Murphy realised. Imagine cleaning all that.

'This looks well pricey,' said Wilcox. He did some taps on his phone again. 'Flats round the corner in Park Terrace are going for six million. Six mil – for a flat! I guess when you're a barrister you can afford to live round here.'

'I guess when you're a barrister you think nothing of complaining to the IOPC' said Murphy, who was busy trying to squeeze into an almost-too-small space. When she had achieved this, the cars either side were effectively locked in place. Getting out again would be a mission, but whatever.

The door was opened by a substantial woman in an apron with multiple rings in her ears and a pugnacious expression, who scrutinised their badges, sniffed and looked behind her, as if for instructions. Murphy wondered if they would be directed to the tradesmen's entrance. She could have some fun with that.

'Who is it?' said a harsh voice. 'The police? OK Karen, let them in.'

The woman opened the door wider and drew aside to let them in, pointing to a room off to the left where a middle-aged couple rose as one to meet them.

Robert Webb was a thick-set man with heavy brows which drew together when he frowned. It was a face that frowned a lot. His wife was a thin-set, fluttery-looking woman. Looking more closely at her, Murphy could see that she had once been beautiful, but grief doesn't do much for anybody's looks.

'So have you arrested anybody yet?' Robert Webb barked, not offering them a seat.

'Not yet sir. We're still investigating,' said Murphy. 'We're looking into anybody who may have wanted to harm Daniel. Do you know of anybody he had any problems with?'

Robert Webb looked like a man just about holding his temper in place. 'Of course he didn't have any problems with anybody. He lived a decent, successful, respectable life. He had lots of friends; they'll all tell you the same thing.'

'Yes,' said Murphy. 'We will be questioning his friends. Does he have any brothers or sisters?'

'We have another son, Marcus. He lives in Australia. He will be coming back for the funeral, but he won't be able to tell you anything.'

'Would you like tea or coffee?' Mrs Webb put in tentatively.

'Of course they don't want bloody tea!' her husband roared, looking as if he'd like to pick her up and set her to one side. 'They're supposed to be doing a job, that's what they're here for.'

'When did you last see Daniel?' Wilcox asked.

It was Mrs Webb who answered. 'I think it was last weekend, wasn't it dear? So about ten days ago. He came for dinner.' Her jaw trembled on the last sentence and tears were suddenly running down her face.

'Sit down Cicely,' said her husband and he turned back to the detectives.

'I don't think there's anything more we can tell you. We saw Daniel last weekend, on the Sunday. He was just the same as normal, we had no reason to think anything was wrong.'

'Did you hear anything from him since then? Were there any phone calls?' asked Wilcox.

'No, I'm afraid not,' said Mr Webb.

'Actually, I spoke to him,' his wife ventured. 'He called to ask if he'd left his sunglasses behind. I said we hadn't seen them and he said he must have left them somewhere else.'

'And how did he seem?' asked Murphy.

Cicely swallowed. 'He seemed fine. There was no problem. He was just calling about the sunglasses. He didn't say anything else.' Her face seemed to crumple.

'What I want to know,' said her husband, 'is why have you not arrested this young woman who was spreading false stories about him? Surely, she has to be the prime suspect. That's where I'd put my money.'

'We have been questioning her,' said Murphy, 'but we have no reason at the moment to think that she had anything to do with it.'

'She might not have done it herself. She might have paid somebody else to do it. Or used a family member. Some of them probably have criminal records. I encounter families like that all the time in my profession. Have you looked into her family? They could have all sorts of unsavoury hangers-on.'

'Yes, we are looking into her family. Believe me, we are considering all possibilities,' said Murphy. 'And I think that's all we need to know for now, so we'll leave you in peace. We'll keep you informed.'

Mrs Webb saw them to the front door while her husband marched off to what was presumably his den and slammed the door.

'I'm sorry for your loss,' said Murphy, realising that she had not yet had the opportunity to say this.

'Thank you.' Mrs Webb tried unsuccessfully to smile and closed the door behind them.

'Funnily enough,' said Wilcox as they arrived back at the car, 'his dad fits the temperamental profile of a killer better than anybody else we've met so far. You didn't ask him what he was doing on Friday night.'

'No, I didn't, did I? I was leaving that to you. Here, you can drive back.' She handed him the keys.

'How on earth did you get it in here?' asked Wilcox as he performed a 36-point turn.

'You got in with me. You can't have been paying attention.'

'He was a bit of a cold fish, our Daniel, wasn't he?' said Wilcox, as they finally extricated themselves and set off down the road.

Murphy nodded. 'I'd say so. I'm sure he knew how his dad treated his mum, but he didn't really care. Only phoned her up to ask after his sunglasses.'

'Maybe he turned out like his dad,' said Wilcox. 'He'd seen that attitude to women and thought it was normal behaviour.'

'Maybe he did', said Murphy. 'Would that explain anything, I wonder?'

Chapter Twenty-Seven

STANLEY AND AUDREY were both in the office when they rang the bell at McEwan and Webb. Stanley Enson and Audrey Wright, as they were reminded, Wilcox having googled them and found nothing significant.

Murphy hadn't paid much attention to them when they had visited the office before, all of her interest being directed towards Daniel, so she had a good look at them now.

Stanley was muscular-looking with short black hair, a neatly trimmed beard and a lot of tattoos. They covered all visible areas of skin. Murphy wondered how far they covered the invisible bits. Surely some areas must be more sensitive than others? When he walked towards them, he was listing slightly to one side and, looking down below his cargo shorts, Murphy saw a foot attached to an artificial leg. He saw her looking and smiled.

'Skateboarding accident when I was a kid' he said.

Audrey had two legs and they were both slim, lightly tanned and unmarked by tattoos. She wore linen dungarees to just below her knees and sandals and her face reminded Murphy slightly of the more famous Audrey. Maybe her parents had liked *Breakfast at Tiffany's* and somehow managed to give her the right genes. Murphy had thought it rather a stupid film, but that was just her.

Both of them looked like they were in the later stages of shock, but Murphy knew how easy that was to fake. They sat down again on the sofas and Audrey switched on the coffee machine.

'We don't know what to do with ourselves, to be honest,' said Stanley. 'We're just sitting here looking at each other. Daniel was kind of the main man. I don't really know what we do now.'

'How is your business set up?' Wilcox asked, when Audrey had handed round the coffee and sat down.

'Architectural practices are usually partnerships' Audrey replied 'and Stanley and I are a partnership in respect of any other work we do, but we set up a company with Daniel specifically to carry out this church project. And we haven't done any other work for the past year, we've just been working on this. The company's called DAS Ltd, from the first letters of each of our names. Bit silly really, I suppose. Daniel had 52% of the shares and we have 24% each.'

Wilcox nodded. 'So he was the major shareholder.'

'Yes,' said Stanley. 'He was the one who put in the capital, so he had to be. I don't know what will happen to his shares now. I guess they will revert to his family. I don't think we could raise enough capital to buy them.'

'Have you met his family at all?' asked Murphy.

'Yes,' said Audrey. 'Once.' A look passed between them.

'Are you aware of anybody who had any disagreements with Daniel, anybody who didn't like him, had a grudge against him, anything like that?'

They both shook their heads. 'Daniel dealt with the contractors' said Stanley. 'And there's always stuff going on with builders isn't there? But problems come up and they're dealt with. I was never aware of any hard feelings. The contractors are doing as well out of this project are we are – were.'

'I don't know of anybody who would have wanted to hurt him,' said Audrey. 'Surely it was just a random attack by some nutter.'

'That's always a possibility,' said Murphy. 'But we try to explore the other options first. Did he have a current girlfriend, do you know?'

'He had been seeing a girl called Leone,' said Stanley. 'I met her once. Nice girl. But he told me a few months ago that they had split up and I'm not aware of anybody else since then.'

'How about friends?'

'I never met any of Daniel's friends,' said Stanley.

Audrey shook her head. 'Me neither.'

'OK' said Wilcox. 'Can you just run through what happened on Friday night?'

'We were here until about 9.30,' said Audrey. 'It was a bit of a late nighter.'

Stanley nodded. 'We were going through some plans. We're expecting another sale to go through in a few weeks – or we were, God knows what happens now – so we were planning for the next building phase, which would be after that money came in.'

'And you all left together?' asked Wilcox.

'That's right,' said Audrey. 'We left together and we locked up. We would sometimes stop for a drink on a Friday night, but we were late anyway, I was meeting some friends and I think Stanley wanted to get home, didn't you?'

'Yes, my partner was making a late supper. He doesn't like it to be ruined.'

'So Audrey, you spent the rest of the evening where?' asked Murphy.

'Macy's Bar in Notting Hill,' she said. 'Do you want my friends' contact details?'

'Yes please,' said Wilcox, pulling out his notebook. 'And we'll need your partner's contact details please,' he told Stanley.

They were both looking a bit subdued now.

'Alright,' said Murphy, ignoring the twinge in her knees as she rose from the sofa. 'I think that's all for now. If you think of anything else, please get in touch with us. We may be back if we need to ask you anything further.'

'OK, what did you think of them?' she asked Wilcox, as they got back in the car.

'I thought mainly that Stanley may have a missing leg, but he has a very powerful upper body,' he answered. 'I'd say he spends a lot of time in the gym. Well able to fell somebody with a blow.'

'Yes, I think that's right. CCTV shows him walking off in the opposite direction but he could have doubled back through the back streets. Most people know how to avoid the cameras these days.'

'But Audrey, well I don't think she can be a suspect,' said Wilcox.

'Why ever not? Because she's female and pretty? Our job is to suspect everybody unless we can rule them out. Do you know what occurred to me?'

'No.'

'Well, there they were, sitting around with nothing to do except agree their stories and work on their alibis, and yet when we questioned them, they managed to make it sound completely impromptu, as if they had never expected to be questioned. All of that referring to each other for confirmation, it was just an act. Unless they're completely stupid, which I don't think they are, they will have rehearsed this whole scenario. Not that any of that means they killed him.'

'If they don't have to repay the money,' Wilcox mused, 'they could do well out of it. The profits will be shared with just two people, not three. Daniel's parents are rich, they might hand the shares over.'

'You've met Daniel's father,' said Murphy. 'Can you see him deciding that these are two deserving young people and they should get Daniel's shares?'

'No. Very much not.'

'And that being the case' said Murphy, 'would you want to get rid of Daniel and risk having his father as your majority shareholder?'

He shook his head.

'There you are then,' she said. 'That's the one big point in their favour. If they offed him, they'll certainly be regretting it now.'

Chapter Twenty-Eight

SOPHIE CARTER HAD GIVEN them the passwords to her phone and laptop and Murphy left Wilcox looking through them while she went and searched the flat. SOCO had been in there again, this time looking for traces of blood or anything else incriminating, but had uncovered nothing. Murphy acknowledged that another search by her was unlikely to turn anything up, as they had searched it once already, but a lot of police work involved doggedly going through the procedures, so she pulled her gloves on and prepared to go through them. Last time, leaving aside the work done by SOCO, they had only been looking for evidence in respect of the suicide note. Now it was a question of murder, so this would be a much wider search. She was accompanied by PC Julie Fraser, who was there, she supposed, to ensure that she didn't plant any evidence.

Julie Fraser had a very methodical approach and seemed to regard everything around her with the correct, dispassionate attitude. Murphy contrasted this with her own somewhat haphazard and over-curious approach. Perhaps Julie would spot something she had missed.

Liam Webster's room had now been stripped and all traces of him had gone. Sophie would have had to do that in order to re-let the room, but there was something sad about it all the same. Murphy left Julie to look through Sophie's bedroom and started in the kitchen. It reminded her of her own kitchen when she was single – a few plates and saucepans, half a dozen glasses. Not much in the way of supplies – tea, coffee, a few out-of-date spices. One cupboard contained stuff that Murphy didn't know much about – collagen tablets, protein powder, creatine capsules, although she was pretty sure creatine was involved in body-building. The fridge held mainly fruit, vegetables and bottled water. Nothing to criticise there. And nothing stuck to the fridge door, no silly magnets, no post-it notes, no photos.

The sitting room had a modest-sized television stuck to the wall and bookshelves covering most of one wall. Murphy started at the top. Textbooks. Maths, physics, chemistry, civil engineering. Subjects that would be forever closed to her. You had to admire the mind that could deal with this stuff. Then a few classic novels – Moby Dick, Mockingbird, some Du Maurier and Poe. A larger number of modern novels and, littered throughout, self-help books. How to deal with divorce, how to recover from divorce, processing trauma, rediscovering the happy you, how to let it go and move on, coping with loss, living one day at a time, coping with sadness, rediscovering yourself, saying no to regrets, being kind to yourself. If you could tell a lot about a person from the contents of their bookshelves, this was a case in point. It looked like Sophie had been badly affected by her divorce.

She moved on and opened a cupboard which contained a yoga mat and a pair of fingerless gloves made from some sort of reinforced mesh with Velcro fastenings.

'Any gym clothes in there?' she called to Julie.

'Lots,' Julie shouted back. 'Leggings, sports bras, trainers, whatever.'

So, probably a physically-strong young woman. Or a young woman working on her physical strength. Not that surprising really. You probably needed to be physically strong to work on building sites. It was interesting though. Sophie wasn't as vulnerable as she looked.

'There are no photos,' Julie remarked, emerging from the bedroom. 'No photos of her, nothing of her with friends, nothing from when she was a kid, with her family, nothing. It's like she's somebody who's recreated herself from scratch.'

'Yet we know that's not true, because we've met her mother,' said Murphy. 'I think she suffered a bad loss when her dad died and maybe again when her marriage failed. Maybe she couldn't bear to keep photos which would have featured either her dad or her husband.'

She headed for the bathroom, wondering if she'd find anti-depressants, but there was no evidence of drugs, prescription or otherwise. What was in evidence was a selection of supplements – D3, C, E, magnesium, calcium. Looked like she was definitely trying to build muscle.

'I think we're done here,' said Julie. 'No sign of anything that could be a murder weapon. No bloodstained clothing. No traces of blood around the water outlets. SOCO have already checked all that anyway.'

Murphy nodded and they let themselves out and locked the door.

Sudden Death

WILCOX WAS SCROLLING on Sophie's phone when they returned and her laptop was open on his desk showing a Facebook profile.

'So what have you found?' asked Murphy, yawning and trying to remember whether she'd had breakfast.

'Nothing particularly significant' he said. 'Daniel appears in her Tinder account, but they weren't following each other on Facebook. Maybe he asked to follow her and she declined the request.'

'Has she mentioned him on Facebook?'

'Not specifically naming him. She posted something last week, saying 'Finally shook off the creep who was stalking me'. That was before she knew he was dead. Would have looked pretty bad for her to make that comment afterwards. There's a friend called Cass who lives in Oxford. This will be the friend that she had spent the weekend with when Liam died. There's a photo of them together in front of one of the colleges on that Saturday morning, probably just before she got the train back and found Liam. Anyway, Cass responded, saying 'Well done, girl' and various other women pitched in with messages of support.'

Murphy read through them:

'Reclaim the streets for women', 'Good for you Sophie', 'Girls together', 'Street sisters rock', 'We're all behind you', 'Stalkers never win' and a number of others in the same vein.

'That was a popular post' she said. 'Lot of likes. Not surprising, really. Anything else on Facebook?'

'About a year ago, she posted a message celebrating the finalisation of her divorce. Lots of girly-support messages of course. Looks like she'd been married three years.'

'She got married young,' said Murphy. 'That's often a

mistake. What about the husband? Have you looked him up?'

'There is one picture of them together, in happier days, I guess. He's called Keith, I discovered, by working my way through mutual contacts. Keith Carter. So, she kept her married name. Sophie hasn't posted anything about him since the breakup, which I guess was two years before the divorce. Here's his Facebook page.'

Keith Carter was smiling in yellow waterproofs, a hard hat and big boots, with his arms round a very large pipe.

'He seems to work mostly on oil rigs,' said Wilcox. 'He's an engineer – I guess that's how they met. Two engineers. I've trawled through his page but I couldn't find anything relevant. He seems an OK guy. He has a girlfriend called Sally and two dogs.'

Murphy nodded. 'Yes, he doesn't look like the sort of guy who would murder somebody to put his ex-wife in the frame.'

'Is that where she is? In the frame?'

'Well, as Bellweather pointed out, until we can find somebody else to put in the frame, she's definitely in it as far as he's concerned. In which case, I think we need to dig a bit deeper. Like, are there no relationships between her marriage ending and her hooking up with Daniel nearly two years later? It seems a long time for her to have been on her own. And if there was someone else, why nothing about it on Facebook?'

'Well it's funny you should say that.' Wilcox picked up the phone. 'There are messages between Sophie and a guy called Richard Agnew, which started two years ago and went on for about a year. Mostly very short, just making arrangements. Then nothing. But there are no emails between them, nothing on Facebook.'

'So he was married,' said Murphy. 'She may have ended her marriage to be with him, or Keith ended it when he found out. Then, sometime later, this Richard probably decided he's not leaving his wife after all. That may have been a devastating outcome for Sophie. It makes sense to me that she would have decided to have a moratorium on men after that. Then she goes on Tinder and clicks on Daniel. Some women have all the bad luck.'

'So do we want to track down this Richard Agnew and talk to him?'

'I think it's at least worth finding out what we can about him. And his wife of course. There's somebody who may think she has a score to settle with Sophie. If she ever knew about the affair. Anything else in the Facebook posts?'

'I just made a note of one she made a few months ago saying a sad anniversary was coming up. A few condolences and messages of support again. Probably something to do with her marriage – or maybe with her dad's death.'

'Something to ask her about,' said Murphy. At that moment her phone rang.

'What? I don't believe it.'

She tapped it off and turned to Wilcox. 'Christopher Dakin. He was mugged last night.'

Chapter Twenty-Nine

ACCORDING to the notes made by the paramedics, Christopher Dakin had been kept in overnight, so they started at the hospital.

'Get him while he's still a bit delicate, might get more out of him,' said Murphy. 'Although of course he's the victim here.'

But stopping at the nurse's station, they were informed that Christopher Dakin had gone home.

'He wanted to leave and we need the bed, so we weren't going to stop him,' said the nurse. 'But he'll need to rest up for a few days.'

Murphy had no particular wish to see Christopher Dakin again. She could easily recall his confident protestations of innocence, his wide-eyed shock that he could be accused of such a thing and his dismissal of his accuser as a fantasist. She had no doubt that he had drugged and raped Molly Wright, not because he was unable to persuade her into consensual sex, he was an attractive man after all, but because he was more excited by the idea of control, of being able to use somebody else's body in any way he wanted.

He was looking less than confident and attractive when he was finally persuaded to open the door of his Islington flat to them. One arm was in a sling and Murphy could see that under his vest his ribs were strapped. There was a large bruise on his temple.

'I don't know why I'm letting you in,' he said, as he shuffled ahead of them. 'Especially not you' he added, looking at Murphy. 'I didn't ask for police interference. I've had enough of that.'

'Yes, I know,' said Murphy, sitting uninvited on the leather sofa. 'But that case is over and done with. And ended pretty well for you, didn't it? It's my job now to investigate this attack, so we need to ask you some questions. Can you start by telling us where it took place?'

He sat opposite them and rolled his eyes. 'Carswell Street,' he said, 'just off the Essex Road.'

'And what were you doing there?'

'Minding my own bloody business. OK, I was walking home. I'd been to a bar in Upper Street. Should have taken a bloody taxi. Streets full of muggers and your lot are too busy pursuing false rape allegations.'

'What bar?' asked Murphy.

'Rizzo's'

'What time was this?'

'Not late. About 9pm, maybe 9.15.'

'And somebody just jumped you?'

'A bunch of somebodies. One of them I would have had no trouble with.'

'So what happened?'

'Somebody grabbed me round the neck. I didn't even hear them coming up behind me. I spun round and they kneed me in the balls. Somebody punched me on the side of the head - really hard,' he fingered the bruise on his temple 'and I went down. Then there were just a lot of kicks, mostly to my ribs, and I think I must have landed on my arm. Some woman saved me. She came running over and they ran off. She called an ambulance.'

'So what injuries did you sustain?'

He waved his bandaged arm. 'This of course and a couple of cracked ribs. And there were signs of concussion, so they kept me in overnight.'

'Nasty,' said Wilcox. 'Can you describe these attackers?'

He shook his head. 'No chance. They were all in black and they had masks on, or their faces covered with scarves or something.'

'Big guys, were they?'

'No, not at all. But hard. One of them punched me in the stomach and I actually couldn't breathe for what seemed like thirty seconds.'

'So they were punching above their weight' said Murphy.

He looked hard at her for a moment, as if he suspected her of laughing, then nodded. 'I'd say so. Literally.'

'And they robbed you?'

'Yes. Phone and wallet.'

'Did anything happen in the bar?' asked Wilcox. 'Did you have any altercation with anybody, anything like that?'

He shook his head. 'No, nothing like that.'

'How long were you in there?'

He shrugged. 'Couple of hours, say seven till nine.'

'And who were you with?'

'What's that got to do with it?'

'Maybe nothing, but they might have spotted something that you didn't.'

'I don't want anybody else dragged into this. It was two guys from the US that I was hoping to do business with. They've probably flown back already.'

'OK,' Murphy began levering herself off the sofa, 'we'll let you know what we find out.'

'You don't need to find anything out,' he shot back. 'You know as well as I do who is responsible for this.'

'Do I?'

'Don't pretend you don't know. It's her – Miss Molly. Stupid bitch. Didn't get her chance to stitch me up in court, so she does this instead.'

'You recognised her?'

'No, of course not. She wouldn't have been involved personally. She got somebody else to do it.'

'OK we'll certainly look into that. You take care of yourself.'

They headed for the front door and he slammed it behind them.

'Let's hit the bar,' said Murphy.

UPPER STREET and Camden Passage were bits of London that you wandered down just for the pleasure of a wander. Murphy hadn't been down here for years and wished she hadn't brought Wilcox. The antique shops were where millionaires bought bits and pieces for their multimillion pound pads, but looking at the stuff cost nothing. And the clothes shops were always full of covetable things. Murphy rarely bought clothes but she did plenty of coveting, not so much wives and asses, but black linen dresses like the one in the window in Toast... maybe she'd just have a quick look inside.

'Guv.' Wilcox was on her heels, just as she was opening the door. 'The place we want is just down here.'

'Good, well spotted.' She turned away from Toast, straightened her shoulders and matched her step to his.

Rizzo's bar had deep red lighting and padded booths all around the perimeter. Just the sort of place an asshole like Christopher Dakin would bring a couple of guys in order to talk business. Murphy hoped the Americans had appreciated the extensive range of cocktails and the app-ordering system. There was nothing like fighting your way into getting served at the bar as far as she was concerned.

A few early lunchtime patrons were already installed and the guy behind the bar was busy with his shaker. He tipped the result out, slid it along to a waitress, and came back to them.

'What would you like?'

'Information,' said Murphy, showing her badge.

'OK.' He was frowning now.

'Were you here last night?'

'Yes.'

'Can you remember three guys, probably wearing suits, two of them American? They arrived about seven, left about nine.'

He shook his head. 'I don't really see most of the customers from my position here. They don't come up to the bar, mostly in this bar we do table service. You'd need to speak to the waitresses.'

'Can we do that then? How many are there?'

'Just two during the week. Jess and Macy.' He looked around. 'Hang on a minute.'

He left the bar and returned a minute later with two young women, who looked at them apprehensively.

'There's nothing to worry about,' said Murphy. 'We're

just looking for information on a group of guys who were in here last night. One British guy, quite tall with blond hair and stubble and two Americans. Do you remember serving them?'

'I think I served them,' said Jess. 'Why? Have they complained?'

'No, not at all,' said Wilcox. 'But it looks like there was a bit of a fight after they left here, so we're wondering if anything happened while they were here. Did they exchange words with any other customers, anything like that?'

Jess shook her head. 'No, nothing like that. Not that I saw anyway. It was all quiet in here last night. A couple of women sitting by the bar looked over at them and laughed. I noticed that. I thought maybe they were thinking these guys looked very straight.'

'Did the women leave just after them?'

'No, they were still here half an hour later, chatting and messaging on their phones. Only other thing I noticed about these guys – they didn't leave a tip.'

Chapter Thirty

KEITH CARTER WAS MOWING the lawn when his wife ushered them through the house. It was a manual mower, one that you had to push, just like Murphy's. One of the things she and Jack had agreed on, in the midst of various things they hadn't agreed on, was that electric and petrol mowers were total overkill for domestic gardens.

Keith agreed with her. 'Bloody noisy they are too,' he said. 'And at least with one of these you get a bit of exercise.' He parked the mower and led the way to a table and chairs set under an awning.

'I gather Sophie is having a bad time. I'm sorry to hear that.'

'She's a person of interest in connection with one of our investigations.' said Wilcox. 'So we wanted to talk to you, as somebody who presumably knows her quite well.'

'Like a character reference, you mean?'

'Well, not exactly, but we are interested in whatever you can tell us about her character. Can we begin by asking how long you were married?'

He frowned. 'Three years – yes, that's right. Got married right after university. We met there – at Leeds. There were only four women on the engineering course and the other three were – well, they looked like they were built for engineering. Sophie was a bit of an enigma, I guess that's why I was attracted to her. She looked kind of arty and insubstantial but she was clever and she worked bloody hard. We did quite a lot of site visits in our third year and she made it her business to keep up. When we started going out, I discovered that she spent a lot of time in the gym – and she was lifting pretty heavy weights.'

'Why did you split up?' asked Murphy.

He shook his head. 'Everything just fell apart after the miscarriage. Oh, you didn't know about that? In some ways, I think it was all my fault. The miscarriage was sad, but I felt that we could get over it, we could try again. Sophie was devastated, she couldn't get over it. I made her go to the doctors in the end and she was prescribed anti-depressants, but she wouldn't take them. It was as if she felt that it was because of her, that she'd brought this about or deserved it somehow. I kept telling her it's just something that happens and it's nobody's fault, but she wouldn't have it. She was still going in to work, she was functioning somehow, but she'd come home at night and she just couldn't even speak to me. She didn't blame me for it, she just seemed to feel that she could never be happy again – actually it was more like she felt she didn't deserve to ever be happy again. Eventually we couldn't stay together, our whole existence had become miserable. I couldn't find a way to help her and she wasn't interested in me anymore. We agreed to separate and then about six months later I met Angela, so there was no going back after that. Sophie filed for divorce but we kept in touch and I wanted to know that she was OK. She took up with some arsehole called Richard. He was married but she said she didn't care about that. Maybe she thought he would leave his wife, but of course he didn't. Then Angela got pregnant and that made things awkward between me and Sophie. The decree absolute came through about three months ago. I really want her to be OK, but I have to think about my own family now.'

'Yes, we understand,' said Murphy. 'Do you think Sophie's capable of violence?'

He stared at her. 'What? Of course not.'

'But she's no seven-stone weakling, is she?'

He hesitated. 'I suppose not. I would say the seven stone's about right, but there's plenty of muscle there. You can't climb a ladder in heavy boots unless you're strong.'

'So she would be able to take care of herself?'

'If she was attacked? Yes, I'd say so. But that's not the same as being a violent person, is it?'

'No,' said Murphy. 'But it's a start.'

'I THINK there's more to know about young Sophie,' said Murphy, as they drove away.

'She's certainly had a rough time,' said Wilcox.

'Yes, she has,' said Murphy, 'but right now she's auditioning for perp, not victim. We already have the victim.'

'I guess she doesn't have an alibi,' he allowed.

'That's right, so we have to investigate her thoroughly. What was the name of that carer? The one looking after her mum? Glenda, wasn't it? I'd like to talk to her. Not much use talking to Sophie's mum but Glenda might give us a more objective appraisal. She looks like someone who knows what goes on.'

Sudden Death

Wilcox pulled into the car park outside the police station and picked up his phone. He scrolled up a few pages. 'Glenda Morrison' he said.

'Good' said Murphy. 'Let's find a phone number for her and arrange to see her.'

Chapter Thirty-One

GLENDA MORRISON LIVED in an ex-council flat just off Bethnal Green Road and the door was whipped open as soon as they rang the bell.

'Come along in,' she said. 'I'll just put the kettle on.'

Murphy saw Wilcox open his mouth to protest. He was particular about his beverages and usually declined anything on offer. She silenced him with a look.

'That will be lovely,' she said and followed Glenda into the kitchen, where the crockery was already laid out. 'Do you live on your own Glenda?'

'Yes,' said Glenda, opening a large tin and lifting out a cake, which she proceeded to slice up. She filled the teapot. 'My husband died a few years ago and we never had children.' She carried the tray back into the sitting room, Murphy followed with the cake and they all sat down.

'But you have a job where you're meeting people all the time, I guess.'

'That's right.' Glenda handed Wilcox a plate and he

took it without demur. 'Some of them are easy to deal with, some of them are a bit more difficult, in that they have more needs, but I enjoy most of the time I spend with all of them.'

'So, you've known Eileen and Sophie for a few years.'

She seemed to stop and think. 'It must be four years now. That was when Eileen deteriorated fast and she needed help. My job comes under the NHS, and I work part-time. I just have four clients. I'm not as young as I was, so I didn't want to work full time. Some patients have complex needs and can be heavy to lift. Not that we're supposed to do lifting these days, but these hoists only exist in hospitals. In the community you have to do the best you can. Eileen is one of my easiest patients because she's not heavy anyway and she's continually making an effort. She really tries to keep her body mobile, she doesn't just sit there. And we have good outings to the park. We both like birds and plants. I know she's really frustrated to be in the wheelchair, but I think that frustration's good — she's not letting it beat her. I think eventually she'll be able to walk outside, at least for short distances.'

'And I gather Sophie's had a bad time the last few years.' Murphy took a sip of her tea and waited.

Glenda sighed. 'That's true enough. Eileen thought she was well settled with that nice young husband then — well, I don't know...'

'We know about the miscarriage,' said Murphy.

'OK. So, I can tell you it really affected her badly. There is a lot more understanding about miscarriages these days than there used to be, it's no longer something women are expected to just put to one side and carry on, but people suffer just the same from them. It's a bereavement and that's how it needs to be regarded. It takes about the same amount of time to recover from as the death of a family member, you can't rush it.'

'Did she get medical help?'

'As far as I know, Keith got her to the GP, but there's not much they can do, is there? They just don't have the time. Thirty-second interview and here's your prescription for the anti-depressants. Maybe it would have helped if she'd taken them, but she wouldn't. And I think she was probably right in the long run. I've seen too many people addicted to those. And then when you come off them, the grief is still there, it's all just been parked to one side.'

'And then she met this Richard' Murphy prompted.

Glenda took up the story. 'Richard, yes. We both knew he was a wrong 'un, but I said to Eileen, maybe she just needs somebody to take her mind off what happened. Maybe it's better than just sitting at home alone and thinking – too much thinking doesn't do anybody any good. At least with him she'll be out and about, going places. Maybe that will help her recover. I didn't think he'd leave his wife; they hardly ever do – well, what man wants to end up paying for two families? – and of course he didn't. I think she was less upset about that than she would have been if it hadn't been for the miscarriage. I mean losing a man is nothing compared to losing a baby, is it?'

Murphy nodded. 'Was she upset when Keith's wife got pregnant?'

'Yes, I could see she was. She hid it well. Nobody wants to resent another woman being pregnant, but it was just another blow. Made her feel a failure for losing the baby, I think. I'll just go and top up the pot.'

She disappeared back into the kitchen and Murphy took a minute to look around the room. Cosy, rather than stylish with thick curtains and several shelves of well-thumbed books. Probably not a gamer. Wilcox had eaten his cake, she was pleased to see.

Glenda bustled back in and resumed her seat. Murphy held her cup out for a top-up.

'I wanted to ask you, Glenda, as a health service professional, how you would assess Sophie's current mental state?'

Glenda seemed to sit up straighter at the 'health service professional' bit.

'She's quite a resilient young woman' she said. 'I don't think she's happy, but she's not disturbed or suicidal. She pushes herself very hard. She's doing a man's job really. I know you're not supposed to say that, but I can't get my head round the idea of a young woman working on building sites. Eileen says she really likes her job, though, so maybe she does. She knows she has to keep up or she'll have no credibility and I think she works hard at making her body strong, lifting weights and god-knows-what, because she needs it to be, but also as a way of pushing negative thoughts out of the way.'

'I suppose that's better than taking drugs' said Murphy, 'or cutting herself.' She looked at Glenda as she said this. Glenda nodded imperceptibly.

Murphy put her cup down. 'Do you think she could be violent if she needed to be?'

'Violent?' Glenda seemed to be considering this. 'No. Although I think any of us could be violent if we needed to protect ourselves or somebody else, but no. She's a soft person if anything, wouldn't hurt anybody.'

'Well thank you for your help, Glenda' Murphy rose from the sofa. 'Can we just ask you – we have to ask everybody – what you were doing last Thursday night?'

'Oh, is that the night it happened? Yes, Eileen told me about that stalker chap dying. Maybe there was somebody else he was stalking and they turned nasty. Has anybody thought of that? Well, makes no odds in my case. I'll have been doing the same as I do every night, sitting in here, having some supper, probably watching Netflix. I like living round here, but it's not an area to wander round at night and where would I go?'

'Yes, I know what you mean.' They made their excuses and left.

'OK, so she's top of the list,' said Wilcox. 'No alibi, probably had means and opportunity – it's all there. And she tried to throw us off the scent by suggesting he was stalking somebody else.'

'What about motive?'

'Let me think. Yes. Didn't she make some remark about losing men didn't matter? Not compared to babies. She hates men, that'll be it.'

'Alright. I'll let you explain that one to Bellweather.'

Chapter Thirty-Two

RICHARD AGNEW WORKED out of chambers in Holborn and, having managed, after a lot of wrangling with the clerk, to secure an interview slot, Murphy decided to visit him alone. This was based on the fact that he was not actually suspected of any offence and, more importantly, that he was a lawyer.

'It's just a cosy chat that will probably yield nothing' she told Wilcox. 'So, we'll keep it low-key. And we know how good these buggers are at drafting complaints to the IOPC.'

Wilcox nodded. 'Best behaviour,' he said. 'Don't let him see you drive up.'

In the event Murphy decided to take the tube. Parking would be a problem anywhere round there and it was within spitting distance (as she phrased it to herself) of Covent Garden, where she hadn't been for at least a year, so she would enjoy the walk from the tube. Covent Garden tube, that was. If Wilcox was with her, they would have had to go from Holborn tube station, which would have been a lot nearer but much less appealing.

When she arrived at the highly-polished front door in Remnant Street, she was carrying a few bags bearing evidence of frippery purchases, which was probably pretty usual for women visiting this expensive establishment. She'd just have to get them into the car back at the station without anybody seeing.

Richard Agnew was a tall man, with dark hair slightly greying at the sides and an expensive tan. She could kind of see how Sophie Carter could have found him attractive. There were no obvious defects, apart from the brusque manner in which he swept her into his office. Not surprising really. There would be no fee note issued after this meeting.

Murphy took the designated seat and hoped she'd be offered coffee. Apparently not.

'Now, what can I help you with?'

She smiled. 'Sophie Carter.'

His expression fell away. 'Sophie?'

'That's right.'

'Has something happened to her?'

'Nothing's happened to her,' said Murphy, 'but she has become a person of interest in respect of a case we are investigating. In pursuance of which, we are talking to her friends and acquaintances. And your name came up.'

She could see that what he really wanted to ask was how his name came up, when he had taken all those precautions, but he was too smart for that.

'I haven't seen Sophie for quite some time,' he began. 'Must be six months at least.'

'Yes, we know that,' said Murphy. 'What would be really helpful would be if you could tell me a bit about your relationship with her.'

He was now looking aghast. 'For instance,' said Murphy, 'can we start with how you met her?'

His face seemed to relax just slightly. He was on safer ground here. 'We met on a construction site' he said. 'My area of expertise is public liability. I had a few meetings with Sophie in respect of a project down in Docklands. I was very impressed with her.'

Murphy nodded in what she hoped was an understanding manner. 'Impressed' was one way of putting it, she thought.

'And you began seeing each other,' she filled in.

He swallowed and nodded. 'Yes, we did. We had a lot in common.'

'So, I guess you were meeting in hotels.'

He swallowed again. 'Yes. Hotels, bars.' He waved a hand airily.

'I'm assuming your wife knew nothing of this. Or were you planning to leave your wife?'

He folded his arms. 'There was no question of leaving my wife. Sophie and I enjoyed each other's company, but that was as far as it went.'

'So your wife still knows nothing about it?' There was silence. Now, she thought, she had him right where she wanted him. He'd be sending nothing to the IOPC.

'We're not really here to enquire into your personal affairs,' she said. 'But we are hoping that you can tell us a bit about Sophie. I gather her life wasn't going that well when she met you.'

He frowned. 'I don't want to betray any confidences' he said.

'You probably won't be doing that,' said Murphy. 'We know about the miscarriage.'

'The miscarriage affected her really badly,' he said. 'She blamed herself, although there was no logical reason for that, there was nothing she could have done that would have caused it. One time she told me that she felt she had let her mum down, I guess because it would have been a grandchild.'

'It sounds like you were dealing with quite a lot of emotional fallout,' said Murphy. 'Did you worry how she would take it when you finished with her?'

He glared at her. 'It wasn't all emotional fallout,' he said. 'We had a lot of fun together and by the time we finished she was in a much better place.'

'What you are saying is that you were good for her,' said Murphy. 'That's a good thing.'

He looked sharply at her as if to see whether she was being sarcastic.

'Tell me, did she ever mention somebody called Daniel Webb?'

He shook his head. 'No, I've never heard of him.'

'Why did you finish with her?'

His eyes swivelled from one side to the other. 'I can't really remember.'

'Oh, I'm sure you can. Good-looking, intelligent girl. No strings arrangement. What went wrong?'

'I decided that she needed somebody who could commit to her more fully than I could.'

'Commit to her in what way? Did she want you to marry her?'

'No, of course not.' He hesitated. Murphy just carried on looking at him. She was good at this. He sighed. 'Well, if you must know, after a while I realised that she was trying to get pregnant. She persuaded me that we could stop using condoms, because it was her safe time of the month. That sort of thing.'

'And you had visions of paternity tests and maintenance? Very scary.'

'Yes, well. That was what happened. She needed a stable relationship and I wasn't able to provide that.'

'In other words, you let her go for her own good.' He said nothing.

'Do you think Sophie's capable of violence?'

He narrowed his eyes. 'Sophie? Of course not.'

'She's a strong girl,' said Murphy. 'Plenty of muscle there.'

'That's just ridiculous. You didn't tell me she was suspected of anything.'

'Well, you know what we're like in the police. We suspect everybody. Are you quite sure your wife never knew about Sophie?'

'Quite sure. My wife has nothing to do with this.'

'In that case,' said Murphy, rising and giving him her best smile 'we won't need to trouble her. We'll leave it there for the moment. I may need to speak to you again, or I may not. Thank you for seeing me.'

She picked up her expensive carrier bags and he escorted her out. He might have had an urge to slam the door behind her but he resisted it.

Chapter Thirty-Three

MOLLY WRIGHT SHARED a flat in Bethnal Green with two other girls and agreed to see Murphy there at 7pm. It was in a council block near Victoria Park, a large part of which was probably occupied not by council tenants, but by private tenants paying rent to former council tenants who had purchased their flat and now become private landlords. And the rent now being paid by these private tenants, as Molly explained, was not insubstantial.

The flat had originally had two bedrooms, which meant that the sitting room was now a bedroom and the kitchen was where everything happened. Everything at the moment when Murphy was shown inside amounted to one young woman sitting by the sink with a headful of foils, issuing orders to a young man holding a can opener, another young woman unwrapping Deliveroo cartons and two cats yowling for their dinner, against the background of some music channel that was striving unsuccessfully to compete with the cats.

Molly told them to leave her dinner in the box and

ushered Murphy up to her bedroom, which had definitely not been tidied up for the occasion. 'Sorry about all this' she said. 'Some evenings there's nobody here at all, it's a bit unpredictable.'

'No problem,' said Murphy. 'It's good to see signs of life.' She thought suddenly of Sophie Carter and wondered if maybe this was the sort of environment she should be living in. Better than that flat all on her own.

Molly pulled up the cover on the bed and sat on it, leaving Murphy the chair. It was a bit informal, but it would have to do.

'The reason I wanted to see you, Molly, was because Christopher Dakin was mugged in the street two nights ago. Have you heard anything about that?'

Molly just shook her head soundlessly. Murphy said nothing. Eventually Molly broke the silence.

'You mean...somebody beat him up.'

Murphy nodded. 'Exactly.'

'Oh my God.' She was silent again. Murphy could almost see her trying to process this. Finally, she got there.

'And you think it was me?'

'No, I don't think it was you,' said Murphy. 'It certainly wasn't you on your own, because he was attacked by three people. We went to visit him afterwards and he was unable to identify anybody involved. However, he said that he thought you were behind it, so I had a duty to come and talk to you about it.'

'How could I be behind it?'

'Well, do you know anything about groups of ... people... who beat up men?'

'No.' Molly looked confused.

'The thing is, we have had a number of cases of men being mugged, and we are anxious to find whoever is behind it. Are you aware of any kind of movement of women, women taking the law into their own hands, that kind of thing?'

Molly shook her head. 'No nothing like that. Only thing I can think of is that when I brought the rape case against Christopher, I remember coming out of the police station and there were a group of women standing over the road. They shouted something like 'Good for you, Molly', but I didn't know who any of them were and I didn't hang about because I was with my mum.'

'Did you post much on social media at that time, about the rape?'

She frowned. 'Yes, I suppose I posted some updates on Facebook, and I got messages of support, but this was all from people I knew, friends, family. It's only natural they wanted to support me.'

'And you will have posted an update when the case was dropped?'

Molly nodded. 'Yes, of course, people would have wanted to know.'

'And did anybody come back and say he shouldn't be getting off, anything like that?'

Molly shrugged. 'Loads of people said that, it was the obvious response.'

'I suppose that's right,' said Murphy. 'I said as much myself. OK Molly, I'll let you get on now. If you have any more thoughts about this, please get in touch.'

They made their way downstairs. The cats were now silent. Dinner must have arrived.

Chapter Thirty-Four

THE MURDER of Jesse Finch seemed to have invigorated Bellweather. He had taken to sweeping in and out of the office, holding tense meetings with the drug squad officers, looking like he was directing operations. Whether the operations he seemed to be directing bore any resemblance to what was actually taking place, was another matter.

'I'm waiting to see him togged out in Kevlar, packing a gun,' murmured Wilcox.

'It could happen,' said Murphy, watching through the glass panel as the drug squad officers exchanged glances and one of them surreptitiously rolled his eyes. 'It's at least taken his attention off us, but probably not for long. So, what have we got?'

'OK. Molly Wright's Facebook.' He clicked and scrolled. 'She has a lot of followers. She works in the beauty business, after all. She posts lot of beauty tips, I guess that's what they're called. How to pluck your eyebrows the right way. How to apply concealer so it doesn't show. Exercises to prevent a double chin, all that sort of rubbish.'

'So how do you prevent a double chin?'

Wilcox sighed. 'The problem is that there are one hundred and twenty-seven followers. Some of them seem to be family, there are some family shots with Molly in them, and some of them seem to be school friends. A lot of them seem to be interested in her beauty advice and that looks like why they're following her. None of them look like the sort of people who go round dishing out violence, but what does that even mean?'

'So there's nobody that stands out?'

He shook his head. 'Nobody has posted anything actually inflammatory. But they wouldn't, would they? They're not stupid. And the people we are looking for are probably not posting on Facebook at all. They might just be acquaintances of people who are on Molly's Facebook and they heard about the case being dropped from somebody just mentioning it. We could put in an awful lot of hours into chasing up everybody on her Facebook, and end up nowhere.'

'OK' said Murphy. 'I don't want to end up nowhere. Nowhere is where we are now. We need to move on from that. OK, what else? Anything more on our main victim?'

Wilcox brought up the screen on Daniel's laptop. 'Surprisingly little. The websites he visited frequently were Amazon, one that sells motorbikes, several investment sites, a restaurant booking site, one that sells ski and snowboard stuff and Tinder. And he's got a number of games loaded of course – Call of Duty etc.'

Murphy nodded. 'OK, mostly boys' stuff. What about the emails?'

Wilcox pulled a pad across. 'I've made a note of the ones that recur frequently. There are a few work emails – exchanged with Stanley and Audrey – but not that many because most of that traffic goes through the company Outlook account. There are a few to family – his mum, his dad and somebody called Marcus, who I think must be his brother – he's in Australia. There are quite a number to a broker who was buying and selling Bitcoin on his behalf – that market seems to have a lot of fluctuations. There are some exchanges with university friends, by the look of it, concerning somebody's stag do, but that was all six months ago.'

'OK. Not a lot there. How about social media?'

'Surprisingly sparse. He's a smart guy of course, not an over-sharer. Not very active on Facebook, just a few holiday photos. And comments from a few guys – one called Ralph Owen and another called Sidney Vincent.'

'OK. Put those two on the list. We need to talk to them.'

Murphy looked at Daniel sitting on a snowy slope with a helmet and sunglasses and his feet plugged into his board, smiling for the camera. She wondered if those were the sunglasses that were the subject of his last-ever conversation with his mother. Another shot showed him sitting on a boat somewhere sunny with two girls in swimsuits and lifejackets.

'Just enough to give the impression of a successful life,' she said.

'Yes.' Wilcox nodded. 'Actually, the boat photo was two years ago, so no summer holidays posted since then. And he has no presence on Twitter or Instagram. I think the smart money is coming off social media. Maybe he's ahead of the curve.'

'Maybe he is,' said Murphy. 'Anybody investing in crypto-currencies has to know all about staying ahead of the curve. Have you been through Outlook?'

'Yes. So much, so boring. Most of the exchanges are between the three directors and quite a lot between Daniel and a guy called Jason Goodall, who seems to be the main contractor. Back and forth about hold-ups on the job, materials not delivered on time, quibbles over overtime rates, extra costs. It just goes on. Also, a lot of other stuff involving a company taking care of dry rot in the crypt. Lots of complicated pictures and diagrams flying back and forth. I couldn't find anything significant in there.'

'How about Stanley and Audrey's alibis? Did you manage to check them.'

'Yes, I got hold of Stanley's partner and two of Audrey's friends. They all said the right things. A little vague on timings, but they all seemed genuine.'

'Alright, so we're now into Daniel's phone. What have we got?

'No Instagram profile, like I said. Browsing history pretty much the same as on his laptop. I've been through his Whatsapp and his messages. A lot of them are just boring stuff, but there is a lot of traffic, well up to about two months ago anyway with a girl called Leone, Leone Freeman.'

'That's the name we got from Stanley. So, she could be the last girlfriend, before he conceived his obsession with Sophie Carter.'

'That's how it looks.'

Murphy stole a glance through the glass panel. Bellweather had risen from his desk. The meeting looked on the verge of breaking up. Time to make themselves scarce.

'Have you found an address for her?'

'I've found where she works.'

'That'll do. Let's get out of here now. We'll call her on the way.'

Sudden Death

LEONE FREEMAN WORKED for a Big Five accountancy firm in Finsbury Circus and agreed to meet them in her lunch hour. At five minutes past one, they watched her emerge from the seven-storey glass and steel building, a tall, slim woman with long dark hair, and they walked together to the nearby city garden.

'I love this place' she said. 'After five hours breathing conditioned air, the fresh stuff is wonderful.'

They sat on a bench and Leone slipped off her shoes. 'I was very sorry to hear what happened to Daniel,' she said. 'And very shocked. Nobody I know has ever died violently like that.'

'How did you meet him?' Murphy asked.

'We met at a party,' she said. 'I can't remember whose party it was now. In fact, I think I never knew the actual hosts, I just went along with some friends. One of those situations. I find parties a bit hard work, all that mingling and introductions and socialising and dancing and drinking too much, and worrying that you'll be left with nobody to talk to. I'm usually looking forward to getting home and falling into bed. That means I often end up in the kitchen. That's where the breakaway party usually takes place – the people who've decided they just can't be arsed. So, I drifted into the kitchen and there were a few people in there and the person you couldn't miss was Daniel. He was sitting at the kitchen table kind of – well – holding court. That's the only way I can describe it. He just sat there and people drifted in and out and chatted to him. He wasn't making any effort, he didn't have to make any effort, people were just coming to him. That kind of social confidence, it's kind of magnetic, and all the rest of us were just the iron filings.'

'That's a good analogy,' said Murphy. 'So that made him very attractive.'

Leone nodded. 'Irresistible' she said. 'At about 1 pm, things were drawing to a close and he stood up, looked at me, said 'Coming?' and that was it. I just followed him out.'

'Just like a movie,' said Murphy, or a sheep, as she thought but didn't say.

Leone smiled. 'Yes, it sounds like a cheesy rom-com, doesn't it? But it got less like a rom-com as it went along.'

'What happened?'

Leone took a deep breath and stretched her legs. 'I have to admit, the sex was OK and we went to a lot of places I wouldn't otherwise have visited – expensive restaurants, theatres, cool bars. But it was really just that. Going places and sex. I felt more like an escort than a girlfriend sometimes. When we were with his friends, he often almost ignored me. He would never have wanted to go for a walk with me, or sit in and watch rubbish TV. He never talked about himself, what he thought or felt, and he wasn't interested in what I thought or felt either. It was like a brick wall. There was no emotional engagement at all.'

'Why do you think that was?'

'I know one mustn't speak ill of the dead, and I'm truly sorry he's dead, but…'

'But you're going to be honest,' said Murphy.

'Yes, I am. He was a very self-confident man, maybe I found that attractive. But I don't think he had it in him to really care about somebody else, and he maybe didn't like women all that much. He probably liked them as bodies, but as people – not so much. I always felt that he would just dump me when the next one came along, or when I got boring. I was always concentrating on not being boring, not making any emotional demands. After a while I realised that I wasn't really enjoying it much anymore. Going along to all these cool new restaurant openings was nice, but it got a bit wearing. I could never relax and I always had to look good.'

'How did it finish?'

'I guess he got bored with me. In the end I must have gotten boring, like I knew I would. He dumped me by text – actually by text, isn't that classic? - after a few months. I wasn't so bothered to be honest, much less bothered than I thought I would be, except that I'd have liked it to be me that dumped him. But why would anybody want to kill him? That's just awful.'

'Can you think of anybody who would want to harm him?'

'No. He probably dumped other women, but I never met any of his other girlfriends and I don't think being dumped would make any of us want to kill him.'

Chapter Thirty-Five

SOPHIE SAT in front of her laptop with a glass of wine. The police had handed it back quite promptly. Hopefully they hadn't installed anything on it. She scrolled through the profiles, looking for one that would make her want to click. It was a big decision, after all. She couldn't afford a mistake.

Andrew: 'The most important thing for me is helping other people.' Yeah, right.

Aidan: 'I come from a big family and I love children.' Well, maybe.

Chris: 'I was in the rowing team at university and I enjoy cycling and rock climbing. I'm training for my first triathlon.' That's the one she should go with, but something stayed her hand. Maybe he's just a bit too satisfied with himself.

But she's not looking for a life partner here, she reminded herself.

Damian: 'I have a math degree from MIT and I've set up my own software company.' Of course. The brains. That was important too. Brainpower was very sexy, no doubt about it, and she could probably have lots of interesting conversations with this guy, but, realistically, quite aside from the fact that he was in the US, that was never going to happen. Don't get seduced by the brains.

'I play piano and acoustic guitar and I'm learning to write music.'
Sweet. A musical one.

But really, whoever this guy was, she'd be using him and discarding him. There was never going to be any future in it. Maybe what she should really look for is someone that's good in a fight, that would be a good bit of futureproofing. But none of them said that.

'I learned boxing in the army and I'm happy to beat up anybody. Particularly enjoy Saturday night brawls and cage fighting.'

That might have intrigued her, sparked her interest. Better than all this Mr Nice Guy stuff. Because the Mr Nice Guys were often not so nice when the going got rough. She knew that. And some of these urbane, sophisticated types could become downright creepy when it suited them. She knew that even better.

That young policeman, DC Wilcox. He looked like a nice guy. The sort of guy she could arm wrestle to the ground. The sort of guy that would be no use to her. No use at all.

Chapter Thirty-Six

RALPH OWEN WAS an economist working in the Treasury.

'I've never been in here before,' said Murphy, as they crossed Parliament Square. 'It's one of the perks of this job, being able to flash your badge and walk into places where you wouldn't normally be allowed.'

'That makes it sound like something illegal,' said Wilcox. 'Actually, I've got a friend who works in the Treasury. He says it's dead boring.'

They gave their names to the man on the reception desk and sat down to wait. Ralph Owen appeared after about five minutes. He was a solid-looking individual with buzz-cut hair and stubble. More prize-fighter than economist, was Murphy's immediate thought. So much for the accuracy of her first impressions.

They stood up and shook hands and Ralph led the way to the door. 'Shall we go into St James's Park?' he said and Murphy nodded. He'd want to keep this away from the office if he could.

'It was a complete shock when I heard about Daniel,' he

said, as they shuffled for places on a bench. 'I can't imagine him being dead. He was always so alive.'

'How long had you known him?' Murphy asked.

'Quite a few years,' he said. 'Since university. Durham.'

'What was he studying?'

'Economics. We were both doing economics. I was doing more of it than he was.'

'Sex and drugs and rock 'n' roll, was it?' asked Murphy. Wilcox rolled his eyes.

He nodded. 'Something like that. Daniel was one of those people who didn't need to work very hard. I never saw him at a lecture and he got through seminars by reading other people's notes at the last minute. Then he did a couple of weeks of actual work at the end of the three years and came out with the same degree as me. I was a bit pissed off about that, to be honest.'

'So, he wasn't really that interested in economics,' said Wilcox.

'No, it was just a subject to do while he was there. University was all about having a good time and he was very good at that.'

'Lots of girlfriends?'

'Yeah. I guess so. He always seemed to have at least one knocking around. But is all this relevant?'

'We're just trying to get a picture of what he was like,' said Murphy. 'At the moment it's difficult to see why anybody would want to kill him.'

'But surely it was just a random attack. We hear about people being mugged all the time, especially in some parts of London.'

'That's one possibility, but we have to consider any other possible scenarios. Did he have any enemies at Durham?'

He frowned. 'Nobody that I can remember. And anything like that would be ancient history now.'

'Ancient history can hang around for a while,' said Murphy. 'Did he have a bad break-up with any of the girls, any of the guys get angry with him, anything like that?'

He seemed to be considering this. 'The thing about Daniel' he said, 'was that he wasn't quite like the rest of us. Of course, we were all young and we could all run wild to some extent, but he was in a different class. He had no fear, no social anxiety, he wasn't trying to fit in with any gang. He was the gang. People just congregated around him. He did and said whatever he wanted to; he didn't care. Some people found him a bit overwhelming and kept away from him. He used to make disparaging remarks about some of those people – the 'weaker vessels' he called them – and the rest of us would laugh.' He hesitated. 'I'm not proud of that. I guess he didn't bring out the best in people.'

'Was there anybody in particular that he was nasty to?' asked Wilcox.

Ralph thought for a minute and then shook his head. 'No, and I wouldn't call it nasty, just a bit dismissive. The people we didn't bother with – well, I can't even remember any of their names now.'

'When was the last time you saw him?' asked Murphy.

'Quite a while ago. It was at a wedding. It would be six months ago.'

'Were there any other friends from Durham there?' asked Murphy. 'They might have seen him more recently' she added.

Ralph scratched the stubble on his head and sighed. 'Yes,' he said finally. 'There were two people that I remember. A girl called Sally – Sally Woodville she was called then, but she's married now, don't know what her current name is.'

'Do you know where she works?'

He started to shake his head, then stopped. 'Actually, yes, I do. She's at the British Library, or she was then, archivist or something.'

'And the other one?'

'Yes, the other one. Lawrence Wade. He was one of Daniel's crowd at Durham. He was there with his girlfriend. I think he works for some legal practice in the City.'

'And you haven't seen either of these people since then.'

'No. They weren't particularly friends of mine. We hadn't kept in touch since university.'

'And you haven't been in contact with Daniel since then?'

He shook his head. 'No. I'm engaged now and I tend to hang out more with people from work – cycling and stuff. Daniel probably has – had - a new set of friends as well.'

'And what were you doing on Thursday night?'

'I was at home with Trish – that's my girlfriend. I must have got home about seven o'clock. Do you want her details?'

Wilcox nodded. Ralph scrolled on his phone and passed it over.

'Thank you Ralph' said Murphy, rising from the bench. 'If we think of anything else, we'll be back in touch. We'll let you get some lunch now.'

They walked across the park, waiting for Trish to answer the phone.

'That seems OK' said Wilcox, as he disconnected. 'She said they stay in every night apart from weekends and he's usually back by seven. She works locally, in a school, so she gets home first.'

'Alright,' said Murphy. 'I didn't really like him as a perp, but we learned a bit more about the victim.'

'Nothing particularly useful,' said Wilcox. 'We'd already decided he was an arrogant arsehole. People don't get killed for that.'

'No, but I thought it was good to have our unseemly prejudice vindicated,' said Murphy. 'You're right. People don't usually get murdered for what they are, but they do get murdered for what they do. There's more we need to discover. What's the other guy called?'

'Sidney Vincent. Works at a hedge fund. He'll meet us at five thirty.'

'That'll be before he heads back in to do the evening shift,' said Murphy. 'Those guys sleep on the job from what I've heard.'

Chapter Thirty-Seven

SIDNEY VINCENT LED the way into a corner booth in the Queen's Head. He was a bit grey-faced but determinedly alert, putting Murphy in mind of a clapped-out whippet.

'I'll just have a mineral water, please' he said. 'I've got a few more hours work to do.'

'I guess these time differences really extend the working day,' said Murphy.

'You bet. At seven am the Tokyo market has been open for hours, so we have to get in early to catch up and the US market will be open well beyond ten pm our time. By Friday I've usually forgotten what day it is.'

'Well thank you for making time to see us.'

He took a sip of his drink. 'No problem. It's good to get out of the office for a bit, get my eyeballs away from the screens. I can't believe what's happened. Was Daniel mugged and they just ended up killing him?'

'That's one possible explanation,' said Murphy, 'but we're keeping an open mind. How long did you know Daniel?'

'We were at school together, at St Matthew's in Watford. We weren't close friends then, not at all. He went on to Durham and I went to Warwick and then, sometime after graduation, St Matthews's held a reunion for our year, intended to get us to give them money, you know, the usual thing. But quite a few of us were curious enough to turn up anyway, and I didn't have any particularly bad memories of school, so I went along. Most of us hadn't seen each other for years, but that's where I ran into Daniel again.'

'Was he different when you met him again?'

Sidney sighed. 'Yes, he was. To be honest, he was a bit of a gang leader at school and I wasn't in his gang, so he never bothered with me. But when I saw him at the reunion we got talking and he was really friendly. I guess we'd all grown up a bit, we weren't annoying schoolboys any more. Daniel was really quite ...engaging. He was telling me all about this church conversion he was doing. He thought I should buy one of the flats. I did think about it, just briefly, but I have other plans for when I escape from financial services.'

'So you're going to get out?' said Wilcox.

Sidney nodded. 'Everybody gets out in the end. We all hang in there as long as possible, see how much money we can accumulate, but it's not a lifetime career. I'm going to open a restaurant. That's what I enjoy doing – cooking. Another few years here and I'll have enough capital.' His face brightened momentarily.

'And what was Daniel's reaction when you told him that?'

'He gave me the usual spiel, you know. Most restaurants fold in the first year. Bloody hard work. Crippling business rates. Having to cope with staff and suppliers. People will rip you off and you won't be able to fire anybody. Tie up all your capital and make losses. Whereas, buy one of his flats, sell it on a few years later, pocket the difference. He was right about that. I'd definitely make money on the flat and have far fewer worries. But it's not all about money. I guess somebody else will be carrying on with his project now.'

'Yes,' said Murphy. 'He had partners, or co-directors rather. When was the last time you saw him?'

He hesitated a moment. 'It was a while ago. Probably six weeks. That was when I told him I definitely didn't want to buy a flat. I don't think he contacted me after that. I probably should have contacted him, but the weeks go by and I lose track. Poor Daniel, what a shock.'

Murphy nodded. 'Indeed. And can you tell us what you were doing last Thursday evening?'

'Normally I work till about ten, except on Friday, but that Thursday was different. I was working till seven and then we all left early and went for a drink because that was the day Nat – one of our traders - left. We went for drinks with him and we didn't go back to the office. We were all in the pub – this pub, actually – till closing time, about eleven pm, I guess. I wasn't in good shape the next day.'

'Thank you for your time, Sidney. We may be in touch again.' Murphy stood up to leave.

'You're welcome. I hope you find whoever did it.'

She nodded. 'I intend to.'

The light was just fading as they emerged onto the street.

'We'll come back here tomorrow' Murphy said. 'See if the bar staff remember Sidney and his mates last Thursday. They're probably regulars.'

'Sounds like Daniel suddenly got interested in Sidney when he found out he had a megabucks job,' said Wilcox, as they walked down Gracechurch Street.

'Exactly.' Murphy executed a swift left turn into Leadenhall Market. 'That's what it looks like to me. We're getting pretty much the same story about him from everybody. He wasn't particularly likeable, but I can't see why any of these people would want to kill him.'

'Why are we going this way? It's definitely not the shortest route.' Wilcox was consulting his phone.

'Silly me,' said Murphy, slowing her pace. 'Never mind, we're going this way now. But it's lovely, don't you think? A real piece of Victoriana.'

Wilcox looked around at the wrought iron and the expensive shop fronts and sniffed. '£125 for a hoodie – I can get three for that on Amazon. Anyway, do you think maybe Daniel was the victim of a random mugging?'

'If he was, it doesn't look like the same muggers as those who attacked Ian Wells and Christopher Dakin.' Murphy was now casing the front window of Reiss. 'Those guys were properly done over and robbed, but there was no attempt to actually kill them. Daniel wasn't beaten up or robbed – just one killer blow.'

'Maybe they just hit him too hard to start with, accidentally, and then he went down and they got scared and ran off.'

'That's always possible, except they do seem to have used a weapon on this occasion. We won't really find out one way or the other until we sort out where these muggings are coming from. I think we will need to put some attention back on that. But first I want to talk to Sally Woodville and Lawrence Wade.'

Chapter Thirty-Eight

SALLY WOODVILLE HAD KEPT her maiden name and was still working at the British Library. Sometimes, things just were that easy.

'It doesn't feel the same as the old Reading Room in the museum,' she told Murphy, as they sat in the noisy cafeteria area of the redbrick building in Kings Cross, 'but it's still a great place to be. At the end of the day, it's about the books, not the building.'

'It's great to have a job you enjoy,' said Murphy, wondering if she felt that way about her job. Maybe, on a good day. 'We're talking to everybody we can find who knew Daniel Webb.'

Sally shook her head and stretched her legs. She was a sporty-looking young woman with a make-up-free face, yoga pants and trainers. None of your power dressing.

'I couldn't believe it when I heard,' she said. 'It's not something you expect to happen to anybody you know.'

'How did you hear?'

'David – that's my husband – saw it on the news. I don't

watch the news much, I'm usually putting the kids to bed. Poor Daniel. Muggings these days are very frightening.'

'I know you saw him at a wedding...?'

Sally nodded. 'Yes. Petra's wedding. There were only a couple of people from Durham there, so we kind of hung out together. Most of the other guests were on Andrew's side – Petra's husband. He had a large family and he's part of a football team – or he was.'

'Was?'

'Oh no, nothing's happened to him. It's just that they don't live here anymore. They moved out to New Zealand a few months after they got married. Still there as far as I know, although I haven't checked in on Facebook for a while. He's a doctor and I think that's well paid over there.'

'So the people you knew at this wedding,' said Murphy, attempting to gather her thoughts, 'were Daniel, Ralph Owen and Lawrence Wade.'

'That's right. And we had all brought partners. Ralph's girlfriend is called Trish, Lawrence's girlfriend was – is – called Julia, and Daniel was with a girl called Leanne, something like that, not that he was taking much notice of her. And there was me and David. That's right, we were a group of eight.'

'Can you remember what you talked about?'

'I remember talking to Julia quite a lot – about babies of all things – and we promised to stay in touch, but I'm afraid we haven't. Sometimes things just go by too fast. Other than that, we all had a few drinks and we laughed quite a lot. I think it was Daniel – yes it must have been Daniel – who was doing character studies, kind of impressions, of some of the other guests – especially the older ones. Bad behaviour really, but amusing. That was Daniel all over.'

Yes, thought Murphy. From what she had seen, that was

definitely Daniel. 'Did you learn anything about what he was doing in life?'

Sally stared at her trainers for a minute, then lifted her gaze. 'He told us he was making a lot of money in property. Then Lawrence talked about a house in Shoreditch that he and Julia were buying. It sounded like a really good deal. Daniel was impressed with that – and it's not easy to impress Daniel – then he went on to tell us about a church he'd just got hold of. A church. Imagine that. As a historian, I worry about the future of historic buildings, but people have to live somewhere.'

'So you've known Daniel for quite a few years, off and on,' said Murphy. 'Do you think he had any enemies?'

Sally drained her coffee and sat back in her chair. 'I think he probably had people who didn't like him. He used to take the piss out of people, he was quite merciless about it. Good laugh and all that, but probably not so amusing for the people concerned.'

'Can you think of anybody in particular?'

'There were people at Durham that he used to make fun of, but they were just people you would see around. I probably never knew their names. Why? Are you thinking somebody mugged him on purpose? I can't see that any of this would drive a person to violence.'

'From what I see every day' said Murphy, 'it takes remarkably little to drive some people to violence, but I tend to agree with you. I don't think that's the case here. Did you ever go out with Daniel?'

Sally smiled briefly. 'I was about to laugh just then,' she admitted. 'Then I remembered he's dead.'

'Yes, he's dead,' said Murphy, 'but the facts are what they are and there's no point gilding them out of some misplaced sense of respect. The facts are what might enable us to find out why he died.'

'Of course. Well, no, I didn't go out with Daniel. Daniel was one of the more attractive men in my year – physically attractive, that is – but he never made the first move. Any woman who wanted to go out with him had to set out to seduce him, and then he'd decide whether or not he could be arsed. In some ways it was quite good – or it should have been quite good – in a feminist sort of way, because it was the women making the initial move, taking the initiative. But in practice it didn't look like that. It looked like he was exercising some sort of 'droit de seigneur' and the peasant girls were lining up to be exploited. Because none of them lasted very long. He had a low boredom threshold.'

'Why do you think he never made the first move?'

'Because he was unwilling to run the risk of being turned down. And he liked the 'control' aspect.'

Murphy nodded. 'That's what I figured. And you weren't up for it?'

'No. I saw how it went and that wasn't for me. There were a number of refuseniks and I was one of them. Daniel and I got on quite well, because I didn't take him that seriously, and once or twice he gave me this kind of, oh I don't know, sexy, come-hither look, as if to say 'wouldn't you like to throw your hat in the ring?' I used to just pretend not to notice and I could see he was puzzled by that. But, you know, he had this dead confident demeanour, but I think it was just skin-deep. I would say that, at bottom, he had reservations about himself. There were probably bits he kept private.'

Like the weird stalking behaviour, thought Murphy. For sure, he would have kept that private. 'I think you're probably right about that' she said. 'Did you say you had contact details for Lawrence Wade's girlfriend?'

Sally grabbed her phone. 'Yes, it must be here somewhere.' She did a few taps and started scrolling. 'Julia, Julia, not that one. Here we are. Julia Banks, here's her mobile number. It makes me feel bad. I never contacted her and now I'm passing her number on to the police.'

'I wouldn't worry about it. 'Overtaken by events' is, I think, what applies here,' said Murphy. 'Can I just ask what you were doing on Thursday night?'

'Oh my God. Am I a suspect?'

Murphy shook her head. 'No, it's just a standard question in these cases. I'll be asking everybody.'

Sally shrugged. 'OK, I would have been doing the same as I do every weeknight. I leave here at five pm, get home by five thirty, relieve the nanny, feed the kids, put them to bed about seven, by which time David is home and we have some sort of dinner. We don't go out again. Bit of Netflix, bed by ten.'

Murphy decided to stand up before her bum went to sleep. 'I think that's everything' she said. 'Thank you for your help. I may need to come back to you but probably not.'

'No problem,' said Sally. 'I hope you find who did it.'

They shook hands and a moment later she was gone, taking the up escalator two steps at a time.

That's the way to do it, Murphy thought.

Chapter Thirty-Nine

JULIA BANKS WAS silent for a moment when Wilcox told her they wanted to come and speak to her and Lawrence about Daniel Webb.

'Ms Banks. Are you still there?' he asked.

'Yes, I'm sorry. Just trying to remember what we have happening. It's OK. We'll be in this evening.' And she gave him an address in Tufnell Park.

'Interesting,' said Murphy. 'Maybe they've changed their minds about the house in Shoreditch. Tufnell Park is not quite so cool.'

'It may not be fashionable, but it's quite a decent area,' she pronounced when they emerged from the tube station three hours later. The address was in a Victorian terrace just off the high street.

'Just one bell,' said Wilcox. 'Looks like they have the whole house.'

The door was opened by a clean-shaven but thick-set young man with brown curly hair. He was wearing suit trousers and a white shirt, and Murphy squinted at the biceps faintly visible through the sleeves. His girlfriend had poker-straight blonde hair with darker roots and looked altogether much less robust. Neither of them looked overjoyed to be entertaining police officers, but Murphy was used to that and smiled as she took the offered seat on the sofa.

'Thank you for seeing us,' she said. 'We're talking to everybody who knew Daniel Webb and it's possible you may have useful information.'

'It's possible,' pronounced Lawrence Wade, 'but not very likely, I'm afraid. I've only seen him once since we left Durham.'

'Well, we'll see how we get on,' said Murphy. 'The one time you saw him was at a wedding, I gather.'

'Yes,' said Lawrence. 'It was a wedding in Sussex. But that was ages ago. We never saw him after that.'

'How did he seem on that occasion?'

He shrugged. 'Much like he always was. Daniel always had plenty to say for himself and it was mostly about himself. I guess I shouldn't say this now he's dead.'

'Oh, don't worry about that,' said Murphy. 'Virtue is not assigned by death, not as far as I'm concerned. What did he tell you about himself?'

Lawrence Wade sighed. 'He told us about his business interests, how well it was all going and his exciting new project involving a church building. He said he was going to take the best apartment, which would include a valuable stained-glass window, for himself. He hadn't changed at all. He was just like that at Durham.'

'In other words, you didn't like him much.'

'We didn't dislike him,' Julia interjected. 'I only met him that once but I'd say he was pretty good company. People who have lots to say are useful in some ways. They break the ice. I thought Daniel was interesting because he had no false modesty. It was as if he thought he was great and he didn't care who knew it.'

'You said he was like that at Durham' said Murphy, turning to Lawrence. 'What was he like back then?'

Lawrence Wade yawned. 'Excuse me,' he said. 'Early start this morning. So, Daniel. I met Daniel early on because we were in the same college and you tend to get to know most of the people in your college. Also, our rooms just happened to be near each other. I think everybody knew Daniel. He was usually the loudest person in the room and the rest of us were always somehow trying to keep up. Looking back, I don't know what we were trying to keep up with. It's not like he was brilliant or talented, but he just had that social confidence that so many of us lacked at that age. If Daniel yelled abuse or something mocking at somebody across a room, the whole room would hear, and probably laugh, because his voice had that carrying quality. I think there were people who avoided him, who would quietly disappear when he walked into a room. He just put them on edge.'

'So he exercised some kind of power,' said Wilcox. 'Did he have any close friends?'

'He had a couple of hangers-on, people who laughed at his jokes,' said Lawrence. 'Not sure I can even remember their names.' He paused a moment. 'Doug. Doug and Bennie. They'd have done whatever he told them to.'

'Like what?'

'Let me see. There was a guy called Simon, Simon something or other. He had some argument with Daniel and the next morning Doug or Bennie, one of them, swiped his towel while he was in the shower. Then he had to walk back along the corridor…'

'Yes. We get the picture,' said Murphy. 'What about women?'

'He was popular with the women,' said Lawrence. 'Worked his way through most of them. He wasn't interested in lasting relationships.'

'He was with a woman at this wedding, wasn't he?'

'Yes, he was' said Julia. 'She was called Leone. Nice person and I think she has quite a good job. He wasn't speaking to her much.'

'Can you think of any enemies he might have had?' Wilcox asked them both.

Julia looked at Lawrence, who shook his head. 'I'm sure there were lots of people who didn't like him much, but I don't imagine he had any actual enemies.'

'Can you tell us what you were doing on Thursday night?' said Wilcox.

They looked at each other. 'That's the night…,' said Julia. She turned to Wilcox. 'I had dinner in Camden with my sister. Camden Brasserie. Got back about ten.'

'And I was here fending for myself,' said Lawrence. 'No-one to vouch for me, I'm afraid.'

'OK,' said Murphy and they both rose.

'This is a nice street,' she said as they stepped outside. 'For some reason I thought you were living in Shoreditch.'

Julia looked at Lawrence. He waved an arm. 'Oh, that was a possibility at one time, but we decided against it in the end. Expensive and overpriced.' They both smiled.

Murphy smiled back and they set off. 'Well, there's something to look into,' she told Wilcox as they rounded the corner. 'Such a lot to unpick there. When people keep looking at each other like that I know they're telling me a story.'

Chapter Forty

'NOW, what was the name of Daniel Webb's tame builder?'

Wilcox looked up from where he was engaged in levering off his cycling shoes. It was unusual for Murphy to appear quite so early. He'd probably been hoping for a few quiet minutes to drink a first cup of tea and check his emails. He dutifully sat up and logged in.

'That came out of our interview with Stanley and Audrey, didn't it?' he murmured as he paged up. 'Here we are – Jason Goodall.'

'Ok, let's get onto him. He may have interesting things to tell us.'

'Well, he's not in the PNC,' said Wilcox a few minutes later. 'His firm is called Goodall's – no surprises there – and the website says they specialise in extensions and basement conversions.'

'Basement dig-outs,' said Murphy. 'So they're responsible for some of the building collapses we keep hearing about. Jolly good. See if we can have a chat with him.'

'He's on site at the moment' said Wilcox when she

returned with the tea. 'Address in Notting Hill. He'll be there for another couple of hours if we want to call round. Didn't sound too happy about it.'

JASON GOODALL WAS SUPERVISING the removal of scaffolding from a three-storey stucco-fronted end of terrace house when they arrived. He was a surprisingly skinny man with a weatherbeaten face, a tattooed neck and a loud voice.

'Watch out with that!' he yelled to somebody on a scaffold several floors up.

Murphy and Wilcox approached and showed their badges. He nodded resignedly, as if they were just one more cross he had to bear today.

'Bloody scaffolders,' he said. 'Turn up three days late and don't care how much damage they do. And it's not as if I don't already have a snagging list as long as your arm. Now what can I help you with?'

'Is there somewhere quiet where we can talk for a moment?' asked Murphy.

Goodall looked around for a moment and then nodded. He led the way round the side of the house and into the back garden.

'Owners aren't here at the moment. Just as well with the mess being made out front. I think we're OK here for a bit.'

They arranged themselves around a conveniently-placed wrought iron table and chairs. Goodall stretched his legs and breathed deeply. 'It's good to sit down for a minute' he said, 'but I can't be away too long.'

'That's fine. We understand,' said Murphy. 'So I'll come straight to the point. Daniel Webb.'

Jason Goodall sighed and slowly shook his head. 'Daniel

Webb,' he said. 'Poor guy. I'm sorry and all that, but what a mess. I'm probably going to end up losing thousands.'

'House in Shoreditch?' asked Wilcox.

He nodded. 'That's the one. Good property. Needs a complete refurb, but that's where the money is. Properties in need of total renovation are like gold dust these days. What happens is, Daniel gets hold of this one, pretty fast completion, he must have had the finances already lined up. We spend three weeks digging out the basement and taking down walls – not load-bearing walls, of course – and that's a big investment on my part. Five guys for three weeks, the subcontractor payments and the subcontractor taxes I'll now have to pay, not to mention the plant hire, those excavators cost a fortune to hire, daylight robbery, be just as cheap to actually buy one, and what happens? The client goes and snuffs it. Sorry to be blunt, but he won't mind as he's dead. So now nothing's going to happen till God knows when, and who's going to pay my bill? I don't mind admitting, I've been having some sleepless nights about it.'

'Have you been in touch with Daniel Webb's father?' asked Murphy.

He shook his head. 'I didn't like to bother the family. I got hold of one of the chaps at his office – Stanley he's called – and he said he'd look into it for me, but I haven't heard back.

'I think Mr Webb Senior is the person you need to get hold of,' said Murphy. 'He's Daniel's next of kin, so he'll be responsible for administering his estate. I'm sure you'll find him easy to deal with,' she added, with as much sincerity as she could muster.

'And there's the church, I guess,' said Wilcox.

Jason Goodall nodded. 'I'm hoping they'll keep that project going,' he said. 'If the company keeps going, that is, if it doesn't get liquidated or whatever. I'm less worried about that project, to be honest, because luckily for me they'd just paid my last stage payment, and of course I pulled the lads off the job soon as I heard what had happened, so I'm not actually owed any money on that one at the moment. But it would be a shame if the project was mothballed when we'd all done so much on it.'

There was a sudden crash out front and Jason leapt to his feet.

'One last thing' said Murphy, as they rushed after him. 'The address in Shoreditch.'

He closed his eyes for a second and then opened them. 'Norman Street' he said. 'Number 65. Just off Old Street. Oh, for God's sake, what the fuck's happened here?'

A man in a hard hat was just extricating a scaffolding pole from a window. It had been a large window.

'See?' said Murphy, as they walked hurriedly away. 'Some people have worse jobs than us.'

Chapter Forty-One

'I DIDN'T FEEL good about it, of course I didn't,' said Shirley Platt, putting the cups down on the coffee table. She was a comfortably-rounded woman in late middle age and the room was festooned in photos of what were presumably children and grandchildren.

She sat down opposite them and took a sip. 'They seemed like a very nice young couple and with her expecting and all, but the sale of the house had to fund my mum's care home fees and those are eye-watering already. She's ninety-four now and I suppose we could have had her here but she's getting to the stage where she needs specialist care, and that's only going to get worse isn't it?'

Sure is, thought Murphy, hoping she'd never make it to the specialist care stage. But maybe you feel differently when you're ninety-four. Maybe you have a whole different viewpoint. How many ninety-four-year-olds did she know? None. Mrs Platt was still talking.

'...and as my husband says once you have somebody in one of those places, you have a hostage to fortune, so to speak. They'll be putting those fees up every year – nothing to stop them, is there? – and the money has to come from somewhere, so an extra fifty thousand pounds made quite a difference. We just couldn't afford not to take it.'

Murphy replaced her coffee cup and nodded. 'And Mr Webb just kind of appeared out of nowhere, did he?'

'I must admit, that was a funny thing. He just phoned up out of the blue. We were a bit surprised, because it had been taken off sale weeks earlier, none of the estate agents were sending anybody round. We'd told them we had accepted an offer, and that was it. So, I don't know where he heard about it. I think my husband asked him, but I don't remember what he said. We told him it was no longer for sale and he said he'd add fifty thousand to whatever price we had agreed.'

'He must have really wanted it,' said Wilcox.

'Yes, he must,' said Shirley. 'It was a good purchase even with the extra money. It's a solid house, big bedrooms. It used to be a bit of a rough area, certainly was when we were kids, but now it's really fashionable, who would have guessed that? It's the house we were all brought up in, so it was sad to let it go, but we have to worry about mum now.'

'And what did the previous buyers, Mr Wade and his partner, say when you told them?'

She shook her head. 'That was the hard part. I couldn't face it myself. My husband phoned up and told them. He said they were very upset. The young man is a lawyer of some sort, I was afraid he'd threaten to sue us for breach of promise or something, but he didn't. My husband said gazumping is not illegal and lawyers are the last people who'd want to waste their time suing anybody and just putting money into the pockets of other lawyers. He's probably right about that. I think the young man said it was dishonourable, something like that, and I can't really argue with that. My husband was a bit upset when he came off the phone.

'Did Mr Wade ask who the other purchaser was?'

'Yes, but my husband wouldn't tell him. He said they don't have any right to that information. We wouldn't want some argument going on between two sets of purchasers, and then maybe they both pull out. Then where would we have been?'

Murphy nodded 'Of course. Thank you for seeing us Mrs Platt.'

She saw them to the front door and a cat rushed in as they went out. 'Must be his dinner time,' said Murphy. 'OK, let's get him in.'

LAWRENCE WADE HAD BROUGHT his own legal advisor, rather than rely on the duty solicitor. Murphy wasn't sure whether that signalled that he knew he was in a lot of trouble, or whether it was simply a way of heading them off. Or maybe, being in the business, so to speak, gave him access to the best and he was using it.

The legal advisor wore a seriously expensive suit. Even squinting hard, Murphy couldn't see what the label was. She also had a seriously expensive haircut, beautifully chopped to frame her face. All that and earning power too. You couldn't fault it. That certainly seemed to be Wilcox's opinion and Murphy had to kick him under the table to stop him staring.

They went through the preliminaries, during the course of which they learned that Lawrence's brief was called Eleanor Madison. The client was looking like this whole business was just a tiresome bore. Murphy hoped he wasn't right.

'We have asked you to come in,' she began, 'because we want to clarify what happened with 65 Norman Street.'

'Nothing happened with 65 Norman Street,' the solicitor shot back. 'My client tried to buy it, the sale fell through, end of story.'

'We're thinking there might be a bit more to it than that,' said Murphy. She turned to Lawrence. 'You were gazumped, weren't you? Nasty business.'

He shrugged. 'It happens.'

'But it's worse when it's done by somebody you know isn't it?'

'This sounds like just a fishing expedition,' Ms Madison replied. 'If you have no serious allegation to make, then we're out of here.'

'Daniel Webb,' said Murphy. 'He found out about the house at that wedding and then he moved in and outbid you. You must have been very angry.'

Wade shrugged again. 'It was annoying.' The solicitor flashed him a look.

'And you were expecting a baby...'

He lunged across the table at her. The constable on duty outside opened the door and the solicitor pulled him gently back into his seat. His shoulders were heaving. Murphy waved the constable away.

A tear was making its way down Lawrence Wade's cheek. 'It was our dream house,' he said. The solicitor was frantically signalling to him to shut up, but he ignored her.

'We'd sold our flat, we'd sold everything we had to get the deposit together and we had arranged the maximum possible mortgage. The whole thing was at a complete stretch. We were really looking forward to moving in. Then he moved in and outbid us, just because he could. It was a really bad shock. We had to move in with my parents while we found somewhere else. Julia was really upset. Then she lost the baby. I don't know whether the stress over the house caused it, maybe not, but it seemed to be all part of the same thing.'

'How did you find out it was him?' asked Wilcox.

'It wasn't difficult. I checked the records at the Land Registry – probably the same as you did.'

Murphy nodded. 'And what did you do then?'

'I think my client needs a break,' said Ms Madison firmly.

'What did you do Lawrence?'

'I went round to see him.'

'At his flat?'

He nodded. 'Yes. I just wanted to tell him what a piece of shit he was. I knew that wouldn't do any good, but I thought it might make me feel better.'

'What did he say?'

'He didn't seem to think it was anything important. All's fair in love, war and business, all that sort of crap. Except to us it wasn't business, it was going to be our home.'

'Was that when you decided to kill him?'

'That's enough.' The solicitor was on her feet. 'My client is saying nothing further. Come on Lawrence, we're out of here.'

But Lawrence was still sitting there. 'I really did want to kill him' he said. 'But I couldn't think how. If there had been a weapon handy, I might have used it. In the event I just did what I could.'

'You punched him on the jaw,' said Wilcox suddenly.

Lawrence turned to him in surprise. 'That's right' he said. 'How did you know?'

'It came up in the post mortem. Hairline fracture, not fully healed.'

The solicitor was now covering her eyes.

'What did you do after that?' asked Murphy.

'Nothing. I felt remarkably better after punching him and after making such a good job of it. I mean, I'd never tried to punch anybody before and he'd gone down flat on the floor. Just like in a saloon fight. It was definitely a moment. I waited for a minute or so, until I knew he was OK. He started trying to get up and groaning, so I left at that point.'

'Did you hear from him after that?'

'No, nothing at all. I wondered if he would call the police or report me to the Bar Association. I was waiting for that to happen. I guess he could have made a lot of trouble for me if he'd wanted to.'

'But he didn't. Why do you think that is?'

'I think he didn't want to go public with the fact that he'd been punched. I also wondered if maybe he had decided that he had deserved it, that he was going to take it like a man. Those are my possible explanations anyway.'

'Did you keep tabs on him after that? Follow him around?'

He shook his head. 'No, of course not. I had no desire to ever see the bastard again.'

'Did you decide that maybe you hadn't hit him quite hard enough and you wanted to have another go?'

'No, not at all. I was done with him.'

Ms Madison stood up. 'Unless you are going to charge my client with punching somebody who never made a complaint and who is now dead anyway, I think we're done here.'

'Yes, I think that's all for now,' said Murphy. 'Don't leave town without telling us.'

She had him out the door in five seconds.

Murphy sat back and stretched her legs. 'The problem is,' she told Wilcox, 'I believe him. I might be wrong about that and I'm prepared to change my mind if more evidence emerges, but that's where I am right now. I'm not sure where that leaves us. Back at square one, I think.'

Chapter Forty-Two

'YOU'VE PROBABLY GUESSED that I have something to tell you,' Valerie said, as the waiter departed with their orders.

'I didn't guess,' said Murphy. 'I just assumed you wanted a decent meal out, same as me.'

'You could have a fantastic meal every night, if you managed to get home for it,' said Susannah. 'Those men spoil you to bits.'

'It's true' said Murphy, sipping her wine. 'I'm very blessed.'

'But wouldn't you like to meet a man you could have a...relationship with?' asked Valerie.

'Sometimes I would – maybe,' said Murphy. 'Other times not. Relationships are not so important when you get to my age. I won't be giving you any more grandchildren, that's for sure.'

'No, I wasn't counting on that,' said Valerie.

'So now, what is it you have to tell us?' asked Susannah.

'Now that we've disposed of Miranda's love life. Oh God, you're not marrying him, are you?'

'Of course not,' Valerie lowered her voice as the waiter reappeared. 'That's lovely. Thank you.'

'So tell us now, before I put this forkful in my mouth and end up choking myself,' said Murphy. 'You're not pregnant, you're not getting married, so what's left? You're going to live in sin?'

Valerie smiled. 'Doesn't seem so long ago that they actually called it that,' she said. 'No, listen. All I wanted to tell you was that I won't be around for Christmas this year.'

There was silence. Christmas had always been at the family home. Murphy recovered first. 'That's no problem for me. We'll probably have a Christmas crime wave, so I'll be working and the kids can spend the day with Jack.'

'You can all come to us, anyway,' said Susannah.

'So where will you be?' asked Murphy. 'Is he whisking you off to the Bahamas?'

Valerie smiled. 'We're going on a cruise.'

Murphy and Susannah exchanged an indulgent look.

'That's lovely Mum,' said Susannah. 'One of those nice river cruises?'

'No, not a nice river cruise. A bit further afield than that.'

'So where are you going? The Canaries? The Caribbean? New York for Christmas shopping?'

'Antarctica.'

Nobody spoke for a minute.

'Bloody hell,' said Murphy. 'On one of the proper boats?'

'Yes. An expedition ship.'

'So you'll get to wear the lifejackets and the big rubber boots?'

Valerie nodded. 'Exactly. We'll make landfall in Antarctica. Such a privilege. You even get to put on a wetsuit and get in the water. I am so up for that.'

Murphy shook her head. 'I am well jealous.'

'It must cost a fortune,' said Susannah.

'Yes,' said Valerie. 'Most expensive trip you can take.'

'So is he paying?'

'Bit of an indelicate question, darling, but yes, he is. Or at least he's paying a bit more than me.'

'Bloody hell,' said Murphy again. 'Can I come?'

Valerie laughed. 'How many years is it since you've wanted to go on holiday with your parents?'

'Does he have an equally rich younger brother?' asked Murphy.

'Oh, you're changing your mind about relationships now, are you?' said Susannah. 'I think that's called gold-digging.'

'Gold-digging seems to have gone a bit out of fashion,' said Valerie.

'Oh, I don't know,' said Murphy. 'Maybe the phrase has gone out of fashion, but we're still world number one spot for high-end divorce. Rich, or wannabe rich, women still flock here for the express purpose of taking their husbands to the cleaners. The ones lower down the food chain have fewer options.' She thought for a moment and a picture floated into her head. 'Maybe they just resort to physical violence.'

Chapter Forty-Three

'I HAD A THOUGHT LAST NIGHT' she told Wilcox.

'Oh?'

'Yes. I don't know why I didn't have it before. If we look at the two mugging victims – Ian Wells and Christopher Dakin – what do they have in common?'

'They're both toerags.'

'Yes, but apart from that. What sort of toerags?'

'A wife-beater and a rapist.' He was silent for a moment. 'Yes, I see what you mean.'

'Sandra Fuller – Ian Wells's ex – has boxing gloves. I suddenly thought of them last night. What if my original instinct was right - there's some group of women picking off men who abuse women?'

'Like female vigilantes, you mean?'

'Something like that. You can see why it would look like a good idea. We're not doing a great job of protecting them.'

Wilcox huffed. 'We do our best.'

'Yes, we do, but we have limited time and resources.

Maybe direct action looks more effective. Probably is more effective, come to that. I want to talk to Sandra Fuller again, and first let's do a trawl and see if there have been any other incidents.'

After about half an hour Wilcox raised his head. 'OK, I've got one here. David Petworth. Two months ago. Beaten and robbed round the back of Angel tube station.'

'Is he in the PNC?'

'Yes. Broke into a women's refuge, threatened to smash the place up and they called the police.'

'Nice. Do we have an address?'

'Yes, we do. It's on our patch as well. One of those streets off the Liverpool Road.'

'Good. Let's pay him a visit.'

THE HOUSE HAD SO many bells it was hard to know which one to ring.

'How many people do you think live here?' said Murphy.

'Bedsits,' said Wilcox, leaning on the bottom bell. 'And possibly multiple occupancy in each one.'

After a few minutes, he tried the next bell and a woman stuck her head out of the window.

'Whaddyawant?'

'Police,' Murphy yelled back. The woman hurriedly withdrew her head.

'Just gone to hide her stash behind the cistern,' said Wilcox and a few minutes later the door was opened. The woman was fronted by a Jack Russell terrier that growled and bared its teeth. Wilcox squatted down and extended a hand and the dog gave a whimper and allowed its ears to be rubbed.

Murphy and the woman exchanged a glance. 'Alright, dog whisperer,' said Murphy. 'We're looking for Dave Petworth, love,' she told the woman. 'Have we got the right house?'

The woman stood aside and nodded. 'Top floor,' she said.

Murphy led the way up the thinly-carpeted stairs and banged on the door.

Dave Petworth glared at them like a man interrupted in the middle of his lunch, which indeed proved to be the case. There it was, laid out on the coffee table. Sausages, eggs and a mountain of sliced bread, in front of *Location, Location, Location* on the TV.

'Planning your next house move, are you David?' asked Murphy, as he turned the TV off and threw the remote down. 'Please eat your lunch, don't mind us.'

He folded his arms. 'What can I do for you?'

'We just wanted to have a chat with you about the attack that you suffered,' said Wilcox. 'See if there's any other details we can gather.'

He sat down heavily. 'Bit late for that, isn't it? Your lot didn't come up with anything at the time.'

'It's possible,' said Murphy, 'that you weren't the only victim.'

He sniffed. 'Victim is right. I had a bruised spleen and a cracked rib. Scared to cough for weeks. I'm still not right, still having flashbacks, panic attacks.'

'Is that why you're off work?' asked Wilcox.

'Of course. Indefinite sick leave. And if you do find who did this, I'll be claiming damages, you bet I will.'

'Very distressing for you,' said Murphy. 'Can you tell us anything about the people – I assume there was more than one? – who attacked you?'

'It was definitely more than one. One I could have dealt with. I'm normally able to take care of myself.'

'I'm sure you are. So how many, would you say?'

He shrugged. 'At least three, more like four.'

'Four? It's a wonder you weren't killed.'

'Well, I fought back, sent them packing.'

Wilcox consulted his notes. 'It says here that it was two young women who drove them off.'

'They came along after, didn't they? I'd already given the bastards what for, they were about to leg it. Then these girls came along and they called the ambulance. I was grateful for that, mind you. I couldn't call the ambulance myself because the buggers had taken my phone.'

'OK' said Murphy, 'and can you describe these assailants at all?'

He rolled his eyes. 'Kids. That's what they were. Just vicious kids. Should be locking up the parents.'

'Did you see their faces?'

'Nah, they had their faces covered and they never spoke, but they weren't big guys.'

'And they took your phone and wallet.'

He nodded. 'That's right. Just been to the cashpoint, too. Hundred pounds cash in that wallet.'

'Well thank you for telling us all that, David. Do you have a current address for your wife?'

'What's she got to do with it.'

'Probably nothing, but she would have been at home when you arrived back, wouldn't she?'

He shook his head. 'No, we'd split up. I was living in the house and she was somewhere else.'

'And is she living in the house now?'

He rolled his eyes. 'No, we let the house go. It was only rented. She's got another flat now. If I was working, I'd probably have to pay maintenance for my son. But not for her. I'm paying nothing for her.'

'Do you have a phone number for her?'

He shrugged. 'Yes.' He tore a strip off the newspaper and scribbled something. 'Here it is. She doesn't take my calls, but you're welcome to speak to her.'

'Indeed. Well, I think that'll do for now. We'll see ourselves out.'

They made their way down the stairs, passing three people coming up.

'He's a real beauty, isn't he?' Wilcox remarked, looking up at the top-floor window.

'Certainly is. But a very different type from Daniel Webb. No social skills there. Anyway, we can contact his wife now, so let's see what she's got to say.'

Chapter Forty-Four

SOPHIE WIPED AWAY a bead of perspiration that was just about to run into her eye and took a large swig from her water bottle. Then she adjusted her hand fastenings and put her gloves back on. She had always had one particular image in her mind when she hit the punching bag, but now the picture was becoming less clear.

Overtaken by events was how she described it to herself, but maybe that made it sound too passive. She had initiated the end game and now she wasn't sure if she had done the right thing, but there was no point thinking like that. He was dead. That was a result, however it had been arrived at. There would be no more creepy notes, no more wondering if she was being watched, no more wondering if he really knew about her and was amusing himself at her expense.

She changed her foot position and struck from a different angle. Important to be able to change the angle of your punch and it was as much about the footwork as anything else. Keeping your weight in the right place, so you didn't throw a punch and then fall over. Keeping on the balls of your feet, able to shift position on a sixpence, so they didn't know what was coming next. She hammered in hard.

'Enough already,' said a voice behind her and she pivoted round on the balls of her feet. 'You've been at it too long. Give it a rest.'

Ritchie stood there, covered in sweat and with a towel hanging round his neck.

'I didn't know you were here,' said Sophie.

'Well, I was, and I've been watching you for the last few minutes. I don't know who that punchbag represents for you, but he's properly dead now. You're just beating up a corpse.'

Sophie removed a glove and wiped under her eyes. 'I'm still not fast enough. I don't think I'm getting any better.'

'Better for what? Are you training to be a cage fighter or something? Come on, let's go for a shower and a coffee. Give somebody else a go on this bag, like this lady here.'

A young woman approached and Sophie smiled. 'Hello Sadie.'

'Hello yourself.' Sadie had two plaits held in place with a black sweatband and a black T-shirt and leggings. 'You've punished yourself enough, piss off and drink coffee.'

Sophie followed Ritchie out towards the changing rooms. 'I've never seen so many women in the gym,' he said. 'Are they all punishing themselves for something?'

Chapter Forty-Five

SHARON PETWORTH WAS at work in a supermarket when Murphy called her and she agreed to meet them when her shift finished. She came out at 4.30, carrying two bags of groceries, and put them in the boot of her car.

'Shall we go for a coffee?' said Murphy, 'or have you got anything perishable in there?'

Sharon waved a hand. 'No, it's fine, all cans and packets. Let's go over here.' She led the way into Costa and Wilcox went to get the coffees.

'We've been having a chat with your husband,' said Murphy when they had seated themselves.

Sharon smiled. 'Well, that was a treat for you. How is he?'

'Not very well, or so he says. He got beaten up. Did you know about that?'

'You bet I did. He actually phoned up and accused me of doing it, threatened to send the police round.'

'Interesting. He didn't tell us that.'

Sharon took a sip of her coffee. 'Naturally he didn't,

because then he'd have to tell you why I might have wanted to beat him up, and he wouldn't want to go there.'

'Do we take it that you didn't beat him up?'

She rolled her eyes. 'I wouldn't want to get that near to him.'

'But you must have loved him once, so what happened?'

Sharon drew a deep breath and rested her elbows on the table. 'I thought I loved him once, when I was young and silly. But you don't stay young and silly forever. After a few years I realised that he was controlling every part of my life. He didn't like me having other friends, he didn't like me going anywhere without him, he always wanted to know where I was and what I was doing. When Freddie was a baby, I didn't really notice, because I was always at home with the baby anyway, I didn't want to be anywhere else. But then Freddie started school and I went out to work, and it was great getting out of the house and meeting other people. But Dave didn't like that at all, he was always accusing me of seeing other men. As if I would have had the time or the energy. Then he lost his job, so I was the breadwinner and I was still having to put up with his stupid behaviour. He beat me up a few times, once in front of Freddie. It took me a while to leave, because he'd always apologise and squeeze out a few tears and promise to behave better and I didn't want to break up Freddie's home. Then one day a woman at work saw the bruises and gave me the contact details for a refuge. I didn't immediately do anything about it. You always think, maybe it won't come to that, but it felt like an option that was there for when I needed it. A week later he beat me again and that was it. I already had some bags packed. I collected Freddie from school the next day and we moved into the shelter. I'd left Dave a note to say we'd gone. I didn't want the police searching for us. But you can't really disappear when you've got a child at school. Next day, he trailed us from the school and came banging on the door of the refuge.'

Murphy nodded. 'Yes, we got called in at that point.'

'It was really awful. I felt so bad that I'd brought this down on them, but the woman running the refuge was marvellous. She said they were used to this and they knew how to deal with it. She spoke to him through the door – she said the number one rule is that you don't open the door – and told him to go away now and maybe a supervised visit could be arranged for another time, or whatever. He didn't like that. He started trying to smash the door down, kicking it and trying to shoulder his way in. By the time the police arrived, which wasn't long, he'd almost dislocated his shoulder. They took him away and gave him a warning. I hoped he'd calm down after that and we could organise things in a grown-up way, but he was so angry. He was still coming to the school gates, so I had to have other people walking back with me. The refuge found me a lawyer and we arranged a legal separation and I found somewhere else to live. I had to be really careful that he wouldn't discover my new address, because he was still creating a disturbance at the refuge and making threats.'

'Then somebody, or a number of somebodies, beat him up,' said Wilcox.

Sharon looked up at him. 'That's right. I haven't seen him since the separation was arranged. I don't know who did that, just muggers, I guess.'

'So you don't have any idea who it could be?' said Murphy.

'Absolutely not. It does seem to have quietened him down a bit, but I don't know anything about it.'

They walked Sharon back to her car. 'You take care,' said Murphy. 'We might be back in touch.'

'So you don't think she had anything to do with it?' said Wilcox.

Murphy shrugged. 'She's got a job and a young child and housework and shopping. Where would she find the time? Plus, I understand how she feels about not wanting to be near him. And this looks like a group endeavour. She probably wasn't personally involved in it. She could have organised the hit, though.'

Chapter Forty-Six

THE DOOR WAS OPENED by a comfortably-proportioned woman with a wraparound apron and bright red hair. Murphy really liked the apron – sort of 1950's retro-cool and probably very expensive these days. What would have made it even better would have been if the woman had tied her hair up in a headscarf knotted on top of her head. The wartime factory girl image. That would be the complete look. Wilcox was now looking at her strangely and she realised they were both waiting for her to speak.

'Ms Welbeck?' She brought out her badge and introduced them both. 'Can we come in and have a word with you?'

Marcia Welbeck widened her stance. 'We don't want any trouble here.'

'No trouble at all. Just something you may be able to help us with.'

Marcia held the door open and they followed her into a hallway festooned in outer garments of every size and description.

'We'll go in the kitchen' she said and Murphy stole a glance into the sitting room as they passed. Three small children were watching a wide-screen TV and two women were watching their phones.

'How many families do you accommodate here?' she asked.

'It varies,' said Marcia. 'There are strict regulations regarding overcrowding and stuff, but I try not to turn people away.'

Murphy nodded. 'OK. Do you remember a visit from a Dave Petworth?'

Marcia rolled her eyes. 'That piece of …rubbish. He damaged the locks on our front door and the locksmith charged me an arm and a leg to get them replaced. Which of course I couldn't claim off Petworth because he was pleading poverty. And the police didn't manage to put him off at all – he carried on hanging around even after I told him Sharon had left. He thought he could scare me into handing over her address. Anyway, that was months ago. We haven't seen anything of him for quite some time now.'

'I think maybe the reason you haven't seen him is because he was attacked and beaten up in the street,' said Wilcox.

Marcia frowned. 'Was he?'

'You didn't know about that?'

She shook her head. 'No, I didn't, and I hope you don't think…'

'We're not accusing you of anything,' said Murphy, 'but we're hoping you might know something. Since the attack on Dave Petworth, two other men have been attacked in a similar fashion. What all three men have in common is that they had hurt or abused women, and what the attacks have in common is that in each case there seem to have been three attackers. They were well-disguised and left no DNA, but we think they may have been women. Women who had had some kind of martial arts training.'

'Well how about that.' Marcia started to smile and then hurriedly switched it off.

'It's possible to think that maybe justice was served,' said Murphy, 'but these sorts of physical attacks don't help the cause of women in the long run – and anyway it's an illegal act, potentially punishable by imprisonment.'

'I understand that, but I'm afraid there's nothing I can tell you. The women who come to stay here usually have children to care for and they often have jobs they're trying to hang onto. When they go out, they're looking out for the abuser, scared of being accosted. There's no way they have the ability, or the inclination, to indulge in any kind of vigilante activity.'

'Maybe not the women themselves, but supporters perhaps. Where does your funding come from Ms Welbeck?'

'Mostly from charitable donations, and fundraising.'

'But probably also a certain amount from the local authority?'

'A certain amount,' she replied stiffly.

'So, if you knew of any criminal activity going on, you would feel obliged to help the authorities?'

Marcia Welbeck straightened up and looked straight at them. 'Of course.'

'OK, I think we're done here,' said Murphy, making her way out. 'If we need any further information we'll be back, but that's all for now. Thank you for your help.'

'Pleasure.' The door with the new locks was slammed behind them.

'I'm wondering' said Murphy, 'whether it's worth

putting a tail on her, maybe just for 24 hours. It's not likely she'll visit anybody in person, life is lived on phones these days, but I'm tempted.'

Wilcox shook his head. 'No budget.'

'I somehow think that if it was to bring to book a bunch of uppity women, Bellweather might be prepared to authorise it.'

Chapter Forty-Seven

'WHAT WAS the name of Sophie's friend in Oxford?'

Wilcox consulted his notes. 'Cass. Cass Phillips.'

'OK. I think we should go and talk to her. Give her a call and see when she's free.'

'She's already confirmed Sophie's alibi.'

'That was just to do with Liam's death, which was not a murder anyway. But I'm interested in what she can tell us about Sophie. I don't feel I understand enough about her. And in the meantime, we need to get to grips with these muggings. They might be random, unconnected events, but they're starting to look like something else.'

She looked up to see Bellweather approaching her desk.

'My office' he snapped.

Murphy followed him in and shut the door. He seated himself behind the desk and cracked his knuckles experimentally. Murphy saw a brief moment of pain flash across his face. More practice needed on the knuckles.

'So where are we at?'

Murphy drew a deep breath. 'We've interviewed Daniel

Webb's closest friends and associates. At the moment, none of them look like likely suspects. We've been looking into previous muggings to see if this could still be a mugging gone wrong, but there are too many differences.'

'Surely these muggers must already be known to us?'

'I don't think so, sir. I think these are new players.'

'How do you work that out?'

'Well, I think it's possible they're women.'

He stared. 'Why would women be mugging people?'

'Not people in general. Men.'

He shook his head. 'What is the world coming to? Has anybody identified them?'

'No, but I have a couple of avenues to pursue. It may require a bit of manpower.'

'Well get on and pursue them. And what about this girl that was involved with Daniel Webb? Surely, she's still the main suspect.'

Murphy nodded. 'Yes, we're still investigating her. I'm planning to interview one of her friends today.'

He sighed. 'Get on with it then. We need a breakthrough on this case. I don't want any more complaints to the IOPC.'

Murphy shut the door and headed back to her desk.

'OK, I think we've got the budget' she told Wilcox. 'See who fancies a bit of overtime tailing Marcia. Did you get through to Cass Phillips?'

He nodded. 'She has a lunch break at one o'clock. We can see her then.'

'Good. Let's head off to the dreaming spires. We can have lunch reclining in the sun on the lawns or lounging on the steps of the Ashmolean.'

Wilcox shook his head.

Chapter Forty-Eight

IT WAS RAINING IN OXFORD, properly raining. The water pounded down from a grey sky and pedestrians hurried past under umbrellas or anything else they could find. The weather had broken when they were halfway through the train journey, leading Murphy to wonder whether it was still fine in London.

Cass Phillips was a stocky girl with curly black hair and a penetrating stare. It was hard to imagine a greater contrast to Sophie Carter, Murphy decided, as they huddled together in a Café Nero with steamed-up windows. Altogether, today was confounding her expectations.

'Thank you for seeing us Ms Phillips,' she began.

'Call me Cass, please. Saves worrying about the Ms and the pronouns.'

'The pronouns. Of course. Well, Cass, I know Sophie is a friend of yours and she's probably told you about all the business with Daniel Webb.'

'A bit, yes.'

'Somehow, Sophie has made it onto the suspect list and

the only way she's going to get off it is if we find out exactly what happened. I don't know if you have any insights to offer, but if you can help us understand a bit better what's going on with her and what went on with Daniel, then that will be helpful.'

Cass moved her bag off the stool next to her to allow a man in a dripping jacket to sit down and then she stirred her coffee for a moment. 'I agreed to see you because I have nothing to hide. I'm not privy to any secrets. Sophie is my friend and I'm not going to be telling you anything that I won't be happy to report back to her, so I'm not sure how I can help.'

'Fair enough. Maybe you can just tell us a bit about her, how long you've known each other, stuff like that.'

'I met Sophie in our first year at Leeds. We had rooms across the hall from each other on campus. I was doing economics and she was doing engineering. I was really impressed by that. Economics has a certain amount of maths component, but it's not a STEM subject, so I always had a lot of respect for people doing maths or engineering. And she didn't look like an engineer, she looked like she should be doing literature or something like that. I guess that made her interesting.'

'Sounds like she's clever,' said Wilcox.

Cass nodded. 'Super clever. And tough. I've managed to stay in academia and she could have done the same, but she's out there doing stuff. Actually, I don't know why I'm saying that. You have to be just as tough to survive in academic life, you have to dodge a lot of knives in the back. Sophie decided to go for the real-life physical challenge instead. I guess, where she's working people will slag you off to your face, rather than behind your back, in print.'

'So you've had a few things to cope with,' said Wilcox.

'Of course,' she said. 'You have to publish fairly regularly to stay in the game – to even keep your job sometimes – and everything you put out there is going to be examined in fine detail by everybody else in your field, mostly looking for something they can take issue with. Luckily for me, I'm well able to look after myself'.

'Do you think Sophie's able to look after herself?'

Cass frowned. 'In many ways I would say she is. She's doing what used to be thought of as a man's job in what is still very much a man's world. She can't afford to show any weakness. She's very physically fit and she has a very tough exterior, but I think she has the capacity to be hurt. Well, I guess we all do. I can't really explain that any better.'

'What did you think of Keith?' asked Murphy. 'How did he come on the scene?'

'Keith was also doing engineering, he was in quite a few of Sophie's classes. As you can imagine, there weren't many women in the engineering faculty, although I think the numbers have grown every year and eventually there will be parity. Anyway, she could have had her pick of any of the guys in the engineering faculty, although we agreed that most of them were not particularly fanciable. And Keith, to his credit, played the long game. She went out with a couple of guys, she said she didn't really want a serious relationship, but eventually she took up with him. And I think they were very happy... until... well ....'

'Yes, we've spoken to Keith, and we know about the miscarriage.'

'The miscarriage happened after we'd all left Leeds, and they were married and living in London. I think Sophie wanted to move back to London to be near her mum. Her dad had died and her mum was practically crippled. I think childhood had been hard, although she never spoke about it. I went to see them, her and Keith, for a weekend soon after Sophie found out she was pregnant and she was walking on air. It was like this was the thing that she had most wanted in life. It's funny, isn't it? She was a brainy high-achiever who had worked very hard, but the thing that brought her the greatest joy in life was something that doesn't require intelligence or hard work – just a fully-functioning reproductive system. Anyway, the miscarriage happened about three months in. Maybe it's not so bad if it happens after a few weeks, but after three months it's a viable foetus, so I guess it's a bigger loss. It was certainly a big loss to Sophie. It was as if she abandoned hope. I went to see them and I was shocked by how she looked. I don't think she was eating, so that didn't help. I felt sorry for Keith, he obviously had no idea what to do.'

'Do you think she changed after that?'

'The marriage broke down after that, so she had a lot of recovering to do. But I think she's done pretty well. She has a good job that she really loves and she works hard.'

'Did she tell you anything about a chap called Richard Agnew?'

Cass nodded. 'He was somebody she went out with for a while. I don't think it was a great romantic attachment, but he provided a bit of a diversion for a while.'

'He was married, wasn't he?'

'Yes, she knew that from the start. There was no lying involved. And I think that suited Sophie at that time. She didn't want any attachments, she just appreciated the company, the sex I guess and the opportunity to get out and go places. Like, going to the theatre on your own's not much fun.'

'Did his wife know about this?'

'I'm not sure. Sophie thought that she probably did, but she had her own stuff going on.'

'Did he end it?'

'Yes, I think it was him. She never had any expectations about it, she never even wanted him to leave his wife. But I think he just decided that it could get serious, and he didn't want that. This is what Sophie herself would tell you if you asked her. I'm not telling you anything she would try to hide.'

'And then she found Daniel on Tinder.'

'Yes. That was unfortunate. I had a bad feeling about it. You have to be really careful on these platforms, there are all sorts of weirdos lurking on them.'

'Is that what you think Daniel was? A weirdo?'

'As it happens, I never met him, so I can only go by what Sophie said. He was stalking her, so that's pretty weird.'

'Yes, his behaviour was certainly weird,' said Murphy. 'Did Sophie show you any of the letters he sent her?'

Cass rolled her eyes. 'Letters. So quaint. I guess he wanted no traces on his phone or hard drive.'

'Yes, that's what we think,' said Wilcox. 'Did you see any of them?'

'She sent me a picture of one of them. Looked like it had been written by a complete jerk. I told her to report it to the police. These weird people can turn nasty.'

'Do you think she was frightened of him?'

'No. It's creepy and unpleasant and I think she was unnerved, but not frightened. And before you get onto it, there is no way she would have wanted to harm him. She's just not that sort of person.' She looked at her watch. 'I have to go now. I have a seminar group at two o'clock.'

'Thank you for your time, Cass.'

'No problem.' She nodded and sailed out and Murphy,

following her direction of travel, saw that the sky had miraculously cleared.

'I think she was a bit in love with her,' said Wilcox.

Murphy shrugged. 'Maybe. None of our business.'

Wilcox squinted at Cass's back retreating into the distance and scratched his head. 'But if we get into the realm of outlandish theories, I could see her smacking Daniel round the head more easily than I can see Sophie doing it.'

Murphy smiled. 'In that case, you can phone her up tomorrow and check her alibi.'

Chapter Forty-Nine

SOPHIE STOOD BACK from the theodolite and stretched her back. Too much time bending forward. Bad for the neck. They were planning a tunnel beneath the main road, which would form part of a cycle lane and, much as she approved of cycle lanes, working out where to route them was an engineering nightmare.

She folded up the equipment and carried it back to the van. It was amazing how little effort that required. A year ago, she had found the physical requirements of her job pretty hard. Now she had arms like pistons, the result of a lot of hard work. If anybody tried to mug her in the street, they wouldn't know what hit them – unless there was a gun or a knife involved, of course. Bit more technique needed in that area.

She climbed into the driver's seat and checked her phone. Missed call from Cass. And Cass had left a voicemail. Voicemails were so bloody tiresome. She'd listen to it later. But then she found herself dialling in anyway, listening to Cass's voice explaining that she'd spoken to the police, but that she wanted Sophie to know that she had not told them anything. It sounded a bit fraught.

Sophie smiled. Poor Cass. Of course, she hadn't told them anything. She didn't know anything. Anything Cass might think she knew was completely inconsequential. Because the important stuff, the stuff that really mattered, that remained well buried. It would be bad to be in the position of trying to remember which bits you'd told to whom. So she told nothing to anybody. Then there was no leakage.

Even Keith, she reflected, there were things he didn't know. She hoped there were also secrets he'd kept from her, that there had been some equilibrium of concealment. That probably said something about the state of her marriage. If the miscarriage hadn't happened, would they have stayed together? If there had been a child, she liked to think they would have made it work. But now, the way things had worked out, she was glad she had kept things back from him. He hadn't needed to know then, and he certainly didn't need to know now.

Daniel Webb had come closest to cutting through to her secret core, to the guilt that would never really leave her. Daniel Webb, with his carefree, mocking smile and his exaggerated politesse. What had he known? Maybe nothing, maybe everything. It had been carefully cultivated, that knowing smile, it was a power play. Was he deliberately keeping her off-balance, or was he like this with everybody? It was the not-knowing that she couldn't bear and it had been clear to her that he was well aware of that. She couldn't have called him out on it – on what after all? She could picture the expression of faux-innocence. And she couldn't have coped with him speaking to her about it – that would have been the worst thing of all. Getting out from under him was what she had needed to do, and then he responded with that stupid stalking performance. Just taking the piss, really. The police pitching in didn't actually help matters. She had known that she would never be able to relax again as long as he was around.

The light was fading. Time for the sidelights. Sophie started the engine, put it in gear and drove off.

Chapter Fifty

SANDRA FULLER HAD BEEN in the middle of plating up chicken nuggets and watching the early evening news when Murphy pitched up.

'This is a bad time' she said when she opened the door.

'Just a few words, between you and me,' said Murphy and Sandra shrugged and led the way in.

'You carry on,' said Murphy. 'Don't let me hold up his supper.'

Sandra carried the plate through to where Finn was watching TV, then she came back and started washing the frying pan.

'The reason I wanted to have another word with you is because Ian is not the only man who has been beaten up,' Murphy said, addressing Sandra's back.

'Really?' said Sandra, without turning round. Murphy thought her back stiffened a bit, but maybe she was just seeing what she expected to see.

She waited until Sandra had dried her hands and

turned around and then she sat at the table. Extra effort required to throw her out if she was sitting down.

'There have been a few muggings which look to me as if the perpetrators were women,' she said. 'In each case the men had abused or were abusing women. Sometimes it's difficult to get a result through the justice system, I'm well aware of that, but if people go down the vigilante route, then that's the end of society as we know it.'

'I haven't been mugging anybody, if that's what you're suggesting,' said Sandra. She sounded unbothered, but Murphy could see a faint flush spreading up from her neck.

'I wouldn't expect you to be mugging anybody. You have a son to look after, and if you were sent to prison he would have to go into care. I don't think you'd want to risk that.'

Sandra was definitely alarmed now. 'I would have nothing to do with anything like that,' she declared.

'No, probably not,' said Murphy, 'but the law would treat anybody who arranged the assault as being equally guilty. I hope you would also have nothing to do with that.'

Sandra shook her head frantically.

'In that case,' said Murphy, 'you won't mind giving me the address of the gym where you do your training.'

'The gym is not involved in anything like this,' said Sandra, scribbling on a scrap of paper.

'That's good, and I hope it's the case,' said Murphy. 'We like to keep an eye on gyms,' she added, not sure whether it was true or not. 'They're places where people hang out together and people hanging out together can get up to mischief. The Kray twins had a gym, a boxing gym, where they used to go in Bethnal Green. Lot of organised crime was planned at that gym. They may have loved their old mum, but they were happy to attack other people.'

Sandra was now looking a bit more worried. 'I've never

seen anything like that happening,' she said. 'I'm sure there's nothing like that going on at my gym.'

'Let's hope not,' said Murphy. 'You take care now.'

IT WAS TOO late to head back to the station, so Murphy went straight home. An evening off. A chance to grab a parking place before the street filled up. Unfortunately, as she remembered when she saw the empty kitchen, Clive and James were out tonight. The only person available to welcome her was Barney. His affection was heartfelt and appreciated, but he wasn't going to cook dinner.

Nor was she, Murphy admitted to herself. Maybe a shower first and then she could think about it. The hot water ran out after a few minutes, so that booted her out and probably made the procedure more eco-conscious. Nevertheless, it restored her energy and to some extent her appetite. She pulled on some comfortable clothes and went down to investigate the fridge. Lots of stuff in there, but most of it looked a bit too unfamiliar. It would be bad to carelessly consume something that turned out to be one of Clive's vital ingredients.

A few hours later she was half-asleep in front of something incomprehensible on Netflix when she heard, as if from afar, the front door opening. She was just looking around for a weapon when the sitting room door burst open to admit Clive and James, wide awake and having had a few drinks by the look of them.

'Murph. You actually got an evening off?' Clive plumped himself down next to her on the sofa.

Murphy nodded groggily. 'You have a good evening?'

Clive smiled and stretched. 'Lovely. A new opening. Friend of James's. Wonderful squid. What did you eat?'

'Beans on toast,' Murphy admitted.

Clive looked shocked. 'Where did you even find such things?'

'Back of the larder. I must have bought them years ago.'

Clive tutted. 'They might have gone off.'

'No,' said Murphy airily. 'Baked beans last forever. In the 60's people were still eating beans canned before the war.' She wasn't sure if this was true, but it silenced Clive.

'Well, you're still alive anyway,' declared James. 'I think if you're basically fit you can get away with eating a bit of rubbish.'

'Baked beans are not rubbish,' Murphy protested. 'They have a lot of protein.'

'I think that's true actually,' Clive conceded. 'Beans are good for building muscle.'

'That and weights, I guess,' said Murphy. 'I'm visiting a gym tomorrow. Maybe I should sign up.'

Chapter Fifty-One

BUT IN THE EVENT, the gym visit went out the window as soon as she arrived in the CID room next morning.

Following an urgent message from Linda Fleming, Murphy found herself attending a meeting in the office attached to the morgue. Also present was another officer introduced by Linda Fleming as DI Simon Raymond. Raymond was tall, spare and middle-aged. He looked like he'd been on the job forever and had no illusions left.

'I wanted to see you both together,' Linda said, 'because yesterday I carried out a post-mortem on a chap called James Wilson. This is DI Raymond's case. Then I looked back and compared the notes I had made on the Daniel Webb killing. It was a bit unexpected and I checked very carefully, but I'm convinced they were killed by the same weapon.'

Murphy just sat and stared. It felt like all the cogs in her brain, which had been whirring away in different directions, suddenly ground to a halt. She didn't know where to start. She had been wrong about everything.

Simon Raymond had not lost the power of speech. Presumably he had only just taken on his case, he hadn't spent weeks making progress in a direction that was now probably wrong.

'But if they were killed by a fungible object, then it's not necessarily the same actual object,' he pointed out. 'For instance, two pieces of lead piping of the same gauge are two identical weapons. They can have been wielded by two different people.'

Murphy's already-confused brain was now shunted in the direction of Cluedo. Colonel Mustard in the Library. She shook her head, hoping to clear it.

'The point is,' said Linda, 'that there are two variables to consider. One is the actual weapon and the other is the way in which the blow has been struck – and, by that, I mean the force, speed and direction. Nothing which involves human beings is ever 100%, but I personally have no doubt that these blows were struck by the same person.'

Murphy had now reassembled her faculties. 'Who is this second victim?' she asked.

It was Simon Raymond who answered. 'As Linda said, he's called James Wilson. Lives in Wandsworth. Killed night before last. Single blow to the head.'

'I'll leave you to it now,' said Linda. 'You'll probably want to pool resources. I'm off to the next corpse.' And she walked out.

Raymond smiled. 'I love her' he said. 'No regard to the social niceties. Does her stuff and walks off. I don't think they're making them like her anymore.'

Murphy nodded. 'You're right there. I think they'll be wanting this office. Shall we clear off back to the station? I must admit, I'm not sure how to tell Bellweather about this.'

Simon Raymond fastened his briefcase. 'I guess it's

thrown your case up in the air? Shall we go and think about it over a coffee before we show our faces?'

'Yes, let's do that. A shot of caffeine to the brain is probably what I need.'

Raymond led the way to a tiny Italian café where the coffee was strong and fresh and served in proper cups and saucers.

'This is so good,' said Murphy. 'So much better than the places serving up gallons of hot milk with froth and chocolate on top.'

'There used to be loads of places in London like this,' he said. 'Before those chains moved in and drove them all out of business. So shall I tell you about the second victim and then you can tell me about the first one?'

Murphy nodded. 'Yes, let's do that.'

'OK. James Wilson, plasterer. Family man. Very much a family man according to Facebook. Two young kids, wife has a part-time job in a call centre, grandparents do a lot of babysitting. Only detail I noticed that contradicts the family man image is that the wife has a few bruises on her arms. So maybe all is not as it seems.'

'So, he could be an abuser?'

He nodded. 'Could be.'

Murphy sighed. 'Let me tell you my vigilante theory.'

Chapter Fifty-Two

SIMON RAYMOND'S team consisted of him and a DC called Wanda Everitt. Wanda was a stocky girl with spiky dark hair and heavy boots. Murphy figured she had plenty of smarts to go with it. That was good, because her own brain no longer felt up to the job.

Wanda and Kevin Wilcox were surreptitiously sizing each other up as the four of them sat in the cramped incident room.

'Well at least it saves on space,' said Raymond. 'We don't need two incident rooms. I'll just run through the main details of the second victim again and Wanda can update the whiteboard.'

'James Wilson. Age thirty-one. He was found in a wooded area near his home in Wandsworth. Area that forms part of the common. No CCTV in the woods of course, and SOCO have found nothing. His wife says he often went running on the common after work. '

'So we're saying he came home from work and then went out again?' asked Murphy.

He nodded. 'That's right. He was wearing running gear. So, somebody knew where he'd be or they followed him from his house.'

'It's a bit hard to visualise this attack,' said Murphy. 'I guess the same thing applies to Daniel's murder, but if somebody's running, how do you catch them up in order to inflict the fatal blow? And Daniel Webb was presumably walking, not standing around waiting to be attacked. In both cases, Linda says the blow was inflicted while they were upright. That means the attacker must have found some way to stop them, get them to stand still for long enough. These were young, fit men, not frail pensioners. Why didn't they fight back? They must have been taken completely by surprise.'

'That's a good point,' said Wanda. 'Suggests the attacker didn't look threatening.'

'Which takes us back to the idea that maybe it's a woman,' said Wilcox.

'I suggest' said Simon Raymond, 'that we put all our energy initially into investigating any possible suspects for this second murder. If we find one that crosses over to the first murder, then we'll know where we're going.'

'On the face of it, the victims look very different,' said Murphy. 'But if Linda is willing to bet the farm on it being the same perp, we'll have to find the connection.'

'Yes,' said Raymond. 'If we don't find anything we'll have to consider the nightmare scenario. You know what that is.'

Murphy nodded. 'The random killer. Please not one of those.'

Chapter Fifty-Three

DETECTIVE CONSTABLE RILEY PRENDERGAST came to stand in front of Murphy's desk and cleared his throat. He was a skinny youth with a prominent Adam's apple and a literal mind. Murphy tried to avoid too much interaction with Riley because she always ended up feeling like his mum. The urge to straighten his collar was sometimes almost overwhelming.

She had been horrified when Wilcox told her he had sent Riley off to tail Marcia.

'For God's sake, couldn't you have found anybody else?'

'Riley was totally up for it. He's saving up for a motorbike. Anyway, it's not exactly a dangerous assignment.'

'What are you talking about? He's not fit to ride a motorbike. And he won't know how to deal with a dangerous bunch of women like that.'

Wilcox rolled his eyes. 'Then he'll have to learn, won't he? He's supposed to be a police officer.'

He was right, Murphy thought. Her attitude was unprofessional.

Now here was Riley back from the field, still in one piece by the look of him, ready to report in. Murphy sat back in her chair.

'OK, how did it go? You can sit down, by the way.'

Riley pulled up a chair and whipped out his notebook.

'I was able to identify the suspect from the description given by DC Wilcox and from the photo on her Facebook profile, and I took up my position outside 16 Caversham Drive, Kentish Town at approximately 18.05. From my vantage point I had an unobstructed view of the front door of the property and at 18.25 I was able to identify the suspect when she opened the door to a caller.'

'Good' said Murphy. 'Can you describe the caller?'

He ran his finger down his notebook. 'Approximately five foot ten, slightly built, maybe 160 pounds, with a beard. Wearing jeans and trainers and a dark brown hooded top. He arrived in a DHL van and handed a package to the suspect.'

Murphy sighed. 'OK. Anything after that?'

'At 19.27 another caller arrived. Female, about five foot eight and 120 pounds, wearing a raincoat and a beanie hat and carrying a Morrisons shopping bag. Accompanied by a young girl, approximately 8 years old. This woman had a key to the property and let herself in, so I did not get a further sighting of the suspect at this point.'

Murphy yawned. 'OK.'

Riley turned a page. 'At 20.42 another caller arrived. This was a woman, an older woman and probably 140 pounds, wearing a dark coat and with an umbrella (it was now raining). She walked with a bit of a limp. She rang the bell and the door was opened, but not by the suspect. The person opening the door looked to me like the woman who had entered the property at 19.27. She was no longer wearing the raincoat, but I recognised other salient features.'

Murphy looked up from her shopping list. 'Excellent' she said. 'Is that it?'

'Almost' said Riley. 'At 21.16 the suspect herself came out of the front door, crossed the road to where I had taken up my position and requested that I follow her. Treating her at this point as a member of the public who had requested assistance, I followed her into the property. She led me into the kitchen and asked me to remove my wet coat, which I did as a matter of politeness. She pointed to a chair and I sat down. The older woman who had entered the property at 20.42 handed me a cup of tea and pushed a tin of biscuits in my direction. I drank some tea as a courtesy but did not avail myself of the biscuits as...'

'Alright! Enough!' shouted Murphy, throwing her biro across the desk. 'The cheeky baggage! No, not you, Riley. You've done a good job, thank you. Send me your overtime claim when you've done it.'

Riley nodded and took himself off. Wilcox was trying hard not to laugh.

'Next time there's a stakeout, you'll be on it,' said Murphy. 'It's my fault, I underestimated them. We need to approach from another direction.'

Chapter Fifty-Four

THE INQUEST on Daniel Webb took place on a grey day, the pavements wet and slippery, a dull mist hanging in the air. Murphy wasn't looking forward to standing up and stating that enquiries were still ongoing, which she knew that his family would translate as the police don't have a clue. Equally, she had little expectation that she would learn anything from the proceedings that she didn't already know.

The room was modern and functional and perhaps designed to dispel the gothic, gloomy atmosphere attendant upon sudden death. Unfortunately, the windows were mere slits, set high up on the outside wall, which admitted very little useful light. On a day like this, the only available illumination came from LED lights set high into the ceiling, which glowed dimly.

Murphy took her usual seat at the back and watched the interested parties file in. The first person she noticed was Daniel's father, striding determinedly towards the front row, with his wife shuffling behind him at a distance. She was looking greyer and more insubstantial than when Murphy had last seen her, and she thought Cicely Webb's uncertain gait and stiffness of movement was probably due to whatever drugs she had been prescribed. She was accompanied by a young man who to some extent resembled Daniel – his brother perhaps? Her husband seated himself without even glancing in his wife's direction. Perhaps attitudes to women were passed down the male line. Murphy thought it would have been kinder if her husband had excused her from attending the inquest, but the poor thing probably felt it was her duty to be here.

The proceedings were opened and the uniformed police officers and paramedics gave evidence about arriving on the scene and finding the body. One of the police officers read out a statement made by the milkman, who had been granted leave not to attend. Murphy thought for a moment about the milkman. What an innocent-looking occupation. What did they know about the milkman? Probably nothing. Had anybody searched his milk float? Probably not. If this was a novel, he'd definitely be the perp. On the other hand, would he have hung around and waited for the first responders if he was involved? No, he wouldn't. Or maybe he would. Enough already. She dragged her attention back to the proceedings.

Linda Fleming was now taking the stand and she gave a dry-as-dust explanation of tests carried out on the body and her opinion as to the cause of death. Daniel Webb was a 32-year-old man with no underlying health conditions. No traces of drugs or alcohol had been detected and death was due to traumatic brain injury following a blow to the side of the head. She was of the opinion that death had been almost instantaneous, but there were further details regarding bleeds and pressure which Murphy hoped Cicely Webb was too sedated to pay attention to.

When her own turn came, she explained that foul play was suspected and enquiries were still ongoing. She made a point of not looking in Robert Webb's direction, but could not avoid seeing the curl of his lip as she returned to her seat. The verdict of murder by person or persons unknown came as no surprise to anybody.

Two journalists had been present throughout, obviously from rival papers as they were stealing surreptitious glances at each other. Murphy made it her business to avoid them both on the way out. At some point they might need help from the press, maybe if they needed to make an appeal to the public. What they didn't want was the press making a link between this killing and that of James Wilson, before they had a chance to fully investigate any link. That would pile on pressure which would come down the line and eventually come to rest on Bellweather's shoulders. The result of that would not be in any way helpful to the investigation.

Heading in the opposite direction to the hacks, she almost ran into the young man who had accompanied Cicely Webb and who now seemed to have escaped from his parents. It was an opportunity to be seized.

'You must be Daniel's brother' she said.

He looked at her for a moment as if unable to place her, then she showed her badge and his expression relaxed.

'You're the police officer.' Murphy nodded.

'Yes, I'm Marcus Webb.'

'I'm sorry for your loss.'

He shrugged. 'I don't deserve condolences really. I hadn't seen him for years. I've been living in Australia. I came back when this happened.'

'I'm sure your mum is glad to have you here.'

'Yes, she is. This is awful for her. It's the last thing any of us could have expected.'

There was a shout and they both turned to see Robert Webb gesticulating next to the open door of a black cab.

'I've got to go.' And he was off.

Pretty impressive, Murphy thought. Robert Webb ran a tight ship. Her own twenty-somethings would have rolled their eyes and taken their own sweet time if she had tried ordering them into a cab.

Chapter Fifty-Five

JAMES WILSON'S Facebook page was full of pictures of family life – silly jumpers at Christmas, beach holidays with his children burying him in the sand, birthday parties with paper hats and singing and blowing out candles. All good stuff.

'It's sad,' Murphy said. 'I'm sure his kids loved him. Hard to lose your dad so young.'

'That's why we have to give them some answers,' said Wilcox. 'He must have been about more than this stuff that he posted on Facebook.'

'That's right,' said Raymond. 'It's likely he was beating his wife, although she'll probably deny it now. He could have been involved in all sorts of other stuff. We have to look into it all.'

'I guess, if we weren't thinking it was the same perp, you'd be investigating the wife,' said Murphy.

Raymond nodded. 'Oh, I have been, believe me. He had substantial life insurance and she'd get the mortgage paid off. I've been looking at all possibilities.'

'Wanda and I have trawled through the Facebook and Instagram posts of both victims,' said Wilcox. 'There seem to be no social media links. Neither of them was following the other or connected in any way. Their numbers were not listed in each other's contacts. It appears that they didn't know each other.'

'I would think,' said Murphy, 'that they moved in very different circles. One was an upmarket estate agent, well-educated, wealthy family, and the other was a self-employed plasterer. I'm not saying one is better than the other, plasterers probably make plenty of money. But I can't see where they would intersect.'

'What this tells us,' said Raymond, 'is that if they did have contact with each other for any reason, it was contact that they were at pains to hide. That in itself would be suspicious. Unfortunately, the likeliest explanation is most often the true one, and the likeliest explanation here is that they didn't know each other.'

There was silence for a moment as they all digested the implications of this.

'OK,' said Murphy. 'If we take that to be true, we have to conclude that either Linda Fleming was mistaken (and I'm not volunteering to be the one to question her findings) or they were random attacks.'

'If they were random attacks, then we're back at square one,' said Raymond. 'I'm not quite ready yet to draw that conclusion. And I'm not ready to tell Bellweather that. Let's keep pushing ahead and see what we can find out.'

'I think we need to look at the people we have already questioned in respect of the killing of Daniel Webb and see if they have any links to James Wilson,' said Murphy. 'And then we can check James Wilson's associates in respect of Daniel Webb. We need to find out whether they have alibis for both killings. That might get us somewhere. And there's a gym that might be worth a visit.'

Chapter Fifty-Six

SOPHIE WAS HALFWAY up a scaffold when Murphy caught up with her. She was pretty sure that Sophie had agreed to see her at work in order to keep the meeting as short as possible. Now she was waiting for her on the scaffold, rather than offering to come down.

There was nothing else for it; she stepped onto the ladder, ignoring shouts from the site manager. At least she was wearing trousers and she didn't suffer from vertigo, so no excuses really. She should have delegated this to Wilcox, he'd have been up the ladder in no time. But that was part of the problem. He seemed inclined to regard Sophie as a young woman in need of protection, rather than a murder suspect. As far as Murphy was concerned, a more hard-headed approach was needed, and that didn't just apply to the safety helmet she had grabbed on the way past.

Arriving on the platform, Murphy stopped to look around and catch her breath. They were at the bottom of the Edgeware Road, opposite Marble Arch and below her was a vast emptiness with a couple of pile drivers at work and two cranes standing idle. There was something to be said for the view. In one direction she could see the top of Selfridges and in the other the whole expanse of Hyde Park.

'I swear to God,' she told Sophie, as she arrived safely at the top, 'last time I came down here there were all sorts of shops – big shops, some of them – where have they all gone?'

Sophie smiled. 'All wiped out. Demolition doesn't take long. Here one day, gone the next.'

Murphy nodded. 'That's the trouble with travelling around on the Tube all the time. You don't get to see half of what's going on above ground.' She pointed at the void below. 'And I suppose this is going to be flats.'

'Luxury apartments, more like.' Sophie repositioned a scaffolding pole that looked out of alignment. 'Not much change out of two mil. That's what I've heard.'

'Blimey,' said Murphy. 'Now tell me, how long have you known James Wilson?'

Sophie looked baffled. 'Who's James Wilson?' The response was immediate but her expression suddenly became more guarded.

'He's a plasterer who lives in Wandsworth.'

'So how would I know him? I don't know anybody who lives in Wandsworth. I don't actually know any plasterers. They don't appear on site until long after people like me have moved on.'

'Let me show you a photograph.'

It was cropped from one of the holiday snaps – better than the face Murphy could have snapped at the morgue.

'He looks like an OK guy,' Sophie said, 'but I don't know him.'

'OK, we'll leave that for the moment. What were you doing two evenings ago – Wednesday?'

Sophie shrugged. 'Nothing much. I was supposed to be going to the National with Freya – a modern adaptation of The Tempest – but she ate something dodgy at lunchtime, so she spent the afternoon and evening throwing up and I didn't want to go on my own. Well, she had the tickets anyway, so we weren't even able to hand them in. We're going to try for it again next week. Probably just turn up and see if we can get in on the door, rather than wasting money on advance tickets.'

'In that case, what did you do instead?'

'You want the full rundown? OK. Freya called me about three pm. I left here at four pm – construction industry starts early and finishes early. I went home, dumped my stuff, went to the gym for about an hour, went home, ate something – just soup and toast, I think – watched a travel program on Netflix and went to bed. Pretty unremarkable really.'

Murphy pulled out her phone. 'Thank you for that. Can I take the details for Freya and the gym.'

Sophie pulled her phone out of her pocket. 'Sure. Check up on me why don't you?' She scrolled up and passed it to Murphy, who copied the information across.

'Thank you for your time, Sophie,' she said, handing the phone back. 'I think that's all for now.'

'Sure.' Sophie nodded and walked off to the other end of the platform.

Murphy steeled herself to begin the descent. Netflix was a bloody nuisance. It was always at least theoretically possible to test whether people had really been sitting at home watching live TV – with Netflix they could claim to have been watching anything at any time and it could be checked, but the records took a lot longer to access.

She arrived at the bottom without mishap and nodded

to the man who had been standing patiently ready to intervene if she had a panic attack or missed her footing. She was grateful to him really, but it was a bit wounding to the personal dignity. She removed her helmet, handed it over with thanks and went in to see the site manager and the foreman, who immediately began quoting the health and safety regulations.

'Apologies' she said, 'but it's a murder enquiry. Have you seen this man before?'

They both stared for a few moments and shook their heads. 'Not on any site I've been on,' said the foreman. 'What's his name?'

'James Wilson' said Murphy. 'Lives in Wandsworth.'

The site manager said 'No, never seen him here. You'd be better off trying south of the river.'

Murphy thanked them and made her way out. There was no doubt about it, this was a challenging environment for a woman and Sophie deserved respect for having made her way in it. She obviously had to be tough, that was a given. Tough enough to kill somebody with a single blow? Probably. She recalled the ease with which Sophie had picked up the scaffolding pole. But that wasn't the thought that was mainly preoccupying Murphy as she headed into Marble Arch tube station. She was picturing Sophie's face right after she denied knowing James Wilson, that expression of complete surprise in the split second before her face closed down. Because that could have been nothing, or it could have been the moment when she realised that maybe she did know James Wilson.

Chapter Fifty-Seven

MURPHY HAD no doubt that she would not be welcome at Daniel Webb's funeral, but decided that she should go anyway, if only to see who else turned up. She slid in quietly after the family had arrived and took a seat at the back.

The funeral was held at St Antony's in Canonbury, a Catholic church built in 1838 to accommodate the increase in the Catholic population due to immigration from Ireland. This much she learned from a leaflet at the door. It was not a large church, which was probably fortunate because she estimated that it was only three quarters full. A half-empty church at one's funeral would not be evidence of a life well-lived, unless of course one had survived so long that all one's contemporaries were dead. Murphy stopped for a moment to wonder how many people would turn up for her funeral, but it was better not to go there. Anyway, she'd be dead, so she wouldn't care.

The coffin had been carried in by four young men, one of whom she recognised as Marcus. The other three she decided must be cousins or friends. Marcus was now sitting in the front row with his parents and a couple of other people and the priest was talking about Daniel in terms that made it clear that he had never met him.

The eulogy was delivered by Daniel's father and had something of the school report about it: 'gifted child', 'so much potential', 'brilliant mind' and then 'wasted'. The tone of his address made it clear that his anger at the loss had in no degree abated. Murphy couldn't blame him. He had suffered the worst loss that can befall a human being (or any living creature) and she, with her two safe, live children, should at least respect that. Daniel's mother was shaking and she saw Marcus put an arm around her.

Murphy slipped out during the final hymn and waited in the churchyard. The coffin was transferred to the hearse and Daniel's parents stood at the door receiving condolences. Marcus had drifted away from the general gathering and nodded at Murphy. She walked over to join him.

'I don't know most of these people' he admitted. 'I suppose because I've been in Australia for five years.'

'So, there are no people you remember from when you were both young?'

He shook his head. 'We didn't really keep contact with people from school. Things change and you move on, isn't that right?'

'So, you won't have seen Daniel for quite some time?'

'No, unfortunately. He never came out to Australia to see me, well I didn't really expect him to, and I was happy there. I didn't want to come back to the UK. I never thought I'd be coming back for his funeral.'

'What do you do in Australia?' asked Murphy.

'I'm a doctor. Doctors are quite well paid there, but it was more about the weather than the money. And Daniel probably made more money than I did anyway.'

'So you went in very different directions, maybe very different people.'

'We weren't close' he said, 'and I can't pretend we were. I was smaller, shyer, a bit of a science nerd, and I guess he used to push me around a bit. Nevertheless, it's very shocking to lose him. We never had the chance to rescue our relationship.'

Chapter Fifty-Eight

WILCOX FELT he should accompany Wanda to the gym, if only to maintain the presence of his side of the investigation, as he rationalised it to himself. Not that they weren't all on the same side of course...

As Wanda was a 'clean skin' – and how much he enjoyed using that expression – they had agreed that she could turn up as a member of the public, so she had booked herself in for a taster session. Wilcox was starring as himself, waving his badge and asking to look at their membership records.

'Why do you need to look at our records?' asked the guy on Reception.

'I'm not at liberty to say,' replied Wilcox, enjoying the feeling of the phrase as he said it. 'But you'll find out in due course,' he added, because the chap was looking a bit belligerent. The receptionist shook his head but sent something to the printer and handed it over a few minutes later.

Looking through the glass doors Wilcox saw Wanda swing out from the changing room, looking not at all like a nervous newbie, which was what she was meant to be. He'd have to point that out to her. In fact, the muscles on her arms and legs made it clear that she spent plenty of time in gyms and after ten minutes she appeared to have shaken off her instructor and headed to where the heavy weights were stored.

'Don't think she needed much of an induction,' said the chap in question, pausing at Reception.

Wilcox returned his attention to the paperwork and absorbed the interesting information that both Sophie Carter and Sandra Fuller were members. There were no other names that he recognised, but those were the two he'd been looking for. Probably best to leave now before Sophie turned up and spotted him. There was no sign of Wanda emerging from the weights room, he'd wait for her in the coffee shop opposite.

'Thank you. That'll be all' he said, handing back the printout.

'Did you find what you were looking for?'

'Yes. Very helpful.' He smiled and made his way out.

It was another forty minutes before Wanda came out, with a relaxed slouch and wet hair. He waved from the window and she came in to join him.

'That was so good,' she said. 'Showers are excellent.'

'You weren't supposed to be in there enjoying yourself,' he said repressively.

'Loosen up, Kevin. If you're going to participate in these things, you have to make a proper job of it. And I had an interesting chat with a girl called Sadie who was giving a lot of stick to a punching bag. She told me it represented her ex-boyfriend. I said, well I guess it's better than punching the real thing and she said punching the real thing can lead to a bit of trouble and she'd be the first person suspected if he got punched. So, I said, you'd have to contract it out and we both laughed. Then she said, well I wouldn't be the first. And I said, no, really? And she backed off a bit then, and said, so I've heard. I said, so if I wanted my cheating ex taught a lesson, I could find somebody to do it? But I think I'd pushed it too far. She was getting suspicious at that point. She said, I wouldn't know really and then she walked out.'

'Interesting' said Wilcox. 'And both of the women we are interested in are members of that gym.'

'Well, that's a result. If we come back again, I might do a spinning class.'

Chapter Fifty-Nine

CHLOE WILSON HAD blonde hair in several different shades, long, intricately-decorated nails and (going by what they had heard through the window) a voice that could strip paint at one hundred yards (or whatever the phrase was). Murphy then parcelled up all these bitchy observations and put them to one side, because this was a woman who had lost her husband suddenly and traumatically.

'Come in' Mrs Wilson said listlessly. 'Conrad, get back in the sitting room now! And take the bloody dog with you!'

Raymond introduced Murphy and they followed her into the kitchen, where the Family Liaison Officer was doing some washing up. Raymond went over and told her to take a break for half an hour. She smiled gratefully, picked up her bag and jacket and was gone. He then put the kettle on and asked if they wanted tea or coffee. Murphy opted for tea and Chloe said she'd had too many cups already.

'You have two children, Mrs Wilson, is that right?' asked Murphy.

She nodded. 'Conrad's three and the baby's eighteen months. She's asleep upstairs.'

'Well, that's good,' said Raymond, coming back with the cups. 'Times when the baby's asleep are very precious, as far as I remember.'

Chloe almost smiled. 'Yes, good for her. Wish I could sleep. Doctor gave me some pills but they don't do nothing.' Murphy could see the effect of the pills in the slow movements and guessed that they had at least taken the edge off whatever grief she had experienced.

'I know we've spoken before, Chloe,' said Raymond, 'but that was in the immediate aftermath of this tragedy when you were still in shock. We wanted to have another chat with you now, because it's possible that you may have more useful information. Things may have occurred to you since that you didn't think of at the time.'

'Don't know what.'

'Had your husband had any arguments with anybody, any business problems, anything like that?' asked Murphy.

Chloe shrugged. 'Nothing that I know about. I didn't know much about his business to be honest. I had my hands full with the kids.'

At that moment the doorbell rang and Chloe stood up and went to answer it. She returned with a thick-set man with a beard and tattoos running up his neck.

'So what's happening, babes?' The man stared at Murphy and Raymond. Chloe made the introductions.

'This is my brother Tony.'

'Hope you're not bothering her,' said Tony.

'We are engaged in finding out who killed her husband,' said Raymond, 'but we are trying to cause no unnecessary bother. Do you live near here, Tony?'

'Yeah. Kind of. Earlsfield. Garrett Lane.'

'And when did you last see James?'

'Dunno. 'Bout two weeks ago.'

'Did you know him well, did he talk to you about anything that was going on with him?'

He shook his head. 'Nah. We didn't have much in common, me and Jimmy.'

'What do you do for a living Tony?' asked Murphy.

He turned his attention to her and frowned as if wondering where she'd suddenly appeared from. 'Personal trainer,' he said. 'Self-employed.'

Tony would be a good person to have a chat with, Murphy thought, he looked like the sort of guy who would know what went on, but they'd need to get him away from his sister first.

'Have you been attacked in the street any time recently?' she asked him.

'What's that got to do with anything?'

'There have been a number of attacks on men over the last few months, so it's something we're asking people.'

He laughed shortly. 'Not likely. I can take care of myself.'

'Do you think Jimmy was good at taking care of himself?'

He shrugged. 'He should have been. But from what I hear, he was attacked with a weapon. That makes it a bit different.'

Murphy nodded. 'Yes, that's right. Can we ask what you were doing on Wednesday night? We have to ask everybody that,' she added as his expression became belligerent.

'Alright. Wednesday. I had one client at six o'clock and another at seven, so I was done by eight. Picked up a pizza and went home.'

'Anybody at home when you arrived?'

'My partner.'

'We'll need contact details for those two clients and for your partner,' said Raymond. 'And for yourself please. And do either of you know Daniel Webb?'

They both shook their heads.

'Who's he?' asked Chloe.

'He's another man who got attacked,' said Murphy. There seemed no point telling them he was dead.

'You mean Jimmy was killed by some random nutter?'

'No' said Murphy. 'We don't think that's what happened. But we have to look at every possibility.'

'Well, I think that's all,' said Raymond. 'We'll be back in touch when we have some news. If you think of anything in the meantime, give us a ring.'

They made their way out, past the sitting room where Conrad and the dog were watching Formula 1, and climbed into the car.

'I'd like to talk to him again,' said Murphy. 'Without her there. That 'didn't have much in common' line says to me that they didn't actually like each other.'

Chapter Sixty

WILCOX AND WANDA sat with their heads together going through James Wilson's phone contacts and social media. Murphy was very happy to delegate this aspect of the investigation. Deciphering all the textspeak and emojis made her brain hurt.

'OK, what do we have so far?'

Wanda sat back and folded her arms. 'He wasn't very active on social media, the usual rubbish on Facebook, pictures of the baby, pictures of the dog, him and the wife looking all lovey dovey on holiday. Just bullshit.'

Murphy smiled. 'If those bruises on her wrist are anything to go by, it probably is bullshit. How about his phone contacts?'

Wilcox pulled up a screen on his laptop. 'I've been cross-referencing them to Facebook where possible. Some of them are people in the building trade, a few are family – father and a sister, plus this woman with whom he's exchanged a number of messages.' He turned the screen around. The Facebook page belonged to a Samantha Bruce, a woman looking a few years younger than James Wilson's wife, who seemed to post a lot of pictures of her scantily-clad bum shown from various angles.

'It's very difficult to photograph your own bum like that without dislocating your neck,' said Wanda, 'but she's given it her best shot.'

'So do we conclude that James Wilson liked her bum?' asked Murphy.

'Looks that way,' said Wilcox. 'I've found her address. And her work address. She's in HR.'

'Well done,' said Murphy. 'We'll get along and see her. When you've exhausted James Wilson, check the Facebook pages of his wife, Chloe, and her brother,' she checked her notes 'Tony Forest -personal trainer.'

'Leave him to me,' said Wanda.

'How about his parents?' she asked Raymond as they left the building.

'Mother died of cancer a few years ago. Father's pretty upset, but not in good shape. Drinks a lot. There's a married sister who lives in Norfolk.'

'I guess we should just check back with his father to see if he knows Daniel Webb.'

'Yes, maybe we can do that after we've seen Samantha.'

SIMON RAYMOND DID NOT FLINCH as Murphy drove down the Balls Pond Road in her usual fashion. She was so used to Wilcox clutching his seatbelt and even closing his eyes, that this was a pleasant change. Even when she came close to ramming a taxi, he remained unmoved.

'I was a joyrider in my misbegotten youth,' he explained, as she spotted somebody leaving a parking place and did an emergency stop to grab it.

Samantha Bruce was more soberly dressed when they arrived at her workplace, the main office of a large DIY retail chain, and she immediately ushered them into an empty office.

'I told my boss that you need my help in respect of an enquiry, but I don't know what it's about. I've had to deal with a lot of jokes about 'helping police with their enquiries', which is upsetting.'

'Thank you for seeing us, Samantha,' said Raymond, 'and I'm sorry if it's caused you any bother. We want to talk to you about James Wilson.'

'James Wilson?'

'Yes,' said Murphy, seating herself. 'A man you've exchanged a number of text messages with and, according to those messages, you've had a number of meetings with him.'

Samantha was looking defiant now. 'So what? No law against it, is there?'

'None at all,' said Murphy. 'The reason we're here is because James Wilson is dead.'

Samantha's mouth formed a perfect 'O'. Then she closed it and frowned. 'Dead? How?'

'He was attacked in the street. Or actually, walking, running maybe, across Wandsworth Common.'

'Somebody attacked him? But why?'

'That's what we're trying to find out,' said Raymond. 'So, we're speaking to everybody who knew him.'

Samantha's eyes were starting to look watery. 'I can't believe it. Poor James. Who would do that? I hope you don't think that I...'

'We don't think anything at the moment,' said Raymond. 'But we would like to ask you some questions.

Can we start with how long you've known him and how often you met?'

She sighed and chiselled a bit of varnish off her thumbnail. 'I met him about six months ago, in a pub. The Dog in Putney, down by the river. I was there with some mates. We hit it off, I guess. He didn't enjoy evenings at home much, said it was noisy with a baby and a toddler and all that. So about once a fortnight or so we'd have dinner somewhere and then go back to my place. I think he told his wife he was doing evening estimates.'

'So what did he tell you about his marriage?' asked Murphy.

'He said he had to marry her because she was pregnant and it was really a bit of a mistake.'

'So, was he planning to leave her?'

'Not as far as I know. Not on my account anyway. Our relationship wasn't that serious.'

'When was the last time you saw him?'

Samantha consulted her phone. 'Last Friday.'

'And where were you on Wednesday evening?'

She shrugged. 'I was just at home, in my flat. Watching TV, I guess.'

'Who else knew about your relationship' asked Raymond.

'Nobody as far as I know.'

'And did you have any other relationships during the time you were seeing James?'

'A few. Now and then I'd meet somebody. Usually online.'

'So, what was in it for you?' asked Murphy. 'I can see what was in it for him. He'd get to spend the evening in some pub or restaurant with a woman other than his wife, escaping all the bath time and shouting and stuff at home and at the end of the evening he'd get sex, which his wife is probably too tired to bother with. What's not to like? But for you?'

'For me it was a bit of a diversion, I guess. It's not that easy these days meeting decent guys. You have to kiss a lot of frogs. So, while I'm working my way through the frogs, I have the odd evening with James, who I know and like. It's – it was – relaxing to be with him because we have – had – no expectations of each other.' She paused. 'I'll miss him.'

'So, if he'd left his wife' said Murphy, 'would you have married him?'

'Good God, no.' She shook her head emphatically and then seemed to realise that further elucidation was required. 'James was a good laugh and I could enjoy his company for an evening once a fortnight, but not on a long-term basis. I mean, we didn't really have much in common, I think I'd soon have got bored. Also, I think he made quite good money, but it's not exactly a career, is it?'

'Did any of the other men you went out with – the frogs – did any of them know about him?'

She hesitated a moment. 'I never told any of them about him. I don't tell them that much about myself. I do remember being with him once and seeing somebody I'd had a date with. He was with somebody else as well, so we just waved to each other across the restaurant. It was no big deal.'

'Did you ever wonder if his wife suspected?' asked Murphy.

Samantha shook her head. 'Not really. We were pretty careful. And it's not like I was trying to take him away from her.'

'Would it surprise you to know that he was beating her?'

'What? No way. He wouldn't have been doing that.'

'Do you know anything about the rest of his family, his friends, people he associated with?'

'No, nothing at all. We didn't talk family or 'shop'. That was our deal.'

Murphy was intrigued. 'What did you talk about?'

Samantha thought for a minute. 'Music, movies, TV, a bit of current affairs – not much. He was amusing, bit too amusing sometimes. He used to crack a lot of problematic jokes and I used to tell him off about them – jokes making fun of other people, you know. That sort of thing is very much not acceptable.'

'That's your HR persona, isn't it?' said Raymond.

She smiled. 'Yes, I suppose it is.'

'Are you a member of a gym?' asked Murphy.

Samantha looked surprised at this sudden change of question. 'Yes. Most people are, I think.'

'Just write the name and address down for me please.' Samantha complied and Murphy stuffed it in her bag.

'Now, tell me, do you know of anybody who didn't like James? Anybody who had a grudge against him, or would have liked to get rid of him?'

Samantha shook her head. 'No, not at all. He just wasn't that sort of person. I'm really sorry this has happened to him.'

'Do you know a chap called Daniel Webb?' asked Raymond.

'No, never heard of him.'

'Well, I think that's all Samantha,' said Murphy. 'Please give us a ring if you think of anything else.'

'Yes, I will do.' They walked out together and she pointed them in the direction of the lift.

'It's a different gym,' said Murphy, as they left the building. 'That was just an outside chance anyway. I can't see that she would have any motive to want to get rid of him. Quite a hard-headed attitude she has – I admire that in a lot of ways.'

'Bit unfair on James Wilson's wife, though,' said Raymond. 'If he's been a bad husband, Samantha has been one of his enablers.' He checked his phone. 'It's not far from here to Mr Wilson senior's house. We can go there now.'

Chapter Sixty-One

DAVID WILSON LOOKED like a man in his early seventies, but Murphy knew from her notes that he was not yet sixty. He had the protruding stomach and shaking hands of the heavy drinker, which she supposed he must be. He was not pleased to see them but the impression she got was that he couldn't summon up sufficient energy to refuse them admittance.

So, they got in by default, into a first-floor flat which looked and smelled like he had not done any cleaning or washing up since his wife died. Murphy selected a wooden chair and gave it a surreptitious wipe with a tissue before sitting down.

Raymond introduced them both and Wilson nodded abstractedly, like he really didn't care who they were.

'We're sorry for your loss, Mr Wilson,' said Murphy. 'And we want to find out who killed James, so we wanted to see if you have any ideas that might help.'

Wilson rubbed his eyes. 'Hardly ever saw him to be honest,' he said.

'When did you last see him?' asked Raymond.

He seemed to be thinking. 'Last month sometime? Maybe month before? He wasn't too interested in visiting me. His mother used to spoil him rotten, he could do no wrong in her eyes. Let him away with murder. Once she was dead, he stopped coming. My daughter comes sometimes, but she's busy with her kids. Maybe James was too. I never saw much of his kids though. I think that wife of his wasn't too keen. I'll drop dead one day and they won't find out for weeks.'

'Mr Wilson, do you know of anybody who might have wanted to harm James?' asked Murphy. 'Anybody who held a grudge, a business deal that went wrong, anything like that?'

He shook his head slowly. 'No. But then, how would I know anything? I never knew what was going on. He never came to see me, told me how things were, asked whether I needed anything, never checked up on my health, nothing like that. Not much point having kids, is there, when they treat you like that?'

'Have you heard of a man called Daniel Webb?'

'Don't think so, but to be honest my memory's not what it was. Sometimes things come back to me clear as anything, other times it's just a blur. I'm trying to get an appointment to see the GP, because I'm sure it's not right losing bits of your memory like that. But you try getting an appointment these days. You can only phone at certain times and they never pick up. If we all just die that will save the NHS some money, I suppose. And my memory's just one problem, there's also my circulation, I have really cold feet all the time and especially in bed at night, and sometimes I feel very tired, exhausted, like I just can't do any more. I drop into that chair and I just don't want to get out again. That's not right, is it? Maybe I need a tonic of some sort, or some kind of rest-cure, one of those health farms. You work all your life, you expect to be taken care of in your old age don't you?'

'Was your daughter close to James?' asked Raymond.

'As far as I remember, they didn't get on all that well. She was quite a few years older and they didn't have much in common. She said she'd be coming down to London when she heard he was dead, but I haven't seen her yet. I don't know whether she thinks she'll be staying here. I'm not really set up for guests, I can't be expected to get beds ready and all that, not with my health problems. I did have one of those social workers coming round after Marjorie died, then after a few weeks she stopped coming. Dropped me just like that. After I've worked all my life and paid my taxes. There's just no respect these days. If I had somebody just to do my shopping that would help. Now that I've suffered a second bereavement, do you think social services, will pull their socks up and give me the support I'm entitled to?'

'I think they absolutely will, Mr Wilson, and you should phone them up immediately and tell them everything you have just told us,' said Murphy. 'We'll go now and let you get some rest.'

Simon Raymond drew in a lungful of air as soon as they got outside. 'Fresh air mingled with traffic fumes,' he said. 'Smells a million times better than the air in there.'

'Somehow,' said Murphy, 'I don't think he's got anything useful to tell us. His daughter's been in touch, hasn't she? Is she still in London?'

'She went back yesterday morning, but she'll be back for the funeral, which she has to organise of course. I'll give her a ring when we get back to the office.'

'Where was she staying?'

'In a hotel – Hilton, I think. I guess she didn't want to see the old man before she had to.'

'More than that' said Murphy, 'I guess she wanted a clean bed.'

Chapter Sixty-Two

'THIS TONY FOREST' said Wanda when they got back, 'guess what? He's got form.'

'Has he really?' said Murphy 'What for?'

'Grievous Bodily Harm. He beat up somebody he said was trying to rob him. To be honest, the guy probably was trying to rob him, but didn't expect to end up in hospital. Forest's brief made much of the fact that he had been a victim of attempted crime, and he got off with community service. Not a man you want to cross.'

'Yes, I figured he'd be handy with his fists,' said Murphy. 'I wonder how he'd react to somebody beating up his sister? Let's get him in.'

TONY FOREST SAT in the interview room and drummed his fingers on the table.

'Can we make this fast?' he said. 'I've got five clients lined up for today and I've had to cancel two of them so far.'

'I understand,' said Murphy, 'and we do appreciate you coming in to help us. Can I start by asking you how you would describe your sister's marriage? Were they happy?'

'I don't know that it's my place to say. None of my business.'

'OK, let me rephrase it. How do you think James Wilson treated your sister?'

'Not all that well, to be honest. She could have done a lot better.'

'Can you explain that a bit more?'

'As far as I could see he wasn't home half the time, he was no help with the kids and he did have a temper on him.'

'Did Chloe tell you that?'

'I'd say it was more what I observed. And she did tell me a few things.'

'What did she tell you?'

He sighed. 'I can't remember too much now, but she felt she had a lot to cope with, she wasn't very happy.'

'Did she think he was seeing other women?'

He shrugged. 'She wondered, of course. There were a lot of evening appointments. But a lot of his clients would have been working during the day, so he'd have to see them in the evening.'

'What did you really think of James?'

'I never thought about him much at all. We weren't mates.'

'That's odd, don't you think? You're both men of about the same age, related by marriage. It would be normal for you to go for a beer together, wouldn't it?'

'I wouldn't waste my time going for a beer with him. He is – was – an asshole. Sorry to talk ill of the dead. I was polite to him for Chloe's sake, but that was it.'

'In what way was he an asshole?'

He was silent for a moment. 'It's a bit hard to explain, but it was like he'd never become an adult. Other people didn't really figure in his calculations. He'd just do whatever he felt like. I think his mother had spoilt him, she thought he could do no wrong. Chloe told me that. Apparently, he had a spate of petty thieving when he was a teenager and his mum used to say he'd been at home all evening with her, whether it was true or not. That meant he never had to take responsibility. It was the same with Chloe and the kids. He'd make sure they had money, he was fair in that way, but he didn't think his role extended beyond that. One evening the baby was ill and she had to get to A&E with both kids. She was there all evening and she couldn't even get hold of him because he wasn't answering his phone.'

'What do you think he was doing when he didn't answer his phone?'

'I think he was probably with another woman, but I couldn't say that to Chloe.'

'So, she didn't suspect anything?'

'She didn't want to suspect anything. Like I said, she wondered, but she wouldn't really look at it. He can – could – be quite charming when he likes and Chloe was besotted. She wouldn't hear anything against him.'

'Were you briefing against him?'

'I certainly had my doubts about him. He tried to interest me in some dodgy get-rich-quick scheme, which nobody with any brains would even have considered and I told him that if he even thought about investing in anything like that, I'd tell Chloe. He thought it was a good idea just because some mate wanted him to do it. "Easily led" is probably the kindest way to put it.'

'Did you think he was beating Chloe?'

'Yes, I thought he'd probably roughed her up a bit, but she wouldn't admit it.'

'Because she was afraid of what you'd do?'

'She had no reason to think I'd do anything, other than have words with him. But I think she'd have regarded it as an admission of failure, the failure of her marriage, if anybody knew he'd beaten her.'

'So, in your estimation,' said Murphy, 'he's not much loss.'

He looked straight at her. 'No, he's not, as far as I'm concerned. But I didn't kill him. I couldn't kill anybody and he wouldn't be worth going to prison for.'

'But you have beaten somebody up in the past, isn't that right?'

He rolled his eyes. 'So that's what this is all about. Going to pin this one on me, are you? Yes, I fought back when somebody tried to mug me. And it turned out I was a lot fitter than my assailant, so he came off worst.'

'He ended up in hospital,' said Murphy.

'Yes, I punched him, he fell over. I didn't intend him to hit his head on the way down and I did stay until the ambulance arrived.'

'So, you're good at fighting,' said Raymond.

'Being good at fighting doesn't mean you go around hurting anybody. It means being able to defend yourself, or defend other people.'

'Point taken,' said Murphy. 'Let's get back to James. Can you think of anybody else who might have wanted to kill him?'

'Frankly, no, unless it was somebody who'd been lured into some stupid investment scheme by him and lost all their money. That would make you want to kill him. But realistically, all I can think is that it was a mugging gone wrong.'

'Very wrong considering they didn't even take his phone or his cards.'

He shrugged. 'They probably panicked. Didn't intend to kill him. Or maybe he fought back. But that doesn't seem like him. To be honest, I'd have expected him to immediately give them whatever they wanted.'

'So, he wasn't a fighter?'

He shook his head. 'No, he wasn't a brave person, I don't think so. He might be well up for smacking a woman or someone weaker than him, but he wouldn't stick his neck out.'

'Did you feel you should rescue your sister from him?'

'There was no rescuing my sister. She loved him, that was her position. She's not having hysterics now because of the drugs they've given her, but once those wear off, she'll be sobbing her eyes out. He wasn't much, not in my opinion anyway, but he was hers and she wanted to stick with him. He did provide for her well enough, I have to admit that. And maybe he would have grown up a bit over time, developed a bit of responsibility. So no, whoever clobbered him did my sister no favours.'

Simon Raymond looked across at Murphy. She nodded imperceptibly. He began gathering his papers. 'Thank you for your time, Mr Forest. I think that's all for now. We may need to speak to you again. We'll be in touch.'

Tony Forest nodded and stood up. A constable arrived to escort him out.

'He fits for motive, means and opportunity,' said Murphy. 'But the motive is not that strong and I don't see him as someone who would appear out of the shadows and just smack James Wilson on the head. A punch to the jaw would be more his style – we know he's good at those.'

'We don't have any evidence to arrest him on,' said Raymond. 'We don't have any evidence to arrest anybody.'

'We're up against somebody who's either very clever or barking mad,' said Murphy. 'And I don't know which is more likely.'

'One point we should note,' said Raymond, 'is that there have been no further victims. So, if it is just a random killer, they're taking a break. And there have been no more similar muggings, have there?'

Murphy shook her head. 'No, I guess that's something. It was quite a clever idea I think, if it was what I think. No woman would be involved in the attack on her own abuser, so she couldn't be identified in any way and she would have an alibi. She would then reciprocate by taking part in one of the other attacks. We still need to find who's behind all that, but it's quietened down. Maybe Riley managed to spook them after all.'

'If nothing breaks, Bellweather will probably have us both on traffic by this time next week – or at least he'll give it his best shot,' said Raymond. 'Shall we go for a quick drink? I think we're done here.'

Murphy looked around. The CID room had emptied. It didn't usually take long once Bellweather had left the premises. 'Yes. Why not?'

They went out past the front desk and wandered next door to the Cross Keys. 'There used to be a lot of drinking done in here when I was first on the force,' said Raymond. 'Today's new recruits are a lot more sober.'

'It's a good thing,' said Murphy. 'Drinking and driving wasn't taken quite so seriously when I was young. But now I have a son who works mostly in A&E, so my viewpoint has radically changed. I'll have a G&T please, then I'll be going home on the tube.'

'Have you left many unsolved cases?' she asked him as they sat down in a quiet corner.

He nodded. 'A couple, no, actually only one. The other one we discovered who had done it, but he topped himself before we could haul him in. The one we never solved, well, I've never forgotten it. I still keep thinking that some evidence will come up on day and I'll be able to nail the culprit. Not likely, but it's how you always think of it. No case ever completely closed.'

'These killings are just so – brazen,' said Murphy. 'You would think the chances of being spotted are really high. Out on the street, maybe not in broad daylight, but not late at night either. It takes a lot of confidence, arrogance, disregard of the odds. Whoever did this was not risk-averse. I'm tempted to say they weren't quite sane.'

'That's right.' Simon Raymond took a mouthful and put his pint down. 'But despite everything, they got away with it. And it's not just beginner's luck because, if we go by what Professor Fleming says, they've done it twice.'

'We just have to keep going,' said Murphy. 'Eventually something will emerge. Lift enough rocks and we'll find something. Just on a different tack, have you heard of a guy called Mark Bingham?'

'No. Do you think he's implicated in this?'

Murphy shook her head. 'No. He's just somebody my mother's taken up with and I'm wondering if I should be worried.'

'Have you googled him?'

'Yes. There's nothing there. I'm probably worrying over nothing. Apparently, his wealthy wife died and there was some malicious gossip that he had something to do with it.'

'If his wife died unexpectedly there will have been a PM. And if anything had been discovered, he would have been number one suspect, so if he's still walking free, I don't think you need to worry.'

'You're right of course. She used to be the one worrying about my boyfriends and now it's the other way around.'

He laughed. 'A friend of mine had a late night out a few weeks back and, when she arrived home at some ungodly hour, she found her teenage son sitting up waiting for her. She got the whole 'Do you know what time it is?' routine. One day, your kids might be doing it to you.'

'I'm safe from that,' said Murphy. 'Mine escaped from home years ago. They only reappear when they're hungry.' A thought came to her. 'This girl Sophie, our one and only suspect, she's a clever girl with an impressive career and her own flat and she's quite tough in a lot of ways, but she seems very attached to her mother.'

'But didn't you say her mother was chronically ill? Maybe it's because she worries about her mother, just like you worry about yours. Which doesn't make her look like the obvious murder suspect.'

'Nothing about her looks like an obvious murder suspect,' said Murphy. 'But, as we all know, there's no such thing. Angelic-looking nurses have murdered babies in hospital. Harold Shipman probably looked like a kindly old gent to most people who met him. Sophie Carter may or may not be our perp, but there's something going on there, just below the surface, and I really want to know what it is.'

Chapter Sixty-Three

IT HAD BEEN one of those days. A glitch in the software that had necessitated rerunning all the calculations. The projected costs had now risen and a whole bunch of people who didn't understand all the factors at play in the project and were frankly unwilling to even try to grasp the concepts involved, were flapping around and making a fuss. By the time she got home, Sophie was too tired and weary to even want to eat anything, although, as far as she could remember, she hadn't eaten anything since breakfast.

She pulled her clothes off and stood under a long, hot shower, finishing on cold, to close the pores and demonstrate to herself that she wasn't a wuss. Then she wrapped herself in a dressing gown, tied her hair up in a towel, poured a glass of wine and opened her laptop.

Having checked that she had received no emails which were worth answering, she found herself back on the site, almost without being aware of it. It was becoming automatic – that was probably not good.

There were some new profiles up. Calum is highly

educated – history at Oxford – and an accomplished pianist. That's good, maybe that's some of what she's looking for. But how good would Calum be in a fight?

David is a molecular scientist with two dogs and three cats. He likes animals, that's a point in his favour. And the brains are important of course. David is definitely a possible.

Archie is a plumber and part-time rapper with 100,000 Instagram followers. Practical skills – that was good too. But maybe not. Too much noise. Would it make a difference? Who knew?

Ben is a student (maths) who runs marathons and plays rugby. That's a possible. Young and healthy. The rugby bit would be good. And the maths of course.

But was she just looking for the sort of person who would be able to protect her? That wasn't what was needed here. Why would she need protecting? She was well able to look after herself and Daniel Webb was now dead, so the threat had gone with him. Was she really looking for someone who'd be able to look after himself? Yes, that was more the issue. She could do the protecting for a time, but then she'd need to know that they were resilient, that they'd be OK.

She sat back and ran her fingers through her hair. It was all bloody exhausting. Her whole life was bloody exhausting. Why did she have to try so hard all the time? What was she really trying for here? And what if it all went wrong? Maybe she should put it to one side for the time being. Maybe she needed some food after all.

Chapter Sixty-Four

THE OPPORTUNITY TO talk to James Wilson's sister came at the end of his funeral. It was held in a crematorium near the North Circular and Murphy was there mainly to see if she could recognise anybody connected with Daniel Webb.

It was a fairly perfunctory service, as the next funeral was scheduled to take place straight afterwards. The room was small and the congregation was smaller. A few people in their late twenties who had maybe been at school with James Wilson, some in their thirties and forties who maybe knew him through business. His father sat in the front row on the left, looking comprehensively cleaned-up. Next to him sat a middle-aged woman who at one point poked him in the arm and seemed to be issuing orders. That, thought Murphy, must be the daughter, who would have been responsible for getting him here.

On the right in the front row sat Chloe wearing a black hat with a small veil. It actually looked quite good, Murphy thought. She was being supported by Tony and next to him sat another young woman and an older couple, presumably the rest of her immediate family.

The eulogy was delivered by a sober-looking celebrant who described James as a 'hardworking family man'. Not much else he could say really, thought Murphy, and probably it was true. James Wilson did have a family and maybe he was a hardworking plasterer. In fact, plastering was quite skilled and you did have to work fast before the stuff dried. She remembered her dad attempting it once and saying it was best left to the professionals, so there would be hard work involved.

None of the relations got up to speak. James's sister had obviously chosen not to, her father was not fit to be allowed to speak and Chloe was in no state to do anything. Her shoulders were heaving, so presumably the drugs had worn off and she was now feeling the loss.

As the curtains closed behind the coffin Murphy and Raymond headed outside.

'There's nobody here who was at Daniel Webb's funeral,' said Murphy. 'But maybe we can have a few words with James Wilson's sister. Do you think she was expecting to see us here?'

'No. We'll just have to ambush her along with her father.'

They emerged a few moments later, her holding tightly to his arm and shepherding him to a car. Raymond stepped out as she opened the car door.

'Mrs Hayes.' He showed his badge. 'DI Raymond. We spoke earlier. As you know, we are investigating your brother's death and we'd like an opportunity to speak to you.'

She looked at them both and sighed. 'OK. I'm staying back at the Hilton. Let me drop my father home and I can meet you there in about an hour.'

'That's perfect,' said Murphy. 'We'll see you there.'

They watched her drive off and turned to see Chloe and her family emerging, Tony with his arm around his sister. He didn't look pleased to see them there.

'I don't think we need to talk to Tony again,' said Murphy. 'Let's head to the Hilton. They'll have really good coffee.'

Chapter Sixty-Five

MURPHY WAS RELAXING in an armchair with the papers when Mrs Hayes reappeared. She had changed from her funeral outfit into a sweater and jeans and was looking correspondingly more amenable.

'Can I fetch you a coffee?' said Raymond.

She smiled. 'Yes please. An Americano with cold milk.'

He went off and Murphy put down the paper.

'I'm sorry for your loss' she said. 'I'm Miranda Murphy.'

'Charlotte Hayes. I'm glad to get out of the black clothes. It's all been a horrible business.'

Simon Raymond came back with the coffee and she thanked him.

'We're talking to everybody connected with James,' he told her. 'We're still trying to find out who could have been responsible for his death.'

'Yes, I appreciate that. I don't think I'll be able to help much, because I haven't seen him for years.'

'So, you weren't close siblings,' said Murphy.

'Not at all. There were six years between us, which doesn't seem much now, but it was an enormous gap when we were kids.'

'So, you were a teenager when he was just a kid,' said Murphy.

'That's right. He was what they call an 'afterthought', so my mother was just delighted with him. I liked him when he was a baby, but by the time I was sixteen and he was ten and I was expected to babysit for him, I thought he was just a nuisance.'

'Naturally,' said Murphy. 'Sixteen-year-old girls have much better things to do.'

'That's right. I was quite an independent kid and when he came along my parents were very taken up with him, so I got to do what I wanted. I didn't run wild or anything, but I went off to university at eighteen and I never came back. Ours was not a particularly happy home so I wasn't leaving much behind.'

'Not happy in what way?' asked Murphy.

'You've met my dad, so you know he drinks. He's always been like that, and if my mum complained he'd knock her about. She died a few years ago and I felt very sorry then, like I should have stayed in touch more.'

'If you left home at eighteen, does that mean you don't know what James was like as a young man growing up?'

She put her coffee cup down. 'I would say that he grew up as a spoilt young man, not in terms of being given lots of stuff, we didn't have much money, but in terms of not much discipline. My mother, as far as I remember, was pretty indulgent towards him, and my father was off his face half the time. That being the case, I think he probably didn't work very hard at school and nobody was there to make sure that he did. I seem to remember him getting into trouble a bit at school, Mum was worried about him going off the rails. She told me that once, but I wasn't really interested. He didn't do 'A' levels or go to university. I don't think he liked school much, but I suppose he didn't go off the rails particularly. He didn't take drugs and he did work for a living.'

'Yes, that seems to be the case,' said Murphy. 'Did you know his wife at all?'

'I came to the wedding with my husband,' said Charlotte. 'Mum had died by then, and the whole thing was organised by Chloe's parents. I got the impression that they weren't too delighted by the marriage. They seemed to think she could have done better, and perhaps they were right. I did try to stay in touch a bit with Chloe, we exchanged a few emails, but I was living in Norfolk and I think from her viewpoint I was just her husband's boring older sister. To be honest, I don't think either of our hearts were in it.'

'Do you think he was a good husband?'

'I don't know. He didn't have much of an example to fall back on, did he?'

'Can you think of anybody who would have wanted to get rid of him, or hurt him?'

She shook her head. 'No, not at all. I've spoken to my dad about it, but neither of us have any idea. I don't think of James as somebody who would particularly make enemies, I don't think he was involved in anything that significant. Maybe it was a case of mistaken identity, or just a random attack?'

'Those are always possibilities,' said Raymond. 'And we are looking into all of them. Thank you for seeing us, and if anything else occurs to you that you think could be relevant, please get in touch.'

Charlotte nodded and they made their way out.

'Obviously we didn't have proper recording equipment,' said Murphy, 'but the coffee and the furnishings were better and so I think this is a much better place to talk to people than those horrible interview rooms.'

'So do I,' he said. 'But I don't think we'll get away with it too often.'

Chapter Sixty-Six

BELLWEATHER WAS OBVIOUSLY TRYING hard to keep himself under control. Wilcox had told Murphy that one of the PCs had told him that Bellweather had been attending an anger management course. That's how rumours get going of course. Right now, they all had reason to hope the course, if there was one, had made some difference. The signs weren't good. His nostrils were flaring and he was cracking his knuckles. He looked at the four of them individually and they all looked straight back at him. Best practice, she had told Wilcox. Don't look away. That's when he pounces.

Then, miraculously, he obviously remembered something from lesson seven, or whatever, took a deep breath, and started again.

'I was planning to berate you all for being useless,' he said, 'but we'll just take that as read, shall we?'

That wasn't right, thought Murphy. You weren't allowed to call your subordinates useless these days. Any one of the four of them could now take out a grievance against him.

Give HR something to get their teeth into. Although HR and teeth didn't seem to go together somehow.

'What we have here is two murders and a series of muggings, and the whole lot outstanding for several weeks. As this burden is clearly too much for four people, I am relieving you of responsibility for the muggings. The reason I am doing this is because I have been informed by the CPS that, as none of the victims are prepared to give evidence, they will not be pursuing any prosecutions in this regard.'

He left a moment for this to sink in. It made sense to Murphy from an organisational and financial perspective, but what sort of message did it send out? That you could mug people in the street as long as they were too scared to face you in court? Yes, seemed to be the answer to that one.

'In respect of the two murders' Bellweather was now continuing, 'I find it inexplicable that so little progress – by which I mean no discernible progress whatever – has been made. What is particularly worrying is that they appear to be linked killings. I did question Dr Fletcher about this and she reassured me that it was undoubtedly the same perpetrator.'

Reassured, nothing, thought Murphy. Linda Fletcher would have ripped his head off for daring to question her findings. Linda Fletcher was the person Murphy most wanted to emulate, but she clearly had a long way to go.

'I would have thought...' Bellweather was moving into his sarcastic mode now. That was fine, they were all used to that. 'I would have thought that having just one perpetrator to look for, and two crimes to their name, would have made the job easier. But apparently not. What is most worrying is that, if we do not find somebody that we can charge over these crimes, the supposition will be that they are random crimes.

And I don't need to spell out – I hope – how that will play out in the press and among members of the public. So I want an arrest made and I want it made in the next few days, or you will all be back in uniform. Have I made myself understood?'

'Yes, clearly sir' said Raymond as they filed out.

'Ignore that 'back in uniform' stuff' Murphy said to Wilcox and Wanda, as they returned to their desks. 'It's just a line he trots out. I think it makes him feel better. Busting somebody back into uniform isn't going to happen on his say-so.'

'I think we need to go over where we are at,' said Raymond. 'We've spoken to pretty much everybody involved. We haven't found any link between these two victims. It's looking more and more like the nightmare scenario.'

'We did consider Sophie Carter for the Daniel Webb murder,' said Wilcox. 'And she has no alibi for the James Wilson murder. But there's no evidence that she knew James Wilson.'

'I did get some inkling that she might know him' said Murphy, 'but it might have been imagination on my part.'

'Maybe she killed James Wilson for somebody else and they killed Daniel Webb for her,' said Wanda.

'The *Strangers on a Train* scenario?' said Murphy. 'It's appealing, I grant you that, but I don't see that she even had much of a motive for getting rid of Daniel Webb. He was stalking her, so what? She's quite a capable girl, she was coping with that, she didn't need to kill him.'

'There must be some link between these two victims' said Simon Raymond. 'We just haven't found it yet.'

'We have gone through their phones and laptops from end to end,' said Wanda. 'There's just nothing there. They had no contacts in common, no groups they were both part of, nothing.'

'We're looking for somebody who wanted to get rid of both of them,' said Murphy. 'But it looks like that must be somebody that neither of them had any direct contact to. How can that happen?'

'It can't happen,' said Wilcox.

Murphy sighed. 'I think Sherlock Holmes had something to say about this. That bit about when you have eliminated the impossible, whatever remains, however improbable must be the truth.'

'Jesus,' said Wanda. 'Things really are desperate when we're calling in Sherlock Holmes.'

'But think about it,' said Murphy. 'If we treat the random nutter theory as being impossible, which we have agreed to do for the time being, then a link lies somewhere, however improbable it looks right now.'

Wilcox shrugged. 'We have trawled all of their social media.'

'But maybe it's not there,' said Murphy. 'Could it be a link prior to social media?'

Wilcox and Wanda looked nonplussed.

'Believe me,' said Murphy. 'There was life before social media. I distinctly remember it.'

'But that would have been years ago.'

Murphy stopped to think. 'Daniel and James are old enough for that. They wouldn't have been able to join Facebook until they were thirteen. Could they have known each other prior to that?'

'Prior to when they were thirteen?' said Raymond. 'That's a bit young for gang membership. Are you thinking maybe they knew each other at school?'

'We don't have anything else,' says Murphy. 'So let's find out where they went to school.'

'Well, they didn't know each other from secondary school' said Wilcox, rubbing his eyes an hour later. 'Daniel Webb went to a fee-paying school, St Matthews in Watford, actually Sidney Vincent told us that, but I'd forgotten, and James Wilson went to a comp. Both of these CVs of theirs look like blatant fabrications, but nobody bothers lying about where they went to school, employers don't care about that.'

'I'm surprised Daniel ever needed a CV,' said Murphy.

'He had a short stint at an estate agent's office after university,' said Wilcox. 'Learning the business, I suppose.'

'Alright' said Murphy. 'We need to check the records of these two schools for the whole period these two guys were there, see if any familiar names come up. Hopefully they'll have computerised their records back that far. Get them to send them over. I'm going to check Daniel's university records, see if there's anybody else that he knew from there that we need to take into account.'

Chapter Sixty-Seven

BY THE END of the day, everybody was clicking more slowly. Murphy could feel a headache gathering over her left eye. A lot of coffee had been drunk, none of it strictly drinkable.

There were a few names from the university of Durham who featured in Daniel's social media, as would be expected, but all of them had been checked out and none of them seemed to have any connection to James Wilson. This had seemed like a good idea a few hours ago, now it was looking like a complete waste of time.

'How's everybody doing?' she asked. 'Have you checked everybody who was in the same school for all those years, staff and pupils?'

'I've done three years, so far,' said Wanda. 'These records are appalling.'

'Databases weren't so good back then,' said Murphy. 'We're lucky it's not all bits of paper in filing cabinets.'

'I can't do this anymore,' said Wanda. 'My eyeballs are going to self-combust.'

'OK. I've done the other four years' said Wilcox. 'No luck.'

Murphy sighed. 'OK, so that's it for the schools. There's nothing significant in Daniel's university records. I guess I'm lucky I even got access to those. So, maybe we need to go back further.'

Wilcox frowned. 'Back to what?'

Murphy spread her arms. 'Back to primary school. You may have to approach the families to find out which schools they went to, it's not normally on CVs. See if anybody else we know was in either school at the same time. And while you're figuring out how to do that, I'm going to have a closer look at Sophie and her family. And that sad anniversary she mentioned.'

WANDA'S ARMS shot up in the air. 'It's the same school!' she shouted. They gathered round.

'Brilliant' said Raymond. 'Now we just need a significant name.'

Murphy pointed. 'That one there – that. That's what we're looking for.'

'You really think so? But there's no evidence.'

She shook her head. 'No. But there's something there and we'll have to dig it out. We're going to need a confession.'

Chapter Sixty-Eight

'I'M NOT SURE ABOUT THIS' said Wilcox.

'Just do it,' said Murphy. Wilcox looked at Murphy and Raymond behind him and then knocked on the door.

It was opened by Sophie, and the look of alarm on her face told Murphy that they might be on the right track.

Wilcox informed her that she was under arrest for the murders of Daniel Webb and James Wilson and read her rights to her. For several moments Sophie just stood there, saying nothing. Shock, Murphy realised.

She stepped up to her. 'Come on love. Let's get your stuff together. Where's your coat?'

Sophie allowed herself to be helped into her jacket. Wilcox took charge of her laptop and phone.

'Have you got your keys?' asked Murphy and she shook her head mutely. They located her handbag and Murphy ushered her out, locked the door and handed her back the keys.

Raymond was driving the police car, Wilcox had

seemed very insistent about this, and Murphy sat in the back with Sophie.

'TOMMY' said Murphy after Wilcox had started the tape. 'Your younger brother. Died aged 10. Suicide. That must have been very hard.'

Sophie nodded and closed her eyes momentarily as if attempting to stem the tears which were running down her face.

'He was being bullied, wasn't he? By Daniel and James.'

Sophie grabbed a tissue and blew her nose. 'I used to see them waiting for him in the playground. They thought it was a laugh. I used to go over and tell them to leave him alone, but I wasn't always around. Then my class was taken off for a trip, for a whole week, and when I got back, he was dead. There were these scars on his arms, my mum thought he was cutting himself, but it was worse than that.'

'They were cutting him?'

'Yes. He must have been so frightened.'

'And no adult did anything?'

'The teacher tried to. She tried to get them both suspended, but the Head overruled her. Daniel's parents were generous donors. My mum and dad would have done something, but he never told them and he made me promise not to tell. He didn't want to worry them, he told me he was able to sort it out himself. I should have done more.'

'And decades later you came across Daniel again?'

'Yes. My family was destroyed by then. My dad never got over Tommy dying. He had a heart attack two years later. Really, I think he died of a broken heart. My mum developed arthritis – the doctors said that the disease had been brought on by the trauma, and it progressed really fast. I met somebody at university and got married. I think I just wanted to get away from all the sadness.'

'So, when you ran into Daniel, you had a different name.'

The duty solicitor stirred at this, but Sophie replied.

'That's right. I kept my married name after the divorce and I was involved with somebody else for a while. That didn't work out too well. Then about six months later I thought I'd have to put myself back out there sometime, and online seemed to be the way to go, so I went onto Tinder, and there he was. I recognised the name, I wouldn't ever forget that name, and when I looked closely, I could see that it was him, still faintly recognisable. And now quite attractive, if I'm honest.'

'So, the moment of reckoning had arrived?'

'Yes, that's what I told myself. I clicked on his profile and we matched, so I went for a drink with him.'

'That was quite brave,' said Murphy.

'I was pretty scared. I didn't think he'd recognise me because I'd changed my name and I had spots and braces last time he'd seen me, but I was still nervous.'

'So, were you going to put cyanide in his martini?'

'That's not allowable.' The solicitor was definitely awake now.

Sophie smiled suddenly. 'I didn't know what I was going to do. The idea of killing him seemed suddenly preposterous. I couldn't think how I would do it and I didn't think I'd be able to anyway. Then I thought maybe I could accuse him of rape, but that often goes pretty badly for the woman concerned. And there were two conflicting feelings that I had, sitting opposite him in that bar, listening to his charming, self-deprecating story of himself.'

'Go on.'

'On the one hand I was a bit scared. This is the man who cut my brother's arm. What would he do to me? Most of all I was frightened that he would tell me exactly what they had done to Tommy. I knew I just couldn't bear to hear it. I didn't know whether or not he recognised me. He had that knowing look which made me feel that he knew something about me, and that was really uncomfortable. And on the other hand, he was really attractive, in a physical sense, quite outside of what I knew about him. I thought, I could go to bed with this man – and what would that make me? I found both of those feelings a bit shameful, actually a lot shameful, so I decided the only thing to do was get out. I messaged him to say I didn't want to meet again, my circumstances had changed, whatever.'

'And he didn't like that.'

'He didn't like it at all. I would have expected him to just brush me aside – a woman of no importance. But instead, he embarked on this campaign of harassment – pretending to be in love with me, following me, sending me letters. All it did was frighten me, and I think that's all it was intended to do. He wasn't really in love with me, that was just crap.'

'I think that's right,' said Murphy. 'He wasn't really the stalking type. He wasn't desperate or needy or in love. I spoke to one of his previous girlfriends and she didn't recognise any of those characteristics. I think that he was probably mostly in love with himself. He was having a bit of fun with it and at the same time he was frightening you off. Because I wonder if maybe he did recognise you, maybe he was smart enough to see past the spots and buck teeth and whatever, and he was curious to see what your next move would be. What he wasn't expecting was for you to just drop him. Just when he was planning to enjoy it. That pissed him off.'

'I didn't kill him, though,' said Sophie. 'I imagined doing it, but I didn't do it.'

'The problem we have,' said Murphy, 'is that you're about the only person we have come across who is connected to both of them. You have no real alibi for either of the time frames involved and you have a hell of a motive. So, you satisfy motive and opportunity, it's just the means we need to establish.'

'Means as in weapon?'

'That's right.'

'But I don't even know how they were killed. And I wouldn't have known where to find James Wilson – it's not exactly an unusual name.'

Murphy sighed. 'I think we both know that anybody can be found these days. People post the most pettifogging details of their lives all over the place, to be read by anybody who's interested. I admit you'd have to sort through a fair few James Wilsons, but it can be done.'

'Yes, I see that,' said Sophie. 'But I didn't do it.'

'Have you called your mum?' said Murphy.

'Not yet. I didn't want to worry her.'

'We'll take a break now and you call your mum. We'll have to search her house for the weapon, so it's best she knows.'

Chapter Sixty-Nine

'THERE'S a bit more stuff now, new stuff.' Wilcox was back to examining Sophie's phone and laptop.

'Like what?' Murphy helped herself to a cup of tea and sat down next to him.

'Nothing incriminating, I don't think. Online pharmacies selling protein powder and supplements. She seems to be into all of that. There's also a site she's been accessing a lot, nearly every day, where men post their details.'

'What, a dating site?'

He shook his head. 'No. They're selling their sperm.'

Murphy frowned. 'Why on earth would an attractive young woman need to do that?'

Wilcox shrugged. 'She wants a baby. Maybe she doesn't want a man, she just wants a baby.'

'I would say' said Murphy, 'that she's not in great shape right now for looking after a baby. She's been under a lot of stress. And babies are a lot more demanding than people realise. She might think a baby's the solution to some problem, but it usually doesn't work out like that. It would be the solution to a problem that then becomes a problem.'

She looked up to see Bellweather padding over in their direction.

'So, you've finally got her in custody. Took you long enough. Has she been charged?'

Murphy sat back. 'Yes, she's under arrest. We just have to make sure all the evidence lines up. Don't want the CPS throwing it out.' That caused him to withdraw, as she knew it would.

'No, no, definitely don't want that. Keep going. Are you charging her with both of them?'

'We've only charged her in respect of Daniel Webb at the moment,' said Murphy. 'But I'm satisfied that the same person killed both of them.'

'Good. Very good. Keep me posted.' He went back to his office and shut the door.

'He's dying to get on the phone to the top brass.' said Wilcox. 'It'll make him look good. If, I mean when, we pull this off.'

'I can't think of anything that would make him look good,' said Murphy. 'Short of a face transplant.'

Andrew Raymond walked in at that moment. 'She's made the call,' he said.

'OK' said Murphy. 'We're on.'

Chapter Seventy

GLENDA OPENED the door to them and led the way into the sitting room, where she resumed her seat on the sofa next to Eileen. They were watching Judge Judy tearing into a large, flabby man who was accused of beating his wife. It was fascinating. Judge Judy was telling him that he was a grotesque piece of lowlife. Murphy couldn't have put it better herself. She would have like to sit and watch it for a bit, but dragged her attention back to the matter in hand.

'I think you know why we're here,' she said.

'Of course we do,' said Eileen, turning off Judge Judy and putting the remote down. 'What's happening with my daughter? Why are you still holding her?'

'She's helping us with our enquiries,' said Raymond. That euphemistic form of words was useful sometimes, Murphy thought.

'Sophie will have told you what we're here for,' Murphy said. 'We'll need to search the flat.'

Eileen rolled her eyes. 'No need to take my place to

pieces,' she said. She pointed towards the corner. 'It's there behind the door.'

Wilcox pulled on gloves and retrieved the cricket bat. He slid it into a long plastic bag.

'It's a lovely bat,' said Eileen. 'Well-seasoned English willow. The best. Belonged to my William. He was a county player when he was young. He could probably have had a career as a cricketer but he gave it up when the kids arrived. He was doing two jobs then, so not much time for cricket. But he was teaching Tommy, said he'd make a good batsman one day.' She shook her head and Murphy saw a tear running down her face.

'It's a murder weapon now,' she said. 'But I don't think you're the person who wielded this.'

'Of course she's not,' said Glenda. 'It was me.'

'You were the teacher.'

'That's right.'

She stood up. Raymond stepped towards her and read her rights to her.

'Get your coat and bag,' said Murphy, 'and we'll be off.'

'They're here ready,' said Glenda and she picked them up off the armchair. She stooped to kiss Eileen on the cheek and said 'Take care now, love.'

'Sophie will be back soon,' Murphy told Eileen, when Glenda had departed with Wilcox and Simon Raymond. 'And in the meantime, you and I are going to have a chat. Or rather, I'm going to chat and you're going to listen. Because I'm not convinced Glenda did it all on her own. Oh, not the physical bit, I'm satisfied she did that, but there's such a thing as being party to an action without physically participating.'

Eileen opened her mouth to respond. Murphy held a hand up and continued.

'What happened to you was awful, losing Tommy like that, and I wouldn't try to minimise that in any way. But your duty at that point was to the child you still had. She needed her mother to help her cope with the loss of her brother and to make it clear to her that what happened was in no way her fault. Because the responsible adult who should have been alive to what was going on was you. Not his sister or his teacher, but his mother. Instead of holding the family together you let it become subsumed in grief. Your husband died and your daughter went off to university and married the first available man, just to get away from the sadness. But she didn't stay away because she still felt responsible for you and your condition. So, she tried to produce a baby, to give you a grandchild and maybe also to give herself a new family, a child she could protect as she failed, she thinks, to protect Tommy. But then she lost the baby, so she'd failed again. Then she started an affair with a married man, trying to get pregnant again. That didn't work. Then she decided to give herself a really bad time by digging up Daniel Webb. If the trauma had been dealt with properly when she was young, she shouldn't have even remembered his name. Now she's trawling sperm sites, so she can have a do-it-yourself pregnancy. And as if that wasn't enough, she's been wondering if she's responsible for Daniel's death, because she volunteered him for a mugging. He never did get mugged because Glenda got there first. And on the subject of bloody deluded Glenda, where do I start?'

'Like Sophie, Glenda felt responsible for what had happened to Tommy. But she'd done her best, she'd tried to get them expelled. You should have relieved her of any guilt, then she wouldn't have dreamed up this mad idea. I don't know how far you were a party to it, and I'll never know, because Glenda is going to nobly carry the can on her own. So, I think you've had all the sympathy you're entitled to for this lifetime. You won't be seeing Glenda again, so you've lost your carer. I'll recommend Social Services sends you somebody else. I'll see myself out.'

Chapter Seventy-One

'I'VE EATEN cake made by a murderer' said Wilcox accusingly. 'And you made me eat it.'

'At least she didn't poison you,' said Murphy. 'She's not a poisoner. And guess what? Didn't you say she was a prime suspect after we went to visit her?'

His face brightened. 'Yes, that's right, I did say that. I was right!'

'There you are, then. We'll tell Bellweather it was a brilliant deduction on your part. Your career might not be on the skids after all.'

The man himself suddenly materialised. 'I've just seen her walking out!' he yelled. 'I thought you had this wrapped up.'

'We're wrapping it up differently now,' said Murphy. 'We have a new suspect.'

'What? That woman sitting in Interview Room Two? She doesn't look like she would be capable of murdering anybody. Isn't this just a mistake? Where's your evidence.'

'We don't actually have any evidence,' said Murphy, realising, as she said it, that it was quite true.

'Then on what bloody basis are you holding her?'

'She's willing to confess,' said Murphy. 'We're just waiting for the duty solicitor, then we're going in to get her confession.'

'Well make sure you do. I don't want this messed up.' And he strode off.

'I think you and Wanda should go now and search her flat,' said Murphy to Wilcox. 'Just in case she decides to clam up and we need a bit of actual evidence. Hopefully her prints are on that bat, but that won't be decisive. She could have picked it up at any time. But as the bat is Eileen's, she can only get off by dropping either Eileen or Sophie in it, and I don't think she'll want to do that.'

'Here he comes,' said Wilcox, as a large, scruffy man bustled through the far door. 'It's Foxy.'

'OK,' said Murphy. 'Take him along to meet the client and we'll give them a few minutes alone. Before we go in and work her over.'

Wilcox gave her a warning look.

LUCKILY SIMON RAYMOND was there to do the set-up. Murphy had forgotten about that when she had gaily waved Wilcox off. It was part of her job description, being able to work the equipment, but it was one of the parts to which she had never devoted any attention.

Glenda was looking relaxed and pronounced herself satisfied with all the arrangements which had been made for her comfort. Timothy Fox looked pleased about this and settled his bulk more comfortably in his chair. Nothing for him to do yet. Murphy hoped he wouldn't actually drop off.

Sudden Death

When Raymond had run through the preliminaries, she addressed herself to Glenda.

'Now Glenda, perhaps we could start with what happened at St Benedict's primary school when you were a teacher there in the nineties.'

Glenda smiled. 'St Bennies. It was a lovely little school. I was really fond of most of the kids.' Her smile faded. 'Apart from a couple of them.'

'And can you give us the names of that couple?' said Murphy.

'Daniel Webb and Jimmy Wilson. Even at that age, there was something bad about them, like something missing. Daniel had rich parents and he'd been overindulged, encouraged to believe that he could have whatever he wanted, that nobody else mattered. We had a lot of trouble trying to persuade him to share equipment and toys and stuff with the other kids. Jimmy wasn't clever, not like Daniel, but he'd do whatever Daniel said, and the other kids were afraid of them. It was really worrying in kids that young. I'd tried to broach the subject of socialising and caring for others with their parents, but they didn't seem to understand what I was talking about. Daniel Webb's dad looked at me as if he thought I was some kind of uppity servant.'

'So can you tell us what happened with Tommy Frensham.'

'Poor Tommy. He was a nice kid. And a bit feisty. He didn't back away from them like all the others. One day Daniel grabbed something off one of the girls and Tommy had a go at him. I saw a look pass between Daniel and Jimmy at that moment and after that it was as if they'd marked Tommy's card. They'd be beating him up in the playground when they thought no teachers were watching.

And the other kids didn't dare intervene. I should have done more. It happened on my watch. And Tommy wasn't the only one they were bullying. I tried to get both of them expelled or at least suspended, but nobody would listen to me. The headmaster and Daniel's dad were friends, same golf club or something.'

'We know what happened to Tommy in the end,' said Raymond. 'But perhaps you can tell us in your own words, for the tape.'

Glenda nodded and took a deep breath.

'Tommy didn't appear for school that morning' she said. 'I didn't think much of it, just asked the school secretary to call his home. I think when she called there was nobody at home, so we thought maybe his mum's taken him to the doctor, something like that. But she'd just nipped out to the shops and when we got hold of her an hour later, we found out he was missing.'

She stopped to blow her nose. 'It didn't take long to find him. In fact, he had been found by a dog-walker before the police even got there. That poor child. What must he have been going through to do something so desperate? I handed my notice in that day and found a post at another school. I couldn't bear to walk into a classroom again and see those two faces.'

'And you left teaching at some point?' said Murphy.

Glenda nodded. 'I left teaching a few years later, I'd had enough. I couldn't feel the same about the kids any more, something had gone out of it for me. I retrained as a care assistant and when Eileen appeared on the list, I decided to take her on. I owed the family that much at least.'

'Eileen knew who you were?'

'Oh yes, Eileen and Sophie remembered me. And they didn't blame me for what happened, although I certainly blamed myself. Their family had really suffered. William Frensham had died a few years after Tommy. They called it a heart attack, but it was a broken heart, Eileen and I knew that. Then Eileen developed rheumatoid arthritis and it worsened really quickly. That's another physical result of severe stress. Sophie was such a clever girl, she kept going and got into university and then she got married and got pregnant and I thought maybe there'd be a bit of a happy outcome for them after all the pain. I thought maybe this grandchild would be somebody for Eileen to love, not to replace Tommy, of course, but another child in the family. But then Sophie had the miscarriage and her marriage broke up.'

'And you'd been keeping tabs on Daniel and James?' said Raymond.

'Yes, I had. It's very easy now. Most people are only too anxious to tell the whole world about themselves. There are so many sources of information and I had access to the NHS database. And of course, it's easier to track men, because they don't change their names. I always knew Daniel would land on his feet, have an easy life. That type always does. James was less intelligent. He was the follower. They hadn't stayed in touch with each other, they hadn't seen each other since primary school, but I'd kind of stayed in touch with both of them. I thought they needed monitoring, and nobody else was going to do it.' She smiled. 'I sat at the back of the church when Jimmy got married and I wondered if, now that he was away from Daniel's influence, he had become a decent person. Then I saw him snarl at his new wife on the way to the reception, and I knew that wasn't the case. Daniel twisted an ankle at university and called in at A&E, so then I knew he was up in Durham. I figured he'd be back in London after his three years, so I kept a watch on his parents' place. The family were still in the same house, they'd never moved. So, yes, it was very easy to keep track of both of them, but I didn't think I was ever going to do anything.'

'What changed?' asked Murphy.

Glenda drank a bit more tea and blew her nose. 'Two things happened. Eileen told me Sophie was being stalked, she'd found a letter in the bin. Eventually she persuaded Sophie to tell her about it and we both recognised the name. I thought Sophie had probably also tracked him down and I was afraid she might do something stupid. And, at the same time, I had been having certain physical symptoms. I went to see a specialist and it was cancer of course. I would say that, as of this moment, I have about three months left to live. When you get a diagnosis like that it's terrifying at first, but then it's liberating. It presents opportunities. I realised I could do this outrageous thing, which would both save Sophie from doing anything that would ruin her life and atone for my failure all those years ago. I decided to just take him out.'

Mr Fox sat up at this and seemed about to intervene, but Glenda held up a hand.

Raymond shook his head. 'How did you manage it?'

'I stalked him, Daniel Webb. I hung around outside his office and his flat and just waited for my opportunity. The good thing about being a woman on the wrong side of middle age is that you are basically invisible. It's a cliché but it's true. You can go anywhere you like, anywhere at all, nobody will notice you. And I had my Freedom Pass, which made the travelling free, as long as I didn't travel during the rush hour. I carried the bat with me at all times.'

'In a basket,' said Murphy.

Glenda looked in her direction. 'That's right. I had a

wicker shopping basket and it fitted in well. And even if anybody had seen it – well it's just a cricket bat, it's not a gun or a knife.'

'You must have quite strong arms' said Murphy.

Glenda nodded. 'You'd better believe it. Some of these patients I have to manoeuvre around are grossly overweight, you either develop the muscles or you get out. In hospitals these days there's no lifting, they have these hoists, but out in the community you just have to do the best you can. So I was pretty sure I could do the job. I just followed them and waited for my opportunity. And it wasn't hard to get them to stop and stand still for me. When some batty-looking old woman says excuse me, young man, they're taken off guard. They don't expect anything bad to happen.'

'But then Sophie came under suspicion,' said Murphy.

Glenda nodded. 'I hadn't planned on that happening, it was the last thing that was supposed to happen. It was really unfortunate that she had become involved with him. Although, I suppose, the only reason I was taking action was because she had become involved with him. I realised I'd have to do something to divert attention from her, so I picked an evening when I knew she would be accounted for. Eileen had told me Sophie was going to the theatre, some Shakespeare play, so I attacked Jimmy Wilson that night. By then I had swapped my basket for a shopping trolley. They're wonderful those things, you know, weigh nothing, transport anything in them. So, I used that when I followed Jimmy Wilson, although to be honest, it wasn't so efficient over rough ground. I knew the police would discover it was the same weapon, I've watched plenty of *Silent Witness*, so that meant Sophie would be in the clear. Of course, then her friend got ill, so they didn't go out. It was a nasty shock when I found that out.'

'Did Sophie and Eileen know what you'd done?'

She shook her head. 'Not at all. Not until I told Eileen this morning.'

'I'm showing you a photograph of the cricket bat which we retrieved from Eileen Frensham's flat,' said Murphy. 'Do you recognise it?'

'Yes, I do,' said Glenda. 'That's the bat I was using. William's bat.'

'And what were you using it for?'

'I hit them round the head with it – Daniel Webb and Jimmy Wilson.'

Murphy sat back and exhaled. Timothy Fox looked like a man in a state of shock, he definitely hadn't dropped off.

'OK Glenda,' said Raymond. 'We'll get your statement typed up for you to sign. We'll let you have a break now.'

Glenda was escorted to the cells, followed by Mr Fox, and Murphy and Raymond wandered back into the CID room, where Bellweather was lurking.

'Good result' he bellowed and clapped Raymond on the shoulder, before retreating to his office.

'Gone to phone the top brass and harvest a few congratulations for himself,' said Raymond. 'I'm afraid you're not teacher's pet.'

Murphy shook her head. 'I gave up on that a long time ago. Him and me, we know where we are with each other.'

Wilcox and Wanda arrived at that moment. Wilcox was brandishing a laptop. 'Top of the range' he said. 'Be interesting to see what's on it.'

'That'll be useful,' said Murphy. 'In case she retracts her confession. But I don't think she will. Find anything else?'

They shook their heads. 'It was just like, a typical ... old person's place,' said Wanda, wrinkling her nose.

Murphy laughed. 'That's why I'm grateful to my young

lodgers,' she said. 'So I won't have to wake up one morning and find I'm living in an old person's place.'

'She just doesn't look like a violent person,' said Wanda.

'It doesn't matter what she looks like,' said Murphy. 'What matters is what she did. It's the ultimate crime, the crime that can never be undone. Because, they may not have been wonderfully likeable people, but Daniel Webb had a mother who loved him, and James Wilson had young kids. So Glenda Morrison, with her convenient terminal diagnosis, doesn't get any sympathy from me. I'll tell you what I'd really like to happen to her.'

'Beaten up in prison?' ventured Wilcox, looking a bit shocked.

Murphy shook her head. 'No, not that. Not at all. I'd like this cancer to go into remission. She thinks she'll have shuffled off the old mortal coil long before we actually manage to get her sent down. Allowing for bureaucratic inefficiencies and all. She's calculated she'll have a few months under guard in a hospice and that will be it. All over. I'd like her to get what all cancer sufferers want – a few more years of life.'

Next in the Detective Miranda Murphy Series

vinci-books.com/dead-drop

Behind every perfect neighbourhood lies a perfect crime.

What do you really know about your neighbours? Probably less than you think.

Turn the page for a free preview…

Dead Drop: Prologue

HE STOOD AND LOOKED at her on the bed, so still, so defenceless. And thought of murder. So easy. No resistance. Nobody would wonder, nobody would even query it. She didn't have long anyway, blessed release they would say, all that sort of thing. So convenient, this end-of-life stage. You could massage it to suit your own ends. The nurses came and went, lots of different faces, overworked and underpaid, looking forward to the end of their shift. Get back to feed the kids and put their feet up. A small mistake with the dosage perhaps, but even that would not be noticed and, if it was, nobody would say anything. Under the carpet. The NHS didn't need any more negligence claims. Death certificate signed by some doctor who would probably never even look at her. Just sign here, doctor. Nobody would ever know. Except him. He would know.

At that moment she stirred and opened her eyes and he smiled and went to hold her hand, caressing the bony knuckles, brushing her hair back from her face. Such a trusting face.

Dead Drop: Chapter One

Francine had that morning come across Nancy Brophy's essay *How to Murder Your Husband*. If anybody looked into her internet history, there it would be. First mistake. In some ways it was an interesting idea. Life without Justin would certainly be less stressful. She wouldn't have to wonder what mood he was going to wake up in, she wouldn't have to cook dinner and hope it met with his approval. She could just eat something simple with Danny, feed Tommy and then go to sleep with the kids. At the thought of all those extra hours in bed a wave of longing came over her. The insurance would pay off the mortgage and probably give her some sort of payout and when Tommy was a bit bigger, she could start taking in more work again. It was definitely something to consider. Well, so much for that. Life was not quite like that. If something was to happen to Justin, she'd probably find she was devastated. She would think of all the good things, not the bad ones. And, of course, the ultimate crime hadn't turned out too well for Nancy.

They were getting near the school now. Danny liked to

Dead Drop: Chapter One

stand on the back of the buggy, which made it heavy to push up the hill, but Francine always walked unless it was raining. It was important to get your exercise when you could and she didn't want the kids to grow up expecting to be driven everywhere. She knew she wasn't a successful school gate mum. There were a number of groups and she didn't seem to belong to any of them. It was a skillset she'd never mastered, standing around, lots of news to exchange, gossiping about other people, or whatever it was that went on. The only people likely to talk to her were Brenda, who was actually a grandmother, and Marion, who was a grown-up rock chick and also avoided the cliquey groups. Right now, Francine couldn't see either of them so she just waited for the bell to ring so that she could beat a retreat.

And now they've got this birthday party tonight. Why did Justin insist on having a party? Is forty really such a big deal? Should she be buying him a present? Probably. Maybe she should. Perhaps if she made a bit more effort, he would be a bit different too. Perhaps they could salvage things for the sake of the boys. After all, he hadn't seemed like that when she first met him. There were none of these moody silences. It's probably all her fault. He just doesn't seem to like her any more, maybe she's no longer likeable. What she really needs to do is to get back to work, but she's not ready to leave Tommy yet. It's not good to be financially dependent on a man she's not sure she still wants.

JUSTIN SAT in his office, scrolling through the market reports. Returns were a bit low at the moment. Could he make that point to his clients? They were as capable of looking at Bloomberg as he was, they'd be expecting a hit to the bottom line. It would give him a bit of breathing room. Cargill's secretary walked past and he smiled at her. She

Dead Drop: Chapter One

didn't smile back. Was that significant? Justin knew he was still good-looking (or he hoped he was). Good, muscular body, brown eyes, blondish hair that flopped winningly across his eyes. Most women appreciated it when he smiled at them. He'd never had any trouble in that department. Had Cargill said something to Julie about him? He had a distinct feeling of being kept at arm's length, no more summons to meetings. Everybody hated meetings anyway, but you didn't like to feel that you were being kept out of the information loop. Maybe Cargill suspected something. No, that wasn't possible. But he would have to manoeuvre his way out of it all at some point, he couldn't just keep grabbing short-term solutions. He was badly over-leveraged. Somehow or other he would have to unwind it, but to do that he needed funds, and ideally, he needed them from a source that wouldn't dig him further in. As long as nobody asked to withdraw, that was the immediate danger. Perhaps he could reduce the rate by half a percent, but then he wouldn't get the new business. These are not stupid people – except in one regard of course – and they all monitor the rates.

His phone pinged. It was a message from Louise. He'd told her not to do this, all he needs is for Francine to see one of these messages. But she wouldn't of course. She's not the sort of woman who would check his messages. Sometimes that worries him – maybe she doesn't care enough to be suspicious. Maybe she's planning to leave him. No, she knows she can't. He's made that clear to her. She knows what the consequences will be and it's not as if he doesn't keep her well provided for. That's probably how he ended up in this mess. He needs to divest himself of Louise – that relationship has really run its course – patch things up with Francine and then figure out how to get out of this much more serious mess. It's all bloody Stanley's fault. Perhaps he'll die soon.

STANLEY SET ABOUT THE WHEEL ARCHES with a scrubbing brush and watched with satisfaction as the soapy water turned grey. A labour of love, that's what it was. Funny to think of love, after everything that had happened. But nothing could dampen his good mood now. He was beginning a new chapter of life – a bit late, but never mind. He was still fit, that's what matters when you get into your sixties. A lifetime of fresh air, exercise and no junk food. But poor Shirley had been fit too, and the cancer had come for her just the same. Maybe luck had a lot to do with it. In which case he would make the most of the luck he had left.

He could remember being a kid with a motorbike, and this feeling is a bit like that. There are men his age who ride motorbikes, but he's not going to be one of them. It's too late now for that. He was sad for so long after Shirley died, it felt like a long black tunnel, but now he's at the other end and it's all thanks to the van. Just like the kid with the motorbike, he's going to spend endless hours working on the van. Well maybe not endless, because it's all pretty much done now, but he can always find odds and ends to get on with. There's always something you can take to pieces.

The van is a converted Ford Transit. A VW microbus would have looked cooler of course, much more Al Guthrie and the gang, but they go for cool prices these days. The Ford has everything he needs – a bed, a cooker, a TV and a shower. It has a side awning for warm days when he'll be parked up in some beauty spot, sitting in a deck chair reading a book. He's studied every video on YouTube about how to convert your van, how to do running repairs, what equipment you need to carry with you. He's researched all the places you can park up, all over Europe. He's ready for the off, he's got everything he needs. Apart from internet, he'll have to go into cafés for that. And he's got the very best fishing equipment, all the expensive gear he's wanted for years, he has it all now. That's an investment, he can write it all off against tax. He's going to be an ageing Jack Kerouc, on the road, maybe without the drugs. And his first trip will be up to London, not quite the sort of trip he had in mind, but he'll do it anyway. He's not particularly looking forward to this party, but it will be lovely to see Francine and Danny and the baby – Justin not so much.

Grab your copy...
vinci-books.com/dead-drop

About the Author

Eva Maclean read her first Agatha Christie (*Death in the Clouds*) at age ten and has been obsessed with detective fiction and writing ever since. After a past life as an accountant, she is finally doing what she wanted to do in the first place.

Eva lives in London with her husband and two cats, her children having grown up and made good their escape.

Her favourite living authors are Kate Atkinson, Donna Leon and Mick Herron. The dead are too many to count.